Hunting Unicorns

BELLA POLLEN is a writer and journalist who contributes to a wide variety of newspapers and magazines, including the *Sunday Telegraph*, *American Vogue*, *Harpers and Queen* and the *Observer*. She is the author of four other novels, *All About Men*, *Daydream Girl*, *Midnight Cactus* and *The Summer of the Bear*. Bella lives in Ladbroke Grove, London.

bella pollen

Hunting Unicorns

PAN BOOKS

First published 2003 by Macmillan

This paperback edition published 2004 by Pan Books
an imprint of Pan Macmillan, a division of Macmillan Publishers Limited
Pan Macmillan, 20 New Wharf Road, London N1 9RR
Basingstoke and Oxford
Associated companies throughout the world
www.panmacmillan.com

ISBN 978-0-330-46077-4

1 3 5 7 9 8 6 4 2

A CIP catalogue record for this book is available from
the British Library.

Typeset by Intype London Ltd
Printed in the UK by CPI Mackays, Chatham ME5 8TD

TO ANDY

who had faith I could do it

TO CAROLE AND SUSIE

who saw me through it

The families who in their heyday were the lords of the earth are now often strangers in their own land. The lions of yesteryear have become the unicorns of today.

— David Cannadine,
The Decline and Fall of the British Aristocracy

We live in strange times. The millennium is upon us. I belong to two worlds, the past and the future. I am what is more or less defunct yet I have not understood what I am to become.

— Daniel Lytton-Jones

daniel

My mother and father drank. Water, whisky, wine. It was all the same to them. Any time, anyplace, anywhere. Curiously they never appeared drunk. Instead they existed in a semi-inebriated world, never allowing themselves to fall below a certain level of intoxication as though to do so would be bad manners — like appearing at breakfast not quite fully clothed. They had two children. Two small boys who watched their parents drink. Both grew up to be deeply affected by this habit. That is to say Rory became a teetotaller, and I, an alcoholic.

The first time I took myself off to a meeting I wrote this down — just in case it was the sort of place where you were pressured into a confession, but it's not like that here. Your peers don't pressure you so much as bore you into submission. The first meeting was so inexcusably dull I swore it would be the last and it would have been had it not been for the eleventh-hour appearance of the fantastically pretty girl. Some gorgeous accident left the chair next to me vacant and one whiff of her scent; earthy, flowery, sold me on the merits of AA and had there been a year's contract

I would have signed on the dotted line there and then. But she didn't turn up to the following meeting nor the one after that. In ten minutes we're supposed to be starting this week's session and there's still no sign of her. I've now made a major management decision. If she doesn't come through the door within, say, five minutes . . . I'm off to the pub. I don't have the energy for this bollocks. There are more pressing matters to be dealt with – the nuts and bolts that actually underpin people's lives. Right now, there's all this stuff waiting on my desk – articles to be written, mail to be opened, bills to be paid . . .

This afternoon, for instance, I was supposed to turn in my piece for the *Spectator*. The editor called, screaming obscenities a couple of hours ago. It's not that it's a difficult piece to write. The subject matter is interesting enough but I seem to have no words to put to it.

For some time now I've been juggling the various incompatible factions in my life but lately it seems I'm in danger of dropping a ball or two. The fact is, I'm having trouble writing under the influence of sobriety. Usually I'm unable to contemplate any kind of work until I've downed a half bottle of red wine. Alcohol gets the blood to the head, unblocks the channels. As words flow, I write them down and print them out. Then I send them off and get paid for my trouble. This is a system and it works, but now that I'm semi-programme, quasi-AA or, more specifically, no alcohol before the six o'clock watershed, the system seems to have crashed.

*

They say that the moment you realize you're an alcoholic is the moment you're scared of living without alcohol. Perhaps this is true for some people but not for me. I have known since childhood I was an alcoholic, since long before I ever tasted the stuff. I am what's known as a genetic junkie. Much of what I have in life is inherited, unfortunately not all of it good. Whatever the distinguishing feature that ties other families together, ours is a gene, a wayward one that has ripped through our family tree like a tornado, dropping the fruit of our ancestors to the ground, leaving generations of us destined to become rotten, pickled and canned.

Rory expends much energy fighting this gene, I on the other hand have embraced it. I don't see the point in not. To spend your life struggling against your own DNA seems pretty damn futile. It's who I am. It's on the swab from the inside of my cheek, it's in my blood, in every bead of sweat and no doubt in every puff of carbon dioxide I exhaled into that police breathalyser last night.

'But we're the generation that can kick it,' Rory says.

But you can't kick it, as you can be sure I'll be telling the group one day, because it ain't no football. Besides, I'm not convinced it should be kicked. Instability is the root of creativity and I like to believe there is a chink in the circle of life – an uneven join on the curve where the top of the genetic pool meets the bottom. This is the place from which flawed geniuses come, where my family, with its mix of the charmed and the damned, belong. Somewhere on this isolated ledge lies the answers to all the contradictions on earth.

*

A dozen people fill the room now, swapping goodwill and drinking coffee out of plastic cups. Attending AA is not unlike going to the theatre. You do it because it's supposed to be good for you – or more accurately, somebody else thinks it's good for you. Your parents, friends, people you don't want to hurt, have almost certainly bought tickets and you go to keep them happy. The theatre analogy doesn't end there. Once in a meeting, there are uncomfortable displays of emotions, an interval between speakers. There are the stars, producers, an audience and prima donnas to entertain them and, oh Good Lord, there's the fantastically pretty girl walking through the door . . .

Her name is Kate. She touches the arm of someone she knows and nods. They give her a brochure, which she doesn't read. Today she's wearing a blue cotton shirt and pencil skirt. I like the way she moves in this skirt. Demure, yet . . . not.

I watch Kate out of the corner of my eye, mentally staking my claim on the chair nearest her. Suddenly, without warning, it's time and the talking stops. I look for Kate but she's disappeared. Everyone sits. I cast around panicked, the mulish child who can't get the hang of musical chairs. There are two seats left, but not together. I'm on the verge of bolting when Kate pushes in through the swinging door from the loo. Her eyes are red from crying. Somewhere along the line, some bastard has been mean to her. I want to be that bastard so that I can make it up to her. She sits down and crosses her legs. There is a ladder in her tights. It starts 5 inches above her knee and disappears up her skirt – God only knows where it might end. Dear Lord she's sexy, I am intoxicated by her beauty, I am overwhelmed by her suffering. If I don't sleep with her soon I will go mad.

The meeting gets underway. Kate was on holiday last week. This I learn from her share: 'Lisbon. Good tapas. A chance to escape.' So far she's given no reason as to why she's slipped on the banana skin of rack and ruin. She flicks her black hair over one shoulder, her eyes are the colour of mulberries.

Who's next? I look around. Whose boil-in-the-bag emotions need reheating this week? Whose family must now carry the burden of their child's dysfunction on top of their own. It's tempting to leap to my feet. *We've had them all*, I could say, *great granny kept a lion, Howard held poker parties dressed as a rat. Uncle Conrad drank himself to death, as did Uncle William. Robert took drugs. Dinah lay on her bed and swallowed pill after pill. Peter walked up to the top of the valley and put a gun to his head. John died of a brain tumour the size of a cantaloupe . . . We're a careless family. We lose a lot of people.* But I keep quiet, holding back for the real loonies and eventually Mad Millicent takes the chair. She has hair like a Brillo pad and believes herself to be Peter Mandelson's bodyguard. We're all a bit bored of her and she soon senses it. Eventually she falls silent then hauls a bottle of Evian water from her knapsack and stares at it incredulously.

Next we get Stan. 'It has come to my attention,' he begins, 'that certain people in this fellowship have been b'littlin' me,' he fixes his eye on Kate who hugs her knees to her chest. She has a fading bruise on her left calf, and intensely white skin through which her veins shine and flow like rivers on a map. 'Well,' Stan continues, 'I should like it known that I am carrying a long sharp knife and should anyone b'little me again, I'll stick 'em like a pig.' He wipes the spittle from his mouth. 'Fanks for listening.'

I have a brainwave. In the break I will ask Kate to be my sponsor. This means I can legitimately ring her up day or night to discuss my disintegration.

'I can't be your sponsor,' she says, eyes narrowing with suspicion.

'Why not?'

'It's crossing the boundaries. You don't even know me.'

'Ah but I don't know anybody here.' I turn my palms up to the ceiling, charming yet helpless.

'This isn't about sobriety,' she says quietly and furiously.

I'm floored that she's on to me so quickly. 'What is it about then?'

'It's about you wanting to sleep with me.'

I've completely gone off Kate now that she's got no sense of humour. If you can't even connect with people on a basic level, what hope is there for any of us here?

'I'll be your sponsor, mate.'

I turn to find a man the size of a small country accosting me.

'I've been sober for a year now,' he says, 'I'm ready to take you on.'

Raymond is black, schizophrenic and has spent most of his adult life in prison. It's going to be hard to say no.

I spend the second half of the meeting contemplating Raymond's neck. The thing must measure minimum a foot and a half circumference. In fact there's no way of deciphering where his neck ends and his head begins.

After the meeting he says, 'Call me anytime you need help,' and crushes me to his chest.

'You can't be on the bloody programme if you're drinking,' Benj says in the pub.

'I'm half on the programme. Half AA. I'm *A*.'

'That's like announcing you're half pregnant. There are certain things you just can't do in halves.' Benj, unshaved and apparently unwashed since the last time I saw him, is doing the crossword puzzle in the *Telegraph*, his third pint of bitter in front of him. When he takes a swig, his Adam's apple rises up and down in his throat like a miniature elevator. Rake thin, Benj looks like someone standing in front of a circus mirror, all extruded. I tear open a bag of crisps.

'The world is full of legitimate halves. Half dead, half decent, half-cooked. Half-witted . . .' I'm having my first drink of the day. A glass of red wine. It tastes pure and delicious and, God knows, I feel like I've earned the thing.

'I don't know why you're bothering frankly.' Benj turns his attention to the obituaries.

I glance fondly at the miffed expression on his face. Benj and I are first cousins, and we've been muckers, drinking and otherwise, since we were at prep school together. He is not taking kindly to my partial desertion.

'Half-baked, halfway, half-cocked.' I scribble with alacrity. The piece for the *Spectator* is flowing.

'They say the moment you realize you're scared of living without alcohol means you are an alcoholic,' Benj says.

'Demi-tasse, demi-cappucine, demi-monde.' I throw down

7

my pen. The piece is finished. I down the glass of wine to celebrate and order two more.

'Does Rory know you're *demi*-AA?' Benj enquires.

'Why? Am I not functioning magnificently on my new ration of alcohol? Am I not coping beautifully under such trying circumstances?'

'Uhuh,' he doesn't look up from the paper.

'Am I not achieving work deadlines, keeping appointments?'

'Speaking of which,' Benj says, 'weren't you meant to be having supper at home tonight?'

Bollocks. I scuttle off. Home, temporarily is chez Rory – not the most ideal of situations for either of us, but a couple of months ago I received one of those estate agent letters. Did I want to rent out my property to some wanker banker and his wife for an extortionate sum of money? If I remember correctly, the original thinking behind agreeing to this (apart from it paying off some frankly pressing, not to mention depressing debts) was that having calculated assignments abroad, weekends at home, and the rest of the time over at my rather obliging girlfriend's flat, I could probably wing it financially for a further six months. When my girlfriend threw both me and my clothes out, Rory seized his chance. I won't bore you with the details of our row but we ended up with a neat exchange of consonants for vowels. B&B from him in return for a commitment to AA from me. Rory, sobriety's bodyguard, has officially assigned himself to my case.

Metaphorically speaking, my little brother and I are

twins. We might be separated by thirteen months but we're the head and tail of the same coin. What I lack, he boasts and vice versa, our weakness and strengths balancing each other out. More importantly I have always lived in his head and he in mine, and thus united we have managed to make sense of the world. But as I drift further over a river he will not cross, things have changed.

Rory doesn't dare be too stony-faced when I finally buzz the door because his fiancée's just arrived from Italy. The purpose of dinner is for us to bond. I suspect neither of them fall for the story I make up about Kate having a breakdown in the meeting but they're gracious enough to pretend, in fact they positively radiate welcome and for a moment I have to muster every ounce of loyalty not to turn tail and flee.

'Would you like to drink something?' Leona says, then blushing adds, 'a Coca Cola?' I grin and kiss her on the cheek.

Leona whips dishes in and out of the oven with strong honey-coloured arms. She's a beauty all right. Cool skin, pale hair, hot Italian blood. Too healthy looking for my taste, I prefer Kate's bruised vulnerability, but at one point I catch the look Rory sends her across the kitchen. I realize the bastard's actually in love and I feel enormously proud of him.

'Are you taking Leona to Hell Hall this weekend?' I ask.

'Over my dead body.' Rory pretends not to see my frown and I do not push it but here we come to the point of separation. Our paths have diverged and discussions about

Hell Hall, about inheritance, matters of tax, our parents, their drinking, their hopelessness, my perceived hopelessness, are all places we no longer go together, emotionally, conversationally, and certainly not physically.

Rory believes he has escaped. Imagines it is possible. He has sworn not to be tied down, and of course, that's his prerogative – but it's also, I believe, his loss. It's different for me. Hell Hall, as our family home has come to be known, is one of the most beautiful places on earth, a place about which I'm passionate – which is just as well really as I cannot escape. I am the eldest son.

The rest of dinner passes pleasantly enough, I badly want a drink but there's just enough Coke to fill my glass, just enough perfunctory gossip to fill the gaps left by other forbidden subjects and by the time we finish it's mercifully late. When Rory takes Leona to bed, he steers her from the room with his thumb and forefinger round the back of her neck.

After an hour or two of television I doze. When I wake, edgy and twitching, it's somewhere between night and day. This has long been a moment of desperation for me. A bad sleeper as a child, irrationally scared of the dark, and now scared of the demons the dark allows me to conjure, I know from the moment my brain registers wakefulness that I will do almost anything for a drink . . .

It takes me a while to find where Rory's stashed it but eventually I triumph with two bottles of wine from the depths of the cleaning cupboard, hidden on a shelf behind the Ajax and Domestos.

*

Later, opening the kitchen bin to throw out the empty bottles, I knock against the drainer. A pile of saucepans clatter to the floor. I stack them back on the sink.

'What's up?' Rory is standing in the doorway looking sleepy and crumpled.

I try to keep the alcohol from my voice when I answer, then I think damn him – why should I? We talk, but as so often these past few months it soon turns to argument and God knows I am weary of it. He tells me I am following tracks in the snow and I tell him I'm no fan of these father/ son style 'chats' because we've been so close all our lives and none of this ever mattered. As he lectures I close my eyes, strip back the years until I see two small boys, arms linked, dressed in woolly jumpers with embroidered initials. R and D. Now I look at him shaking his head angrily and I wonder what the hell happened to us. Two things occur to me. The first is that somewhere along the line, wires have been crossed. Rory seems to have responsibility whilst I have the responsibilities and the second is my fear that Rory is growing up whereas I am clearly regressing and I know then and there that I have to get out of the house before I either cry or end up clocking the little bastard.

As I'm unchaining the bike from the railings I remember that I meant to tell Rory he will not escape his roots, no matter how hard he tries. There is something of the father in every son. The gene might be dormant, but it's lying in wait. Then I recognize the fear and indecision in his eyes as he hesitates in the doorway and I see that he knows this already.

I head for Highgate, for the cemetery. The street lights are fading, the sky lightening. I pass an old man sweeping dust from one side of the road to the other and a dumpy matron jogging, her grey tracksuit stained greyer with sweat. Past Primrose Hill, the streets are empty and the city belongs to me. The exertion of pedalling sends all remaining alcohol straight to my head. Despite the freezing temperature I feel gloriously warm. Tabasco is running through my veins. My brain spins with all the things to do in life and in this one perfect moment all of them seem possible.

Then the moment passes. Crosswinds blow against my face. I put my head down, grip the handlebars – peddle for all life's worth up the hill. It's late autumn and the leaves are whirling. They fall against my face, slight, light, like oiled pieces of skin. Dawn breaks quickly as if the tip of a paintbrush had touched a dab of orange to wet blotting paper. I look into the sun's weak rays to suck some warmth onto my face.

Wait a second, where did that bastard come from? A white van has shot over the crossing and through the give-way sign. I squeeze the brake lever, nearly projecting myself over the handlebars. The bicycle stops, leaving just enough space for the van to swing through its turn. I give the driver a nod, but he doesn't nod back. In fact he doesn't wave, smile, salute or show appreciation of any kind – he just revs off down the street belching fumes from his exhaust. I stay still, breathing heavily, balancing the heel of my boot against the tarmac. As a spectator at this scene I might have an impending sense of doom. I might watch my face, catch the flicker of irritation that becomes a slow burn of anger at one human being's total lack of consideration towards another. I might warn myself that to seek revenge, given the disparity in our chosen mode of transport, is to dice with death but from where I'm standing it doesn't seem that way at all. Fuelled by the mix of self righteousness and idiocy that only the truly pissed can muster, it just seems like the right thing to do.

It takes only a minute to catch the van. A taxi stops to eject its passenger, the van slows behind. I pedal out into the middle of the road, fly past his open window, shout, 'Manners, you wanker.'

The driver's head turns but I am sailing on through the dawn chill, laughing, untouchable.

Or at least so I think.

By the time I see it, the bus is virtually on top of me. Christ, CHRIST, what happened? It swerves, I swerve and for a split second I think I'm home free but I haven't accounted for its tail end, haven't accounted for the fact that the thing moves together, has no mind of its own. It is, of course, just a bus, a thirty ton piece of metal, and I realize absolutely that it's going to hit me and I know too that whatever happens I don't want to go down. Up is an option, down under this monstrosity is not. If I'm going to go, let it be through the air, like an eagle, not squashed underfoot like some irrelevant bug.

The bus hits. There's no pain, it's all too big for pain. There's just a tremendous force, like being fired from a cannon, and really not so unpleasant as you might imagine. There's an explosion of red, a deep, deep red, and a colour too vivid to be borne. I close my eyes but I can still see through the skin. I can see through the windscreen of the bus, into the driver's black eyes, through his body into his beating heart. For a second, suspended in time I can see everything, all that defines my life, everything I love.

Overhead the air darkens, the weather changes fast and furious. Clouds hurtle through the sky. I feel a great burst of passion towards life, and its momentum carries me home. I am standing in the lake-field. The soil is damp between my toes. I can smell the earth, smell the honeysuckle lifting off the river breeze. I see the woods, the park, the great oak tree bowed in the fox cover. I see my father, stripped to the waist, axe in hand. I see the elms falling. There's a rushing in my ears, the sound the wind might make as it blows through the flowers of a horse chestnut – then there is nothing.

maggie

I have to confess that my basic knowledge of London's geography comes from playing Monopoly. My father, never the most switched on of shoppers, mistakenly bought the English version for Christmas one year. My mother disapproved of the game – vaguely distrusting it as a training in capitalism – but I loved that the makers identified places by colours. It reminded me of a car game I used to play with my dad. He would describe in detail a city he had worked in, then make me blur my eyes and tell him what colour it represented – Madrid, for instance, was brown, Bangkok was orange, Washington white and New York was . . . well one of the reasons I love living in New York so much is that we could never pinpoint its colour. It's a kaleidoscopic mix of shades, smells, sounds and race. Millions of multicoloured stitches that make up one small but fantastic pocket of humanity.

Maybe it wasn't the ideal present for an only child but I loved Monopoly. I saw it less as a training in capitalism than a crash course in survival. It's surprising what tips you can pick up from a game. How to land on Chance and grab Opportunity. How to get out of jail free. I can still feel the adrenaline buzz of being down to your last buck and making a run for it through those lethal trouble hotspots – the triple-hotelled properties.

I remember the colours of every card. Fleet Street was red, Piccadilly was yellow. Now, peering through my cab window at the damp streets of London, I assumed due to the grand nature of the offices to which I was heading they'd be situated in the royal blue hues of Park Lane and Mayfair. Turned out they were somewhere called Edgware Road, a street not actually featured in the game at all, which, as I wound down the window to take a better look, was unsurprising. With its shops selling carpets and lanterns, its profusion of hookah smokers sitting around outside juice bars playing backgammon, it felt more like some souk in Beirut than a mere traffic jam from Oxford Circus.

'It is very . . . ah . . . *Arab*,' Alexander Massey confirmed looking furtively behind me to the dark hallway as he opened the door.

Overweight, old school and upper class, Massey was the author of five anthologies of obituaries and a leading expert on Burke's Peerage (a publication listing everything you always wanted to know about the titles of England's aristocracy but were too afraid to ask) and I was praying he was going to be able to help me.

It was January, the first month of the Millennium and the world was recovering from its conflicting feelings of relief that earth hadn't exploded and its disappointment that nothing had fundamentally changed. I'd been in London for less than a week and already run into trouble. My crew was arriving in a couple of days but I had nothing to film.

I work for *Newsline*. You probably know it, most people do. *Newsline* is a current affairs, news and issues program that leans towards story journalism rather than information journalism – sort of a younger and smaller cousin of *60 Minutes*. We specialize in exposing scandal and exploding myths. We target corrupt government bodies, insensitive public companies, institutions and monopolies. I love working there, as a show, it just isn't afraid to kick ass.

This all started last November when I was running to a meeting in the *Newsline* offices. It was the Thursday before Thanksgiving weekend and New York was in its usual bi-thematic state of shivering outside and sweltering inside. Thanksgiving always feels like the practice run for Christmas and true to form the Santas were out in force, hitching wide leather belts over even wider beer bellies. It seemed that the whole of Manhattan was making the rush to Grand Central, off to family weekends and stuffed turkey dinners, but my parents had never been big on family occasions, and public holidays tended to prompt special derision for the over-commercial, greeting-card sentimentality of the American People. Besides, Alan Soloman, *Newsline*'s senior producer, had called me in for a meeting and when Alan scheduled meetings no one went home early.

A week before Thanksgiving, I'd made Alan a presentation; a story I really wanted to pursue in the Middle East. Alan had been ambivalent about letting me go, but now I was hoping to get it green-lighted.

A big man, weathered and broad, Alan pulled down the shutters in his office then perched on the side of his desk, tapping dried cranberries from the packet – a token nod to his high cholesterol. A CBS executive was sitting in on the meeting. I couldn't remember his name but since the sale of *Newsline* to CBS a year ago, network grands fromages were becoming a familiar sight around the place. The television fizzed then cleared. On screen were scenes of mayhem. I recognized them straight away. This was footage taken when England's Labour Government had finally succeeded in pushing through the abolition of the hereditary peers in the House of Lords. My grandfather had been Irish and ever since the British Parliamentary channel had been made available on cable I'd been alternately horrified and amused by the antics of the Houses of Parliament. I assumed Alan was inviting criticism of somebody else's rough-cut, a trick he pulled from time to time to keep correspondents on their toes. This segment looked like Ed's work. With his hand-tooled leather shoes, fussy little dogs and penchant for antiques, a piece in England would be right up Ed's alley.

The action cut to the chambers where tempers seemed more frayed than usual, in fact it looked as if a fist fight was on the verge of breaking out between members. The shot changed again to a line of aging peers handing in their security passes. One had tears in his eyes. Alan freeze-framed the image with the push of a button.

'Up until now the House of Lords has had the power to pass and initiate laws purely through their hereditary right. So it got us thinking . . . with the loss of this last vestige of political power, what influence do the aristocracy of England have left?'

Only then it dawned on me this wasn't a rough at all, Alan was pitching me a story.

'Wait a minute,' I glanced at him suspiciously, 'what about the piece I proposed?'

He didn't meet my eye. 'We have enough people out there right now, Maggie. Instead, we thought it might be revealing if you went over and interviewed some of the heads of England's more influential upper-class families . . .'

I couldn't believe I'd heard him right. The story I'd pitched was on honour killings in the Yemen.

'But England is cold, wet, formal.' I pleaded. 'Couldn't I please have desert, heat, scorpions? Couldn't I at least have something a teeny bit more relevant?'

'One thousand years of aristocratic rule. This is the end of an era, Maggie, this is *historically* relevant.'

'Added bonus we get a nice tour round England's country houses,' the executive threw in, 'keep the female viewers on the hook.'

Alan must have caught the look on my face. 'I know, Maggie, I know,' there was regret in his voice and it stopped me short of total rebellion, 'but the hard reality is, we have to chase the ratings like everybody else. Look, deliver me this piece and next time round you'll get the assignment you want but for now, go revisit Brideshead in the twenty-first century.'

Revisit Brideshead in the twenty-first century. That was my brief – whatever it meant. I guess it could have been worse. In television it seemed to be happening more and more – hard news stories were being ignored in favour of mushy high-rating segments. At least I wasn't being sent to see how some mother in Baltimore was coping with quintuplets or how Buttons, the heroic dog, had pulled a kid out of a hole. I'd never been to England and besides, when I'd calmed down enough to think straight, I realized I had a heady ulterior motive for spending a little time in Europe. I figured I'd just go and make the best of it.

Course, it hadn't turned out that simple. I'd done meticulous research in New York, but as soon as I arrived in London, permissions I'd spent weeks negotiating had been cancelled. The British, it seemed, were notoriously camera shy.

Access, to a journalist, is like blood to a vampire. If you cannot get to the people you're interested in, you try to get to their friends. If you can't find a whistleblower you're dead in the water.

At that point I could have called in to *Newsline* with a blank. It sometimes happens, you chase a story as far as you can then it dies on you. 'The dog won't hunt' as Clinton would say. You might have thought I'd be happy to find a legitimate reason for backing out of an assignment I'd felt railroaded into in the first place, but I couldn't do it. I hated giving up on a story.

Despite the market feel of the Edgware Road below us, Massey's offices offices were dry, stuffy and very small. Books and paperwork were strewn on every surface, and a stressed-looking assistant was struggling with a copying machine in the reception area. Through an open window came the resonant wailing of middle eastern pop music. 'The . . . er . . . *ethnicity* makes it very tricky at lunchtime you know,' Massey said leading the way down the narrow corridor to his office – a box-sized room smelling of pipe tobacco and decorated cheek to jowl with framed cartoons from *Punch* magazine. 'I've tried some of these places, but I never know what to *order*. I can't tell you how intimidating it is *not to know*.'

I took one of the leather-bound volumes of Burke's Peerage from his shelf and opened it curiously. Alexander Massey was reputed to know the names and genealogy of every great family in England – if he couldn't help me, then nobody could.

'Do you mind me asking, is anyone actually interested in this stuff anymore?'

'Oh you'd be surprised,' Massey said affably. 'Hotels, shop owners, that kind of thing. The sort of people listed here,' he tapped the front cover, 'can get very shirty about being wrongly addressed, you know.'

'You publish this annually?' The book weighed a ton.

'The great problem with the war,' Massey regarded the ringing phone with something approaching dismay, 'apart from bombs coming down of course, was a shortage of paper, that's when we decided to bring it out every five years instead of three. Now it's growing in popularity all the time.' He plucked the receiver gingerly from its cradle.

There was something a little Graham Greene about Alexander Massey – Our Man In The Edgware Road, keeping watch on his tiny piece of the empire, wearing his white linen suit in the perishing cold of a London winter. Actually, Massey was punctiliously dressed in neat fawn-coloured pants and corduroy jacket. In a way he was disappointing. I'd been hoping he was going to be a fantastic snob, instead he was gentle and self-effacing.

'Quite so, quite so,' he was saying into the receiver, 'to read of one's own death, whether over breakfast or not is, naturally, terribly distressing, but a genuine editorial mistake I can assure you,' he threw me a pained expression. 'No, no I'm quite sure that's not the case. I feel confident that your son must have been as distraught as everybody else . . . ah . . . sent a removal van for the furniture did he? Yes, I do see. That does present things in a slightly different light . . . yes, yes of course I'll send a written apology.'

'Well, rings the changes I suppose,' he positioned the phone back on his desk. 'Usually get it in the neck for leaving out births.'

'Don't people mind their addresses being printed?' I scanned through the tiny print of the book. 'Aren't they worried about getting robbed or stalked?'

'Dear me,' Massey said vaguely, 'well yes, I suppose there is a danger, but in my experience the criminal fraternity prefer browsing *Hello!* magazine for that sort of thing.' He took the list from my hand. 'Now these are the people you're interested in, are they? Let's see,' he switched on the brass light by his elbow and studied the names. 'Fermoy . . . yes, made their fortune selling black crêpe for Queen Victoria's funeral. He thumbed through the wafer-thin pages, 'Hartfield, oddly enough I was at prep school with. Just been voted out of the Lords. Makes cider now I believe . . . Bevan, as I'm sure you're aware, is cousin to the queen.'

'Really? A close one?'

'Oh yes.' He smoothed his finger gently along the book's binding. 'Eighth Earl of Bevan, family name Lytton-Jones, Danby also of Clandoyle. Issue two sons, eldest recently deceased—'

'Look, I know it sounds really pushy,' I rummaged in

my tote bag for a pen, 'but is there any way you could help get me in with these people?' The idea was to visit some of these fallen lords in their homes. See how they lived, find out what they stood for, what they believed in.

'Well now,' Massey cleared his throat, 'I'm only interested in genealogy, I'm a bit of a dry stick when it comes to the people themselves. Besides I think you'll find that the real top dogs, the sort you're after, would never allow themselves to be filmed.'

I pondered on this. I live in an age and a country consumed with celebrity. It's simply a national obsession. People will bare all and usually for nothing. The very idea of discretion seems archaic. When you ring up sources in America and say you work for a television show, you can barely shut them up.

'Do you have *any* influence? Could you get me any kind of access?'

'You'll have to find someone who's familiar to that world,' Massey said, 'someone they trust. It would of course entirely depend on the thrust of your piece but I'm afraid the answer is you probably won't get access. Why would they agree? What could you possibly offer them?' He closed the book. 'I'm sorry.'

As I headed out through the corridor I remembered something and doubled back.

'Moutabal,' I said.

Massey turned from the shelf.

'It's like an eggplant dip, and hummus is really nice too. Also check out the lamb kebab in pitta but make sure you order it with the chilli and sesame sauce, and don't touch the mayonnaise.'

Massey's brow cleared. 'Right,' he said beaming, 'splendid, thank you.'

'You're welcome.'

'Hang on.' He patted through the debris on the desk for a pen and scribbled a name on a piece of paper. 'Look, take this . . . an acquaintance of mine. I can't guarantee it, but it's just possible he may be able to help you.'

I want to see them starving,
The so called working class
Their wages weekly halving
Their women stewing grass
When I ride out each morning
In one of my new suits
I want to find them fawning
To clean my car and boots.

— Philip Larkin

daniel

It's wrong to say that time is a great healer. It isn't. What happens is that you get used to things. It's a question of survival and to survive you adapt. Rory is only beginning to understand that now. 18 October 1999. The price of petrol rose, a BSE outbreak was confirmed in France, twins were born to a sexagenarian, and a lesser-known journalist went down under a bus.

For over a year now, Rory's been living in a state of arrested insanity and how much longer it might continue he has no clue. All points of reference are gone. How many ounces to the pound? How many weeks in the year? How many inches to the foot? Oh God, let someone push back the clock for him because nothing makes sense any more.

Death results in isolation for the living and there are days when he must resolve to hang on until he returns to the safety of his own home, when it's all he can do to keep his temper at bay, when he considers himself a danger to society at large and if the authorities only knew what kind of lunatic was roaming the street they'd have him whisked straight off to a secure unit before any damage was done. These are the days that induce much self-pity, but Rory can be excused from wallowing because ask anybody who knows about these things – grief can bend your knees. Grief can bring you down.

As he sets off to the bakery where he buys his breakfast every morning he wonders whether people can actually see the fuse protruding from the cannonball that doubles up as his head – and if so, whether some mischievous child might do him a favour, take it upon themselves to light it then, cheers, it would all be over. On bad days he wonders why, on looking at his reflection in a mirror, he doesn't see the actual iron ball or the hand grenade with its accompanying pin, but the face that stares back at him is always the same bland mask and he considers himself a tribute to that great English skill of hiding emotion. Having said that, it's a bloody unreasonable way to live. If you're blind, you get a white stick. If you've got a gammy leg you get a disabled sticker for parking on double yellow lines. A hand grenade for a head is a genuine disability and it would be easier if the general public were made aware of it. Perhaps he could start a trend – the lovesick could stitch a heart on their sleeve, the bitter, tape a soggy chip to their shoulder. If there were more obvious clues to why people behaved the way they did, the world would surely be a nicer place.

Tomorrow it's Rory's thirty-eighth birthday but he feels ten thousand years old. His life has split in two and the chasm he's slipped into has fundamentally changed him. Leaving aside the loss of his sense of humour, which both he and I are praying will return shortly, Rory, in his best moments, used to be someone who believed in love at first sight, who thought that the hole in the ozone layer might self-heal. Now fate has flipped him up and landed him wrong side down on the face of pessimism. It's not that he doesn't get angry, just that he feels he must restrain it; or that he doesn't have passion, only that he feels he should conceal it. His irritability is taken out on things and events he can't control, pigeons that shit on him or stupid phone operators. Only last week, infuriated by drunk party-goers repeatedly ordering a taxi from the phone box outside his window, he took an unloaded shotgun and told them if they didn't bugger off, he'd blow their heads off. This was no solitary incident. Over the last year the list of people he'd like to kill has been endless and varied, and though gradually diminishing, still includes, for the record, most of his clients, all members of his immediate family, Alison his secretary and, very particularly, the lady in the bakery, who has persisted in asking him every day since the accident whether he's feeling better.

They find him surly, of course. A year ago he would have flirted with the baker lady good-naturedly, a year ago he would have flirted with the sticky bun had it been the good lady's day off – Rory's charm is natural and used to be applied indiscriminately. Now it is held strictly in reserve.

He shovels a sausage roll into his mouth reflecting that today looks set to be one of those days. He's just spent the night on the sofa, and on waking this morning found the channel changer wedged between his knees and the screen a buzzing pop art of black and white. He hates these endless nights. In his dreams I am laughing, full of life, always dancing away from him, out of reach while he can neither move nor speak. In these dreams it is Rory, not I, who is dead.

maggie

'*The middle classes view us as profligate and idle, nothing short of money-grabbing buffoons hiding behind our family's coat of arms . . .*'

'Wow.' I pushed my glasses further up my nose and took a closer look. I was in the bowels of the BBC watching footage of an old aristocrat, and whoever had executed the camerawork for this piece of film had done a stunning job. You could almost see the spider veins on the man's cheek pulsing with indignation.

Massey's acquaintance had put me in touch with a producer called Simon Brannigan who'd made a documentary about politicians' wives. 'Slaves to their Class'. Simon was a defensive left-winger with a media crew cut and a muscular intensity that hinted at daily gym workouts. He reminded me of an activist my mother hung out with for a while when I was a kid, who spent a disproportionate part of his day standing on his head against the wall.

My mother was one of the original pioneer feminist film-makers – and when I say pioneer, I'm not joking. Her devastating documentary about female circumcision in Somalia had strong men fainting at its Academy screening.

Needless to say, it didn't win, too controversial or maybe, as Mom always maintained, the board were guilty of anti-female bias.

Simon Brannigan's documentary was not exactly partisan itself, guilty of just about every kind of bias – class, wealth and gender – but it was also compulsive viewing. 'I can't get anyone to talk to me.' I told him. 'Where's aristo.com when you need it. How did you get this kind of access?'

'With great difficulty. Your problem is that you're trying to set up a lot of people fast.' He grimaced. 'Don't forget my film took two years to make. You've got to keep chiselling away . . . by the way, what is the thrust of your piece? What's your hook?'

The thrust of my piece. Massey had asked the same question.

The thing was I wasn't really sure.

Were the English aristocracy a dying breed who after centuries of appalling behaviour were finally getting their comeuppance?

I didn't know, but probably.

Was I sympathetic to the loss of their immense houses from death duties?

Not particularly.

Was I worried that they might forfeit the right to wear sharply tailored red jackets and tear foxes limb from limb?

It wasn't keeping me awake at night.

Would this attitude endear me to the landed gentry?

Well obviously not.

'Though, funnily enough, what you just said . . .' Brannigan was frowning.

'What did I just say?'

'Your quip about aristo.com.' He tapped his pencil against his forehead as though trying to dislodge some snippet of information. 'I did hear, well apparently there *is* now some agency.'

'There is?' I said hopefully, feeling around in my pocket for a Kleenex. I'd managed to contract a really first-class cold since I'd arrived and had been begging Tylenol stand-ins and hot drinks off the long-suffering hotel staff for the last couple of days.

'What you have to understand,' Simon said, 'is that these old farts are increasingly having to face the commercializing of their estates.'

'Yeah right,' I grinned. 'Poor destitute things,' The vast residence of Brannigan's indignant peer had now filled the screen. 'So what does this agency do?'

'Takes advantage of just that. The guy who runs this business is supposedly brilliant at getting a foot through the door in return for cash or, in your case, a few million viewers who might—'

'One day be paying tourists?'

'Exactly, that's about the gist of it.'

'Great. So do you know how I get hold of this guy? What kind of set-up is he running?'

'As I said, the agency wasn't around when I made *Slaves* but I imagine he's some new dot-com e-commerce wide boy who's bought himself a well-cut suit, learnt his dukes from his earls and is now busy exploiting them both. And frankly,' Simon looked at me and smiled broadly, 'the very best of luck to him.'

daniel

Outside number eight Connelly Mews, a small street tucked discreetly into a corner of south west London, Rory trips over a bunch of cable lying on the cobbled ground. 'Mind out,' shouts the builder switching off his drill. He repositions a sign *'Incorporating Stately Locations'* under the existing sign 'R. L. Jones' and moves aside to allow Rory to enter.

'Oh dear, you look terrible,' Alison says.

Rory grunts.

'Nice cup of coffee?'

'No thanks,' Rory throws his jacket on the table.

'How about tea? I've just heated the pot.'

Rory shakes his head.

'Breakfast? I could pop out.'

Rory doesn't bother to answer.

Alison looks crestfallen. Twenty-six going on forty, Alison could almost be pretty if it wasn't for the slight squint that made her appear as though she was permanently in bright sunlight. Alison is Rory's 'assistant' for want of a better word and every morning she arrives early to open up the studio and tidy the place. Every morning she snaps the blinds, makes fresh coffee, sometimes she even puts flowers, bought out of her own pay cheque, into a vase on Rory's desk but my little brother, in his current mode of self-pity has yet to notice these minor acts of worship. He has yet to really notice Alison at all, though with her placid brown eyes she reminds him vaguely of an orphaned heifer we once rescued as boys. We named her Ginger Rogers and bottle fed her for nearly two months. Every day we led her round the lake-field on a rope and scratched the velvety space between her ears. One Sunday about seven months later, Rory asked what we were having for lunch. 'Ginger,' my mother replied, her upbringing on the West Coast of Ireland having given her an entirely unsentimental outlook on life.

'You've had four more calls,' Alison says. 'Lord Carnegie, the Marquess of Nanthaven, uh, your mother twice about her dry cleaning and . . .' but as Rory takes the messages from her hand she feels the brush of his skin and it starts. Deep inside her the heat wells up, registering first as a tingling in her stomach then around her breasts. Gathering speed, it creeps up her neck before finally hitting her face full on. The colour that suffuses her cheeks can only be imagined because by the time she normally escapes to the loo to check in the mirror it has generally subsided.

'And,' she says shakily, 'your ten o'clock appointment is a little bit . . .'

'Cancelled?' Rory says hopefully.

Alison glances warningly towards the office door behind which the sound of muffled crying can be heard.

'Upset,' she says faintly and, as Rory turns, it takes all

her strength of character not to remove the tiny piece of shaving tissue glued by blood to his neck. Instead she takes herself off to the bathroom and weeps three or four mascaraed tears before wiping them away in a practised manner with the palm of her hand.

In Rory's office a couple in their late fifties perch upright on the tightly upholstered sofa. They look apprehensively to the door as it opens. The Penningtons both wear an identical expression, that of people who don't deal with disappointments, but instead simply absorb them. They are reasonably new clients for the reasonably new business of Stately Locations. Rory took them on two months ago but since then, they've been to see him a staggering nine times. There's not much to set them apart from Rory's other clients — many of whom once represented the great names of England, but who are now lost individuals, virtual foreigners in their own country, and the journey that has brought them to Rory's door is littered with death duties, bitter sacrifices, noblesse oblige and Lloyds. All Rory's clients have different stories to tell, but their endings are identical and are faced with the same look of bewilderment, the same gentle sense of defeat. They're all Penningtons, Rory's clients, and in every Pennington, Rory sees our parents.

'My boy, good to see you.' Lord Pennington pushes himself to his feet and rings Rory's hand. 'You're looking well.'

'Thank you.' Rory says, but he has decided the problem of these people must be faced head on.

'Look, Lord Pennington, as I mentioned before, you really mustn't trouble yourself coming in so often, I'd be more than happy to discuss potential bookings on the telephone.'

'No trouble at all, dear boy,' Lord Pennington says blithely, 'I'm sure you're far too busy to waste time telephoning clients all day long.'

Rory grinds his teeth and stretches for a file on his desk which is, I note, strewn with sob story letters from 'Venice in Peril' and 'Friends of Highgate Cemetery' etc. It's hard to believe Rory has become a soft touch for this sort of thing – but then let's be honest, Rory views his life differently now – and this is just as well. These days he has inherited the role of eldest son and all the fun and games that go with it.

'Right well. ITV are looking for a location for *Middlemarch*,' Rory reads from his file. 'A couple from New Jersey will die happy if only they can sleep in a king's bed. Apparently any old king will do . . . the splendidly loaded Mr and Mrs Lieberman from Palm Springs are interested in buying a title and are willing to pay really exciting amounts of money for it . . . and an American TV team are researching some icky Anglophilic piece.'

The Penningtons bow their heads, predictably uncheered by Rory's unique brand of sarcasm. 'Dell computers are looking for somewhere to host a retreat.' There's no attempt to keep the boredom from Rory's voice, 'and finally some gossip magazine needs a ballroom in which to photograph a "quality" soap person.'

He glances up. Until now he's managed to avoid the

ludicrous expression of misery on Lady Pennington's face, which is taut with the effort of not crumpling.

'Look,' Rory relents, 'I know it's a nightmare having strangers in your home but . . .' Rory tries in vain to dredge up the mitigating circumstances that have forced him to commit to this hellish job but finds himself at a loss.

The truth is the business of Stately Locations has not panned out exactly as Rory foresaw. When conceived eight months ago in a reckless bid to help the parents, it made sense. People like the Penningtons desperately needed money if they were to keep their homes. In return interested parties with cash would be able to appreciate the history and beauty of some of England's great houses, not normally open to the public. This notion proved depressingly naïve. The reality is that Stately Locations appeals to rich Americans prepared to pay for their slice of culture, or worse, scabby journalists intent on a scoop. Oh the business is lucrative all right, but it's repellent.

'It's not that,' Lord Pennington interrupts, 'it's . . . well . . . you see . . .' He falls into an uncomfortable silence.

'The thing is . . .' Lady Pennington attempts to clear her personal puissance for the second time.

I hope and pray with every fibre of my body she will not burst into tears. Last time the Penningtons came they brought with them an envelope of receipts. 'Life is so costly,' they said, 'bills so high, capital almost gone.' Tears had flowed, handkerchiefs had been wrung out. When Rory suggested they write down their major expenses it transpired they still had a cook, a chauffeur, a housekeeper and a butler.

When he instructed them to fire three out of four, I thought the paramedics might have to be called.

'We've tried to economize as you suggested. We got rid of the car,' Lord Pennington finally gets it out, 'oh . . . this is all so embarrassing,' he hangs his head.

'The thing is,' Lady Pennington looks beseechingly at Rory, 'taxis home have proved *surprisingly* expensive.'

'But Lady Pennington,' Rory is aghast, 'home is over two hundred miles away.'

'Yes, of course it is,' she says, wide eyed, blinking rapidly, 'but you said—'

'When I suggested public transport, I had in mind uh,' he looks at their uncomprehending faces, 'well . . . uh . . . a coach.'

Lord and Lady Pennington could not look more shocked had they just been informed of the second coming of the Lord.

'A coach?' they repeat blankly. It really is a revelation to them that this degree of cost cutting might exist.

'Well, well.' Lord Pennington gets to his feet. 'What a weight off the old shoulders.'

He grips Rory's hand, 'Always feel so much better after these little sessions, don't we, my dear?' He pats his wife clumsily on the shoulder. She, in turn, beams mistily at Rory.

'Lord Pennington, Lady Pennington . . . with great respect,' Rory breaks off, 'look you really must try to understand,' he says wildly, 'this is a locations finding agency, not a bloody counselling service.'

'Absolutely.' Lord Pennington says, 'Quite right, quite

right. Point entirely taken, totally understood.' He steers his wife towards the door. 'Same time next week then?'

Believe me, if I had the power, I'd go down there, take hold of Rory's head and bang it against the wall for him.

maggie

When I got back to my room in the Cadogan Hotel, Jay was lying on the bed. 'Jesus,' he said. 'Do these trolls in congress actually believe the bumper sticker drivel they spout?' He was stretched out on top of the chintzy counterpane, reading the *Wall Street Journal*, glasses on his nose. His hair was flat where he'd been sleeping on it, and he'd been using his old leather briefcase as an extra pillow. His beat-up Nikes had been tossed onto the floor by the armchair. I sat on the bed and grinned at him. There was no point in asking him how he'd broken into my room. Hotels were, after all, his speciality.

Jay was my lover. We'd met at a human rights convention at the Kennedy Centre in Washington. Before I worked at *Newsline*, I spent five years at WKM TV, a small but respected local station up in Maine, where I did time writing, producing then field producing before I finally made correspondent. Anyway, a local counsellor with whom I'd become friendly while researching a story was speaking and had invited me to come along. It was going to be one of those off the chart scary evenings so I don't know how I talked myself into saying yes, let alone turning up. Some people have an irrational fear of spiders and mice, but my own room 101 is filled with people in tuxedos drinking champagne and engaging in small talk.

Even the time I picked up an award for a story I'd worked on I was at the ceremony, crouching in the loo with a cigarette for most of the evening, so when my name was announced I didn't hear it. Coming back into the room I couldn't think why everyone was looking around expectantly and clapping. I was so discombobulated that when I eventually staggered up to the mike I could only admit that I had to pee rather than say I had to smoke. For obvious reasons that night still ranks as both the best and worst of my life.

So when I walked into the Kennedy Centre that evening a couple of years ago, I wished for a moment that I'd come with a guide, someone who would hold my arm and steer me through. But a career in television, its accompanying obsession with stories and weeks spent holed up in editing rooms, not to mention the sheer amount of travel – well being single just seems to go with the territory. It was OK. Manhattan is one of the few places you can live alone and not feel lonely. People are all around you, life is happening everywhere. If you're on a Kansas farm, hours from the nearest town, you might be excused for microwaving puppies or pickling the heads of wayward hitchhikers. Real loneliness mitigates all sorts of crimes. In fact, if you think about it, a crime of passion must be a luxury for a lonely person.

Anyway the point was that I had this *moment* standing alone in that big room. What if I was one of those women who never had long relationships, who never got married or had kids? I'd always loved being attached to nothing and no one – considering it an incredible freedom – but for ever?

The talk began. Courtesy of my friend I'd been placed in the front row so there was to be no escape. After nearly two hours of speeches, I became aware of the man next to me shifting uncomfortably in his seat. The speaker had just shown slides of mass graves in Rwanda and there was a prolonged and uneasy silence in the room during which my fidgety neighbour leaned towards me and produced a partially inflated whoopee cushion. 'Would it be inappropriate do you think,' he whispered, 'if I were to let this off now?' This was so out of left field that by the time I recovered he was up on stage. He introduced himself as Jay Alder. He was valedictorian of the event and admitted, almost sheepishly, that he had worked for Doctors without Borders for twenty years. He then proceeded to speak for forty minutes without notes and I was totally mesmerized.

By the time I'd come out of my trance the evening had descended into the kind of social maelstrom that leaves me stranded. I stood in its hub, conversation and laughter washing over me, and clutched the program of speakers I'd found on my seat. Jay's picture was on the back. He had thick grey hair and looks that were strong, rather than handsome. He'd drawn himself a Biro goatee and scribbled the caption 'In need of major refurbishment'. I felt my face heating up. It was as though he was already asking me to move in.

He appeared at my elbow. 'Do you know what you look like standing there?'

'What?' I accepted the glass of red wine he was holding out.

'Like an alien who's landed on earth and only just discovered they don't know how to breathe oxygen.'

He was staying at the Elliot Hotel. It was late by the time we got there. The restaurant was virtually empty. My shoes were pinching. My shift kept shifting.

He said, 'You don't look all that comfortable.'

I told him I thought I might be a freak of nature.

'How so?'

'Because when I'm dressed up as a butterfly, all I want to do is turn back into a caterpillar.'

He laughed.

'Besides . . . I borrowed this dress and I hate it.'

'There's a simple solution to every problem,' he said and nodded to the waiter for the check.

Later Jay said, 'Of course this would be an entirely inappropriate relationship.'

I was already having inappropriate thoughts about the word relationship so I didn't answer.

'Although I realize a man of my age must be almost irresistible for you.'

Lying in the darkness I couldn't see his face but I heard the irony in his voice.

'OK, so just how old are you?'

'Old enough to know better,' he said.

'What do you suggest then?'

He lit a cigarette. 'Maybe I can adopt you.'

The next morning, packing to leave, he said he would try to call, but it might be difficult.

'Sure,' I said lightly.

'It won't be for the usual reasons.'

Round up the usual suspects, I nearly said.

I assumed he couldn't call me because he was married. When I discovered he wasn't, I didn't feel relieved. Instead I was shocked to discover I hadn't felt guilty in the first place. I soon understood why a relationship would be impossible. His life was crazy, genuinely crazy, his world unrecognizable. Half his time was spent bearing witness to some of the world's most atrocious crimes, the other half, to keep a semblance of normality, he had to force himself to pretend those crimes weren't happening. Whenever I saw him, I wondered at the huge effort required to move seamlessly from one reality to the other.

Soon after I got back from Washington, I found an aeroplane sick bag amongst my post. On the back was a stamp from Nicaragua and on the front he'd scribbled, 'Can I get you out of my mind? The hell I can, but I'm working on it.'

Please don't work too hard, I thought.

daniel

Look I don't want you thinking that Rory is just some pastiche of a Hooray with a loser's job, because he's not. Stately Locations is not his first choice of career, truth be told it's not his choice of career at all. What he was by trade, and continues to be whenever he gets the chance, is an archaeologist, and a pretty good one at that. An obsession with age, which began in childhood with counting rings in trees, teeth in horses, layers in sedimentary rock and even the dry wrinkles on our mother's elbow, grew into a passion for dead things, restoration and travel, but despite being consultant to the V&A, it's a job that has never paid much, and certainly not enough for his current needs. So when the first telephone call Alison puts through to his office this morning is from the museum who want to know whether he'd be prepared to go to Turkey on a three month dig, his inability to accept leaves him even more frustrated than when he arrived.

Frustrated he should not be. Last night, I can report, he spent a night of unadulterated passion with Stella — at least let's qualify this phrase by describing it as a night of reasonable although uninspired sex. Still, this is not to be sniffed at – representing as it does a grand breakthrough for Rory. It would not be an understatement to say that Rory, since the sudden departure of Leona from his life, has been no Tom Jones. There have been precious few pants slung onto the sweaty stage of his libido. Stella is a beautiful, sharp girl who paints and works the London scene with equal ardour though somewhat less equal skill. Unfortunately Stella is also a girl who must take before she can give and I can tell you from personal experience that a sexual encounter with her might be fulfilling for the body but tends to leave the mind emptier than ever. When she asks him, whilst applying toner to her neck, whether he thinks she looks older in the harsh light of day, you can almost see him mentally scarpering off in the opposite direction.

By the time Rory has extricated himself from Stella's morning neurotics and made his way through the rain to Connelly Mews it's ten o'clock and a parking ticket is waiting on the windscreen of his Rover. As he peels it off, a garbage truck rolling through a puddle sprays him with the dregs of London's sewage. Now, hanging up the phone on the V&A, he sits at his desk and in general thinks evil things of the world.

On the other side of the glass partition Alison looks at him longingly. The more broken he seems, the more she yearns to fix him. Her dreams are feverish, peppered with images of stroking away his pain. She imagines clasping him to her bosom as he cries himself dry, at which point she will lead him to bed, remove his clothing and perform a little gentle oral sex in a further effort to exorcise his demons. In her fantasy he is the innocent who's languished twenty years in jail, the castaway marooned on an inhospitable island, or even the shell-shocked soldier returning from war. Whoever he is, she is there for him because he is, apart from his rotten temper, nearly perfect and she sometimes wonders whether her heart might burst with love.

In the meantime she pours a mug of coffee, spoons in four sugars then securing the morning's post under her arm, scuttles timidly to his office. She speculates whether a knock is appropriate, decides it is, but is not rewarded with an answer. Plucking up courage she turns the handle.

Rory barely looks up. Alison places the coffee on his desk and finding no further excuse to stay, has little choice but to go. Then luck smiles on her. Her gaze falls on the small pools of water gathering upon the floor.

'Oh,' she says happily, 'you're soaked.' She advances on him fussily.

'No, no,' Rory pushes his chair back and holds up his hands, 'I'm fine.'

'You should take those off you know, you'll catch a cold.'

'Back off, Alison,' Rory gives her a look.

'Or even flu,' Alison quavers.

The look turns to a glare. Rory points at his chin, 'See this?'

Alison creeps a bit closer.

'What is this?'

'A chin?'

'And on the chinny chin chin?'

How she hates him at moments like this. Her verbal artillery is not armed with the necessary warheads to combat such nuclear sarcasm.

'A spot . . . uh no . . . a hair?' She takes a deep breath. 'OK I understand what you're saying. You have stubble, you're not a baby.' She attempts a dignified exit.

'Thank you,' Rory calls after her. 'Thank you for being so, so understanding.' He is in fact behaving exactly like a baby but doesn't care. Alison is maddening. He lobs the mail into the in tray and is in the process of ripping into a brown paper package when the door opens for the second time. Alison is again bearing down on him.

'Give me the trousers,' she says.

He looks at the towel in her hand. The pile has been rubbed bare but he can just make out a pattern of frolicking highland terriers.

'I'm not putting that on.'

'You've only got that girl for the accounting job.'

'I don't care.'

'Your trousers will be dry by then, I'll put them on the radiator.'

'Absolutely not.'

'Someone has to look after you, Rory.' Bravely, Alison stands her ground.

'Oh for Christ's sake,' he explodes.

Alison waits patiently while Rory yanks down his trousers. He snatches the towel from her and wraps it round his waist.

Alison plucks the wet trousers from the floor and turns away triumphantly.

'I have a mother,' Rory shouts after her. 'God knows I don't need another one.'

He reaches for a pair of scissors and stabs at the brown package. Inside are two silver foil containers, one marked 'bread and butter pudding' the other 'cheese and onion pie'. Rory's face lights up. He reads the accompanying note, 'To keep the wolf from the door! Happy Birthday, Love Nanny'.

maggie

Jay was gone by the time I surfaced. I pulled the pillow towards me and groaned. Almost always he had to leave before I did. Almost always I wished he could stay. These trysts left me with nothing more tangible than the imprint of his hands on my skin, his smell on the sheets.

I had never once asked how he managed to track me down so successfully. With anybody else, the assumption that I would always be pleased to see him might have seemed like gross arrogance, but not with Jay.

Before Christmas, Jay had left for East Timor where the previous summer Doctors without Borders had been evicted along with all other humanitarian organizations. He re-established health care facilities for the displaced population before travelling on to Bosnia, where he was now based. London was a lot closer to Sarajevo than New York. Jay was a pretty good ulterior motive for staying in England.

All I wanted to do was drift back to sleep but I'd been in negotiations with Simon Brannigan's aristo 'wide boy' and was supposed to be meeting him at his agency to pick up an itinerary covering the next few weeks. I crawled out of bed and padded into the bathroom, standing under a cold shower to force myself awake. There'd been a time at *Newsline* when we would not have been put up in hotels with marble bathrooms and gold shower fixtures. Those were the days when *Newsline* was struggling and when some of the stories it ran caused advertisers to yank their budgets. A segment Alan once put out about abortion lost him three hundred thousand dollars and it took a long time to prove to advertisers that contentious subject matter delivered viewers. Contentious subject matter was the reason I went to work for *Newsline* in the first place. Jay was right. To hell with the puff piece.

'So how's it going?' he'd asked. We'd been lying on the bed, the television tuned into CNN. The crew had finally showed up that morning and I'd whisked them straight from the airport to the Houses of Parliament where we had an appointment to film Lord Canaver. He was a stately old peer and supposedly an expert on Northern Ireland. He'd agreed to be interviewed when I'd done the original research but the minute we started filming he pulled out just like all the others. I was beginning to panic. I almost didn't care what we got on film as long it was something. We ended up trailing him halfway across London before eventually being turned away at his club.

'Is it because I'm not wearing a jacket?' I asked the porter. OK so I was being facetious. I knew full well White's was a gentleman's club.

The porter gave me a supercilious once-over.

'Madam,' he said, 'Jackets are for potatoes, gentlemen wear coats and ladies are simply not welcome.'

'You got to hand it to these people,' I reached for the water by the bed, 'for dinosaurs, they've lasted pretty well.'

Jay was channel-hopping looking for the same report from a different source. Jay's daily media diet consisted of snacks of NBC, ABC, CNN before embarking on a main course of newspapers, the *New York Times*, *Wall Street Journal* and the *Washington Post*. 'If there's more than one version of the truth, that means there is no truth,' he was fond of saying.

'I'm surprised Alan sent you. *Newsline* is built on reliable typecasting. He must know he's better off keeping you on the front line with an Uzi.'

'Well, I guess I got the sticky end of the lollipop this time.'

'I tell you why you didn't get your Middle East piece.' Jay switched off the television. 'Some advertising focus group had told CBS to tell their executives to tell your boss that a puff piece shot in grand old houses is exactly what's needed to recapture the twenty to thirty demographic.'

Jay's current *bête noire* was America's obsession with demographics – and to be fair he had a point. I recently heard even Barbara Walters say on *20/20* that once you've reached the age of forty-nine it is statistically proven that you use the same toothpaste for the rest of your life.

'I like your White's club story. There's opportunity there.'

'Like what?

'Like, let's see,' he rubbed his fingers around his temples, a habit he had when he was tired, 'there's snobbery, debauchery, Christ, there's even lunacy if you want it. Come on, you said it yourself, this is the English aristocracy we're talking about, a group of people living in ivory towers whose time has come and gone. Just what is their point any more – if any?'

'They're hardly falling over each other to tell me. I'm having problems enough with access as it is.'

'So do a little sleuthing. Ask the right questions, do what you're good at and blow a little smoke up their butts. Give these people enough rope, Maggie, and sooner or later, I guarantee you, they'll hang themselves.'

daniel

'What do you mean you didn't allow them in to any of the main rooms?' Rory asks. 'Surely that's what they were paying to see?' He presses his Biro into the notepad. 'Yes, but you must understand, you *are* doing this for the money, Lady Harcourt . . . no, it's because you *are* broke . . . quite penniless in fact.' From the other end of the line come the unmistakable sounds of his client's impending breakdown. Lady Harcourt is victim of the usual: heavy taxes, bad investments and an astonishing ability to bury her head in the sand. She has inherited a large but severely encumbered estate to which Rory recently organized a visit by a busload of wealthy Japanese widows prone to extravagant tipping. From the sound of it this outing has not been a resounding success.

'No, no, please, Lady Harcourt, I beg you, don't start crying again. Let me have a word with Benj, I'm sure we can sort something out.' He endures a few more tearful burblings before he lucks out with the dialling tone.

'Where the fuck is Benj?' He slams out of the office. 'I *told* him to go with them. Lady Harcourt is *not* used to dealing with, and I quote, "*The Great Unwashed*". She's a die-hard Grade One for crying out loud.'

Grade One and Grade Two in Stately Locations does not imply, as you might be forgiven for thinking, the architectural integrity of clients' houses, but rather, their owners' level of skill in dealing with the General Public – Grade One being the most inept. Rory looks with exasperation at Benj's empty desk, overflowing with coffee-ringed paperwork. 'Why am I insane enough to employ him?'

'Because certain of our clients find me rather reassuring,' Benj says. He has been unwilling, during Rory's tantrum, to move from his position on the floor, primarily because it affords him a great view up Alison's skirt. This has to be one of the better early morning views Benj has enjoyed for quite some time.

He's not in a good way my cousin, Benj. He's been a fuck-up all his life, who wouldn't be with his background. An only child, the product of generations of stifled upbringing, it's not surprising he's lost and feckless; what *is* surprising is that he's lost and feckless with quite so much charm. He's always had a drinking habit, but recently this habit has sloshed over into the more hazardous category of dipsomania. Most evenings he quaffs himself into a stupor then wakes the next morning in a strange place, no memory whatsoever of how he got there. When this happens people tend to rescue him. Like a puppy, they feed him, check the name on his leash and someone, usually Rory, is called to fetch him home.

A few months ago, having driven all the way to Wimbledon Greyhound Track, only to find half a dozen canteen ladies ironing Benj's rumpled jacket and frying him a second egg, Rory decided enough was enough. He bought him a desk, gave him a chair and forced him into some compulsory hard labour.

'Well most of our clients can't find you *at all*,' Rory says, grabbing him under the arms, 'you're about as bloody competent as a bag of snot.'

'Yes, you're quite right, Rory,' Benj allows himself to be heaved into a sitting position. He rummages in his coat, whose pocket bag has finally given way and deposited its contents; a corkscrew, one honeyed date and a paperback edition of *Lord of the Flies* into the lining where they now sit, evenly distributed along the hem like old-fashioned tailors' weights.

'Did he sleep on the floor?' Alison whispers. Not privy to the full depravity of Benj's lifestyle she is aghast at such a notion, 'Has he been *drinking*?'

And for a moment Rory looks helpless.

Had he been drinking? They'd asked him the same question at the morgue. The problem is you can't breathalyse the dead. A post-mortem reveals me to be only twice over the limit but over whose limit pray? Was it not Winston Churchill who said, 'I have always taken more out of alcohol than it has taken out of me.' Considering all the lethal things you get up to when really plastered, to be exiled from life when you're only partially tipsy surely qualifies for the cliché of being hanged for the crimes you don't commit.

Benj has now found the remains of a kebab he'd stowed in his coat last night. He fails to notice the disgusted expression on Rory's face until he's mid-chew.

'Sorry, Rory,' he says meekly, offering it up as though it

were a quarter pound of fine Iranian sevruga. 'Have you had breakfast?'

Rory grabs the kebab from Benj and hurls it to the other side of the studio – at which precise point the outside door to the office opens and a girl walks in. Benj and Alison stand open-mouthed, like a couple of wax dummies. The kebab looks set to hit her but she dodges athletically and it smacks against the wall leaving a grease mark on the paint. Rory recovers first. He looks at the girl by the door, then double takes and stares at her. Despite the messy ponytail, the face scraped clean of make-up, she is unusually pretty for an accountant. 'Yes?' he says, sickeningly pleasant all of a sudden. 'Can I help you?'

He sits her down at the chair in front of his desk. 'So . . .' he begins then stops almost at once, at a loss apparently for an intelligible follow-on. Mechanically his finger goes into the bread and butter pudding. 'You're an American!'

'Uh. Yeah,' she says, eyes busy taking in the damp shirt, the bare legs sprawling loosely under the desk.

'Been in London long?'

'Uh, no. Not that long.'

'Like it so far?'

'Oh sure . . . it's great.'

'It's a good city to live in and . . .' he trails off, seemingly mesmerized by a tiny piece of skin on the left-hand side of her neck, 'But ah . . . you're all legit and everything I assume.'

'I beg your pardon?'

'I mean you've got your papers and everything?'

'Well I've got everything I need right here,' she pulls her knapsack onto her lap, 'if that's what you mean.'

'Good, perfect,' Rory says, 'because we don't want customs and immigration dragging you off your first day do we?'

'Uh . . .' she narrows her eyes questioningly, 'no . . . not really.' There's a long pause. Her ponytail has worked its way loose. She sweeps her hair into a knot and secures it with the elastic. 'The thing is,' she says carefully, as though weighing up the possibility that she's dealing with the village idiot, 'I'll be pretty much ready to get going in the next few days. So I was wondering, really, well . . . is everything under control, I mean . . . are you organized?'

'Organized?' Rory queries. 'Well, no, not really. In fact I would have to say, truthfully . . . not at all.' He leans over the desk, 'You see if we were organized chances are we wouldn't really need you now would we?'

She's openly staring at him now, clearly thinking that her original assessment was correct – he *is* a little simple . . . then suddenly she twigs.

'You have absolutely no idea why I'm here do you?'

'I . . .' Rory is completely thrown. 'Of course I do.' but he's looking at the wide forehead, at those strange eyes, brown, even hazel in the light and almost slanted really and he's thinking, *Forget no work papers, forget customs, it would be plain distracting to have her around the office.*

The telephone starts ringing. 'They'll get that next door.' Rory shifts uneasily in his chair

They don't.

The ringing continues.

Rory straightens a single piece of paper on his desk in

an effort to regain control of the meeting – and still the ringing continues. The girl's eyes slide towards the telephone.

Rory snatches it up. 'Yes.'

'Benj here,' comes the stage whisper. Benj is sitting on the floor in the reception area, his body hunched around the receiver. 'I'm actually still on the premises . . . and I realize of course that you're busy.'

'Yes.' Rory swivels his chair towards the wall.

'I was just wondering whether now would be a good time to tell you that—'

'Yes.' From the corner of his eye Rory watches the girl as she wanders over to the bookshelf and begins inspecting the spines of his archaeological books.

'Those uh . . . Americans are coming for their itinerary today as opposed to uh . . . tomorrow.' Benj clears his throat. 'As I might have perhaps originally led you to believe.'

'I see, how very helpful of you, thank you so very much.' Fuming, Rory places the receiver down. He tips his chair back and gropes for a package in the in tray on the ledge behind him. 'Maggie Munroe.' He reads off the label. The girl turns from the bookcase. She's wearing khaki combat trousers and a standard white T-shirt. Up until this point Rory has been oblivious to his own rather more eccentric form of dress. Grimly he tightens the towel around his waist. 'Robert Jones,' he says, putting out a hand, 'well, Rory most people call me. Maybe we'd better start again.'

'Fine by me,' she shakes it. Then things get a little awkward. He has of course meant to let go of her hand in the traditional manner but as she sits down he finds he's still holding on to it — moreover for a short moment it looks like it's all he can do not to clamber over the desk and sink his teeth into her neck. In the nick of time he pulls himself together.

'Right then,' he gives his head a little shake, 'you're with *Newsline*, and you're here to do a piece about the aristocracy for which you have given us . . . ah yes,' his eyes scan the paperwork, 'the usual brief — pomp, circumstance, some grand interiors and a duke or two.'

'You seem a little surprised.'

'Let's just say you weren't exactly who, or rather what, I was expecting.'

'Really,' she smiles, 'what were you expecting?'

Well for this not to be batted back at him for a start. He is now confused. Is she being direct, or is she flirting? He's played this game before of course, it's just that he's forgotten the rules. 'As a matter of fact,' he says, 'you're a great deal older than I was expecting and frankly a lot uglier.'

There's a flash of a grin, but so quick he can't be sure. 'How disappointing for you.'

She crosses her legs.

'Disappointment has become something of a hazard in this job.'

'In that case should we maybe dispense with the . . . uh . . . well . . . whatever, and get down to business?' She pulls a black file from her knapsack.

'Fine by me,' Rory shuffles through the paperwork in his hand. 'I've done a bit of work on the list you sent in and so far, of the people you requested, the Roxmeres have turned us down.'

'Pity.' She draws a line through their name.

'Balmoral is a little unlikely, as you might have guessed. Blenheim's a definite no.' He looks up, 'Where on earth did you get this list from?'

'Why. What's wrong with it?'

'You don't think you set your expectations just a little high?'

'I was told you could get a foot through the door.'

'Well, yes, some doors and it depends whose foot. Most of these people would rather have red hot needles poked in their eyes than be filmed.'

'Maybe so . . . but we have twenty million viewers and that kind of advertising you can't buy.'

'Hmm.' He looks at her closely, 'OK, well Hartingdon is actually not on our books, but I've called them – they might be interested.'

'Wait a minute, you missed one.' She frowns. 'Page four?'

'Hartingdon is page four.'

'Bevan is my page four.' She turns the papers to show him a photocopy of a newspaper article. A couple standing on the steps of an imposing eighteenth-century house. 'The Earl of Bevan? The queen's cousin?'

Before Rory is forced to respond, Benj provides a handy diversion by pushing through the door with a large tray. He's lost weight, Benj has. When he walks his trousers flap against his bony shins as if they're hanging on a washing line.

'Morning,' he says cheerfully. 'Coffee?' He positions a cup in front of Rory and a mug in front of the girl. 'One espresso and one Americano.' He utters Americano with great flourish, as if he were announcing the name of a Broadway musical. 'Benjamin,' he introduces himself.

'Maggie,' she says. 'Hi.'

Benj perches on the edge of the desk. 'Do carry on,' he says graciously, wrapping his grandfather's checked overcoat around him. Like most drunks, Benj is permanently cold.

'So, Bevan . . . cousin of the queen,' The girl turns back to Rory, 'famously beautiful house.'

'Er, right, Bevan,' Rory interrupts, 'actually Bevan is not a possibility because the house is,' he pauses, 'well as a matter of fact the house is—'

'Closed,' Benj says.

'Closed . . . right,' Rory repeats gratefully. 'Exactly. Thank you. The house is closed.'

'Couldn't we set something up with the Earl? From what I hear, he's some character.'

'Some character . . . Is that what they say?' he mutters.

'Yes, what do you reckon? Can you fix something up?'

'No.'

She blinks at him.

'The fact is,' Rory casts around, 'he's not . . . look the Earl is not—'

'There,' Benj says.

She looks from one to the other.

'The Earl's not there,' Rory repeats slowly, 'because he and his wife have gone—'

'Mad,' Benj says simply.

'What?' the girl says. 'Both of them?'

Rory glares at Benj.

'Both of them,' Benj ignores him. 'Mad as baboons.' He

hugs his arms round himself as if in a strait jacket and makes a gormless face.

Maggie Munroe starts packing away her things. 'Look,' she says, exasperation creeping into her voice, 'I don't have a lot of it, but you guys clearly need more time.'

'I'm sorry.' Rory shovels the last of the bread and butter pudding into his mouth and follows her through to the main office. 'The truth is one or two people *have* let me down recently.' He sends a draconian look back at Benj before wrenching open the door. 'But I'll deliver everything to you tomorrow. I promise.'

Outside the rain has stopped. A tiny ray of sun shines up the wet tops of the buildings. 'To your hotel,' he adds. His feet are turning blue on the wet pavement. 'Deal?'

But the girl is distracted by something. 'Jesus,' she says, apparently revolted, 'I wouldn't want your neighbours.' Rory inclines his head. Suspended by the neck, two dead birds are spinning slowly at the end of a rope attached to the door frame of the house next door. This, as it happens, is the other half of the mews building, where Rory lives. The pigeons, shot at the weekend, have been hanging for a couple of days and Rory wonders whether they are ready for plucking.

'January's a dismal month,' he suggests. 'Perhaps they were depressed.'

'Excuse me?'

'Look.' Rory drops the empty foil container in the bin. 'I'm truly sorry for the delay, I hope we don't seem too unprofessional.'

'Well,' the girl considers him, 'you didn't know I was coming, you haven't got my itinerary, you're wearing a skirt printed with,' she peers closer, 'some kind of rodent, and you've been eating something I wouldn't allow in my apartment, let alone my stomach. I can't imagine why I might have that impression.' Then she smiles prettily and sashays off leaving Rory staring after her, clutching his damp towel, looking not unlike a disgraced Roman legionnaire stripped of his shield.

Benj sits at his desk eating stem ginger.

'Fat lot of help you were,' Rory says, swiping the jar from him and digging out a chunk.

'I thought we didn't do "fly on the wall",' Benj says.

'We do this time.' Rory licks his dripping fingers then retrieves his trousers from the radiator.

'Why?'

'Rich flies.'

'How much?'

'Plenty much.' Rory rubs his thumb and forefinger together.

'Goodee.' Benj screws the lid back on the jar. 'In that case what's your problem with Bevan? Why can't they be normal clients like any others?'

'Because, as you so subtly put it earlier, they're not really very normal are they?'

'So,' Benj says, 'none of our clients are normal.' He leaves the ringing telephone for Alison. 'Presumably you've checked out the luscious Miss Munroe, and it's not like they couldn't do with the cash?'

Alison murmurs something then puts her hand over the receiver. 'Rory?' she says tentatively.

'You're actually suggesting putting them in front of a camera,' Rory says.

'Why not?'

'You don't think that might be just a tiny bit foolish?'

'Rory?' Alison tries again.

'What you have to understand, Rory, is that the kind of Americans we deal with love the aristocracy,' Benj says. 'They can't help themselves, it's a sort of compulsion to be impressed by breeding and culture, I mean the word "lord" is so dazzling to them they can't see the woods for the trees as it were. If I were you, I'd take any money you can get for Bevan.'

'Rory,' Alison interrupts timidly.

'What?' he snaps and takes the receiver she's holding out to him.

'You've always been a little over-sensitive about Bevan,' Benj continues oblivious to the darkening look on his cousin's face.

'After all, how embarrassing could it be?'

The definition of a waste of time must surely be getting people repeatedly out of trouble. As Rory noses the Rover onto the dual carriageway he feels like he's being regularly screwed out of time and energy. The police hadn't been specific on the phone but they didn't need to be. Their tone was familiar enough.

There isn't much traffic on the M1 and he finds himself close to the exit for Stockton on Tees roughly three hours later. A flashing sign over the bridge announces the reduction of the speed limit to 20 miles an hour. Cars have slowed to a crawl. Rory's thoughts turn instead to the girl. OK so she might have been a witch but she'd had a smile that serious face hadn't prepared him for. When she'd grinned it had been wide and wicked, like someone had just told her an unbelievably dirty joke. Then he rounds the bend and all thoughts of her disappear. A line of bollards cordon off the slow lane in which, to Rory's growing apprehension, he sees three cars welded together in a mess of disfigured metal. Angry drivers stand beside the vehicles, gesticulating furiously to policemen who, in turn, are taking notes. Ahead, an RAC truck turns through the gap in the bollards. Rory follows suit. A policemen shoves his hand in front of the windscreen. Rory gives his name and the name of the detective he spoke to earlier. The bollards are moved aside and a quarter of a mile further on Rory parks the Rover next to a service truck. Slamming the door shut, he notices that the bank to his left has been torn up, the bushes on the top flattened to reveal a ploughed field where a dozen uniformed men from the Motorway Services Department are milling around. Two more policemen stand on the edge of the hard shoulder, charting their progress and barking unintelligibly into walkie-talkies.

'So what ploughed? Don't know which crop. Mud with weeds looks like. Well stand by. Who? Oh he's here, is he? Where?'

'Excuse me?' Rory says.

'Got him. Yes. Now.' The policeman turns to face him. 'You're the gentleman my superior spoke to earlier?'

Rory nods.

'I see,' the policeman says. His colleague stares out over

the field across which the MSD are now tramping, arms linked like Morris dancers.

'Let me see if I have this correct, sir,' the first policeman says. 'This *thing* that has caused a multiple pile up on the motorway – this *creature* that has wasted four hours of police time, not to mention head-butted two members of the emergency services, belongs to your *clients* and is moreover being kept in their grounds for its *milk*?'

'Well yes,' Rory concedes, 'although not so much milk apparently, more . . . er . . .' he breaks off. The men in the field have started running. Rory and the policemen stare mesmerized as the large shaggy head of an American buffalo careers into view over the ridge. Panicked, the men split as the creature gallops through their ranks and charges towards the mangled hedge. Its pursuers, abandoning all attempts to maintain their line, resort to chasing after it in ragged chaos.

'As I was saying, not so much milk,' Rory says and does some brutal coughing. 'Cheese. Mozzarella cheese to be more accurate.' He can already visualize the headlines. *Saintly widowed mother mauled by buffalo, Siamese twins brain damaged by single kick. Handicapped busload of refugees . . .* Christ. He does a quick spot check. No bodies, no ambulances, and so far, thank the Lord, no press. Damage by the creature should be covered by Bevan's third party insurance, in the unlikely event of it being paid up to date.

The second policeman is looking sceptical. 'Is mozzarella cheese not traditionally made from the milk of the *water buffalo* rather than the American buffalo, sir?'

Rory digests this. Quite honestly he has never considered

whether mozzarella came from an American buffalo, a giraffe or was grown on trees.

'I'm sure that is technically correct, yes,' he says carefully. He looks into the faces of the two men and gives up.

'The thing is . . . it's actually rather hard to explain.' The expression on both policemen's' faces remains politely enquiring. 'My clients, themselves, are also . . . a little hard to explain.'

'And your *clients* would be, sir?' The second policeman who we shall now refer to as PC Fuckface, gazes at Rory with a faux deferentialism that makes Rory want to punch him in the kidneys.

'Alistair and Audrey Bevan,' Rory says. Thinking that by not giving their full name there is a chance, a tiny, insignificant, one-in-a-million chance that these two bastard pigs won't inform the press. A chance that next week will not have to be spent fending off journalists, that he will not tomorrow read the dread headlines in the *Sun*, but a chance that promptly dies a death with the knowing looks the police are busy exchanging. The first policeman carefully puts his pencil and notebook away. PC Fuckface itches a leg with his baton. 'That would be the Earl and Countess of Bevan, would it, sir?'

Rory is impotently furious at the large bold font of 'sir', but he's again diverted by the noise of thundering hooves. The buffalo, looking more pleased with itself than it has any right to, appears over the hedge. The policemen take a step back. The creature gazes down as if contemplating the wisdom of such a long jump – but it's a pause too long. There's a crack. The buffalo looks round in mild surprise and more than a little reproach at the emergency services, whose ranks have now swelled to twenty men, one of whom is hastily reloading his stun gun.

'As I was saying, sir,' says PC Fuckface. 'If the Earl and Countess are unable to keep their . . . er . . . little business ventures under control, they are very likely, next time, to find themselves behind bars.'

There's a screech of tyres as two vans side swerve the bollards. The press have arrived. Rory watches with loathing as men jump out trailing wires, cabling and a video camera which they point at the bank with feverish excitement. And now we can see why. A late-middle-aged lady in gumboots and tweed skirt has appeared on the scene. Positioning herself between the stun gun and the buffalo she calmly slips a leash over its head then leads the newly docile creature off over the ploughed fields. Rory turns back to the police. 'Do me a favour,' he says wearily, 'why don't you just arrest them now.'

maggie

When I was born the doctor's big joke was to tell my parents that I looked like a savage. My eyes were black, my face purple. Oh yes, the midwife had agreed, I'd come out whooping and hollering, all but carrying a tomahawk. The midwives were prone to laughing at the doctor's jokes because they thought he was pretty cute. My parents just thought he was a bigot. My colouring came as no surprise to them. My mother's great grandmother was Native American, a Kiowa who married a farmer from Oklahoma and with my sticking out cheekbones and black hair, I had obviously inherited her blood. As a child I loved to show off about my maternal ancestors, less interested in my father's more pedestrian Irish roots. When everyone else was hooked on Eloise and Stuart Little, my mother was busy reading me *Bury My Heart at Wounded Knee*. At school I argued the case for the Indians like the whole of their race depended on me.

I guess I should explain. As a child I was subjected to a degree of political conditioning. If I told you I had seedless grapes snatched from my hands because exploited Mexicans had been forced to pick them you might get the picture.

No weekend was complete without a protest outside City Hall and I went to my first anti-Vietnam march on Dad's shoulders, a sort of variation on a take-your-daughter-to-work day. Our photograph ended up in the *New York Post*. The next afternoon when a friend came over to play she asked me what a draft-dodging hippy was. My mother was incensed and quoted from Art Buchwald's column in the *Washington Post*. 'Do you realize,' she said, 'that with the amount of money required to kill each Vietcong, you could fly him first class to America, buy him a Cadillac, a membership to the most expensive country club in Connect-icut – you could turn him into a bona fide capitalist and it would still be cheaper.' OK so that may not be entirely accurate paraphrasing, but I was only four years old at the time.

'Doesn't matter what you do with your life,' Mom finished up, 'so long as you make a difference.'

I was thinking about this as I walked into the Cadogan Hotel following my appointment at the locations agency. The truth was I was pretty pissed. I stood on the squared-stone floor of the lobby looking around for Wolf and Dwight, watching the receptionists behind the front desk swipe credit cards and deal with enquiries. It was a nice hotel, friendly and welcoming with heavy curtains and deep fabric covered chairs. The clientele were mostly tourists, American from the look of them, sixty/seventy-year-old ladies holding Burberry umbrellas and booklets of theatre reviews, their short grey hair under baseball caps. It was all very white and polite, all very *comfortable*. I didn't want com-fortable. I wanted to chase stories that meant something, it was like Jay said – I *was* happy in the trenches with my Uzi. Instead I'd been sent to cover a goddamn tea party.

Dwight and Wolf weren't in the lobby, or the breakfast room. When I rapped against their door upstairs, I heard the sound of joint snoring and felt better. I knew every peak and trough of that particular concerto. Dwight and Wolf were my crew, my crack team. I'd been on assignment with them both many times and Wolf in particular had become a real friend. We first met while I was working on the film for my degree. Political corruption was the subject of choice and it was, as I bored anyone foolish enough to listen, going to be so lid-blowing that American politics would reform itself overnight. Somehow I'd been granted permission to follow a New York senator with a dubious reputation, filming him going about his business, fly on the wall style. After two days trailing him from the Oak Bar to the Rackets Club to the Plaza, he finally had to attend some trifling matter of government in his office but this meeting had only just begun when the building was stormed by a ABC news team headed up by the infamous Philip Grigson. Grigson was a reporter I'd always admired but he turned out to be a real asshole, ordering both his crew and me around in an overloud voice. Some story had obviously broken but whatever it turned out to be, I was as determined to get it as he was. Things soon got ugly. Philip kept shoving huge furry microphones into my shot, trying to queer my pitch. I put enormous radio mikes on everybody in the room claiming them as mine. It was pretty academic because as soon as the senator's press aide arrived the whole lot of us were thrown out, but it was my wire that was pinned to the senator's righteous bosom and I prayed he'd fall for the oldest trick in the book, forget he was miked up.

And hallelujah he did.

Philip, his crew, my 'sound recordist', a friend from college and I were all hanging around outside the office. I was trying to act cool, my lens pointed carelessly at the floor, because as long as I was getting sound, and I was – it didn't matter what I had on film. I could run it over footage of a duck marrying a Great Dane in a Mormon ceremony if that's what it took, but Philip's enormous cameraman, taking up most of the bench next to me noticed my red record button was lit up. 'Hey,' he said accusingly.

Philip stopped pacing the corridor and looked up suspiciously. My heart was in my mouth. The senator was being accused of a gross misuse of funds, but if this giant exposed me, I would definitely be thrown out of the building. The cameraman looked at Philip, then back to me. 'Your lens could do with a polish,' he said and passed me a cloth which I used to cover the record button just as Philip walked over.

It was his voice that really made me notice him. Wolf has a beautiful voice, like oil running over pebbles. I don't know what his parents were thinking calling him Wolf, he should be named Bear. Even with the curve at the top of his back, the cameraman's permanent stoop, he's six foot three and broad with it. He doesn't walk so much as *lumber*.

Later that week, I bought him a coffee. He told me he disliked Philip intensely but was too lazy or, I thought privately, too stoned to do anything about it. When I went to work for *Newsline*, I tracked him down.

The noise inside the crew's bedroom reached a crescendo. Wolf might have a beautiful voice, but he had a real ugly snore. I decided to leave the boys to sleep, they were jet lagged and besides, now we had an extra day in hand. The door opened opposite and a breakfast trolley was pushed out. I was just snitching a piece of leftover toast when it opened again and this time a man in a towelling robe deposited a handful of eggy Kleenex onto the dirty plates.

'Morning,' I said, embarrassed to be caught.

The man sighed deeply, dug into the pocket of his robe and stretched across the trolley.

'Oh.' I looked down at the couple of pound coins in my hand. 'Thanks a lot.' As he shut the door hurriedly, I looked down at my T-shirt and army trousers. If I was going to infiltrate the upper classes, I really had to get myself a more subtle uniform.

daniel

If you were fortunate enough to be given a helicopter tour of some of England's more green and pleasant lands, chances are you'd be impressed by the approach to the Bevan Estate. Flying deep into the county of Yorkshire you eventually dip into a valley whose stone- and bracken-covered hills mark the boundary of the grounds. Descending over woods and parklands you can follow the curves of the river until you eventually spot the house, built in the seventeenth century from stone quarried locally. With its annexes, wings and turrets, you might suppose you were about to land on one of England's statelier homes run by an immense hierarchy of staff. Circling the north-east side of the house you might also imagine that one of the more eccentric members of the family, perhaps nursing a passion for hybrid architecture, had whimsically added a folly of darker stone – or was it some kind of unusual walled garden? By now you might conceivably be confused by the morass of greenery in the centre of this folly, and as you draw in closer you might question why much of its stonework seems to be missing, why corners don't meet in the traditional manner and why height levels are so worryingly haphazard.

Possibly it would have struck you by now that something was terribly wrong. What you've been admiring is not a folly at all, but an integral part of the house, the east wing. Except its roof has caved in, while its smoke-blackened walls have crumbled and pigeons, constantly circling its perimeter, spend their days depositing guano on anything that remains between them and the ground. In short the place is a ruin.

Rory, however, approaches Bevan via the more conventional route of its drive. Despite slowing to the sign-posted 5 miles per hour at the pillared entrance, the next couple of miles must be negotiated with extreme caution. Numerous switchbacks are layered with stones so lethal you might be forgiven for thinking they had been hand sharpened to render maximum damage to tyres. Gaping potholes are filled with muddied rainwater and just when you feel it is safe to speed up to a whopping 6 miles an hour your exhaust is nobbled by random sleeping policeman built to discourage local drivers from practising their rally racing skills using Bevan as a short cut from the railway station to the village of Skimpton.

As he draws up to the house Rory notices some recent state-of-the-art repairs. Guttering, eroded to splitting point has been spliced together with twine and wire. An old wooden tennis racquet has been nailed over the drains to catch leaves. Alistair and Audrey Bevan, roused by the noise of wheels on gravel, hurry out. Alistair is a bluff man of seventy-five dressed in corduroys and a checked Vyella shirt which carries the faintest smell of mothballs. Audrey wears her usual uniform of tweedy skirt covered by a sleeveless padded jacket, zipped up over a long sleeved version of the same garment. Alistair is also wearing a padded jacket, but his is new, ordered as a nod to modern times from a farming catalogue to which he subscribes. They are accompanied by a vast grey setter, all tangled hair and elastic strings of saliva, which bounds down the steps in front of them.

'Get down, Lurch,' Rory thunders as the dog makes its leap. Setters are a neurotic breed, attracted to the person who pays them the least attention, so Lurch merely slobbers a little more industriously before throwing himself into a grateful heap on top of Rory's boots.

'Mrs Emery claims Lurch has been worrying the sheep,' Audrey says. 'She had the nerve to ring up and get quite snippy on the phone but Lurch has never been interested in sheep.'

'Besides he was locked in the outside room all day,' Alistair says. 'Bloody woman, must have been somebody else's dog.'

'Or maybe it was somebody else's buffalo,' Rory says.

Alistair takes off his glasses and wipes them on his cardigan. Audrey examines the mud on her gardening gloves.

'Don't you think it might have been sensible,' Rory says, 'after the oyster bed fiasco, following the surprise failure of the stone-polishing business, to run the *Genius of Mozzarella* by me first?'

'We didn't want to bother you, Robert,' Audrey pats his arm, 'You have enough on your plate already,' she adds soothingly.

'Would have all been perfectly fine,' Alistair says, 'it's just that we failed to take one or two little extra expenses into consideration.'

'This stuff came out of its nose,' Audrey explains, 'bright

green, absolutely beastly, we could see he wasn't at all well, poor old thing.'

'Then what with the vet's bills, the general anaesthetic . . .' but Alistair, catching the expression on Rory's face, loses momentum.

'You see, Robert,' Audrey says confidingly, 'buffalo are not really indigenous to the north of England you know.'

Rory feels the familiar quicksand of nonsense sucking at his feet.

'You are aware that mozzarella comes from the water buffalo and not the American buffalo, aren't you?' he says.

This trump card leaves them silenced.

Rory presses his advantage. 'Well what arrangements have you made to get rid of it?'

'Get rid of it?' Alistair says astonished.

'Well yes, surely—'

'Don't be ridiculous, Robert,' Alistair says testily, 'Your mother's grown far too fond of it.'

Alistair and Audrey would do rather well in prison Rory muses as he wanders up the path to the church. There's something about the ingenuous that makes them indestructible. A favourite story about our mother proves this point. Before getting married she'd travelled to Boston to see friends. At the airport she'd taken a taxi as instructed but discovered halfway through the journey that she'd misplaced her purse. The driver unceremoniously abandoned her in *Bonfire of the Vanities* territory – and there she'd stood, a white woman with her sensible shoes, headscarf and neatly strapped luggage, waiting patiently for help to come along

– which it soon did in the form of a purple limousine bursting with Puerto Ricans, flick knives wedged between their teeth . . .

'You los', baby?' they'd drawled. 'You wanna lift?'

'How thoughtful of you,' Audrey said.

She furnished them with her friends' address and the car sped off. History doesn't relate as to the conversation en route, though I've always had this vision of her, in an identical though possibly shorter skirt than today, squashed between the sweaty vests of her rescuers, uttering such gems as, 'You seem like a nice young man,' and 'What do *you* do for a living?'

When the car cruised to a stop in front of a deserted warehouse, Audrey looked out the window and remarked, 'But this is not at all where my friends live.'

'Sowhat, Lady?'

'Well,' she'd said severely, 'They'd be most awfully upset if I were late for dinner.'

The Puerto Ricans were so taken aback by this apparent lack of concern regarding her forthcoming rape and brutal murder that they promptly drove her to the address she'd given and firmly refused a tip.

From time to time Rory strokes Lurch's head as the dog trots by his side. Above their heads, rooks are screaming and cawing, the spiky pods of their nests lodged in the leafless boughs of the sycamores. The sky rumbles with an approaching storm. The path narrows and mud squelches under his feet. It's wet. Again. Grey, wet and warm. Not that I approve of Rory's disinterest in the English country-side but global warming really has seen an end to decent weather. Newspapers are apt to quote statistics about average temperatures remaining the same, but God knows, seasons used to know how to behave themselves. Winters were cold, summers were hot. There were Christmases when the countryside froze. You can't conceive how beautiful Bevan is in the snow. That moment when you turned into the front drive was like stepping through the back of the cupboard into *The Lion, the Witch and the Wardrobe*. The magic kingdom of Bevan, preserved in ice, ignored by road gritters, untouched by the outside world. There are so many memories here, so many of them good. We used to toboggan down this bank off the church walk. We built a launching pad at the top. We'd start screaming, end crashing, wind caught in our throats. God but we were brilliant too. Headfirst, sitting, backwards, kneeling, crouching, we'd steer straight for obstacles, the bigger the better. Rory blinking back tears of fear because we were the Bevan Boys Daring Double Act. The fearless undisputed champions of the sled. And then there were the summers – when the air was thick and hazy with the smell of roses and burnt hay, when the heat drugged you, when you could only just muster enough energy to collapse on the lawn or lie in the boat listening to the water slap against the bottom.

As he walks alongside the wall, Rory touches the velvety edges of emerald moss on the stone. I will him to peel it off, to remember how it feels – as satisfactory as a scab off the knee – Christ, how can Rory not think about these things? If he were to stop right now, if he were to just *try*, he might hear the drone of the hornets, he would remember clipping sweet peas into a basket, remember licking their sticky dew off his finger. He would remember crawling under the strawberry net in the kitchen garden – but Rory doesn't stop and he doesn't remember. Rory doesn't do nostalgia at the moment.

The avenue before the church was once a topiary of yews planted by my great-grandmother's gardener, Bindey. Bindey was a hunchback and famous locally for his ability to hold the largest number of clothes pegs in one hand, winning first prize at the village fête for thirty years running. He was a splendid character, almost a distillation of old England really and he used to fuss over the yew trees as if they were the batch of unruly children he'd failed to conceive with his wife. Mrs Bindey worked in the house and Bindey was inconsolable when she died. Up until that point the bushes had always been the best-tended things on the Estate. Now they've been left to grow into bouffant affros, but when we were children they were clipped into precise shapes, peacocks and pheasants, hollowed out in the centre, some large enough to hide in.

'Seen the boys, Bindey?' Great-Grandpa would ask.

'No sir,' Bindey would lean on his shears, 'given you the slip have they?'

My great-grandfather was a passionate gardener. He spent all his time in the potting sheds and greenhouses. He walked the grounds with his stick every morning checking for frost damage. A gentle man, he reserved most of his aggression for the deer that ate the bark off his trees. He smoked sixty cigarettes a day and nicotine had streaked the skin yellow on his fingers. When he talked, he had to interrupt himself to cough. He refused to accept that there was any connection between his cough and the amount he smoked: 'It's a little cold I've picked up,' he would say, or 'The pollen count is high.' One winter, he became very bad. The doctor told him he had a clear choice – give up smoking or die of emphysema. Great-Grandpa listened quietly. As soon as the doctor left, he went to the gardening shed and smoked ten cigarettes in a row. Two years later he was dead.

Rory stands now before the headstone in the churchyard. The flowers from his previous visit have drooped tiredly over the edge of the jar as if, having realized the impossibility of being decorative any longer, they might as well take a well-earned rest. I've been wondering lately about this custom of leaving flowers on graves. Why not something more interesting? Photographs or favourite foods for instance. An apple and game pie from Paxton & Whitfield, or even potted shrimps would go down nicely but Rory has picked me some early crocuses. He props them up in the jar and whistles for Lurch who is conscientiously digging up Mrs Bindey a few rows away.

On his way back to the house he meets Alistair trudging up the hill, his walking stick making soft plops in the mud. Since Rory's arrival he's drunk a half bottle of whisky but this does not make him completely unaware of his son's disapproval. Awkward in each other's company neither speak till they reach the car.

'Are you coming down this weekend?' Alistair asks.

'Probably not, Pa.'

'Right then.' Alistair is a little disappointed, but at the same time, a little relieved.

Rory's got the engine started and is crunching gears into reverse when there's a knock on the window. Alistair's face looms comically close.

Rory rolls down the window. 'Quick,' Alistair says, 'before your mother sees.'

From behind his back he hoists an item which at first glance resembles a tree stump but on closer inspection turns out to be the waste paper basket from the South bedroom. It's about a foot and a half high and made from a scooped-out rhinoceros hoof. There are no words to describe the depths of its hideousness.

Alistair glances anxiously towards the drive. 'Take it up to London, could you?'

'Dad, keep it, it's worthless.'

'You know, I do believe that old urn has got a crack.' Alistair squints towards the pillar by the back drive where the urn has sat, cracked, since 1971.

'Dad, honestly, you might as well put it back.' Rory doesn't begrudge Alistair's selective deafness, believing it to be one of the great perks of old age.

'Nonsense,' Alistair says stoutly. 'If Sotheby's got a couple of hundred for that moose's head this'll definitely be worth a little something.'

Rory knows this is a fight he will not win. He hears Lurch barking. Audrey, on the home-stretch of her afternoon walk, will appear any minute around the bend in the drive.

Sighing heavily, he pings the lock on the boot.

The pigeons are still swinging from their makeshift gallows when Rory arrives back at Connelly Mews. He unhooks the string and drops the birds into the rhino bin before humping them up the stairs and into his flat where he casts helplessly around for an available corner.

In the home decorating style favoured by our mother, things do not get thrown away. The verbs *to jettison* or *to discard* are against her religion, which decrees that objects, irrespective of size and state of repair were invented to be accumulated. In fact it would be fair to say that Audrey does not officially acknowledge the concept of mess.

Take the kitchen worktop at Bevan. At any given time you might find the following: a selection of chipped porcelain items, a damp sock, a dozen virtually empty jars with accompanying fungus of marmalade and chutney beneath their lids, one dead animal. Amongst these larger objects nestle old coins, (shillings, farthings) matchboxes, a nob of rancid butter, tiny exotic-looking shells, shreds of paper with illegible, though vital telephone numbers and inky pen tops – all of which are welded together by that special sticky paste made from dust, cooking grease and decomposed flies found exclusively in large English houses left uncleaned for twenty years. On top of all of this there would be the normal debris from daily food preparation. It's a wonder we didn't both die of E-coli as children.

As a result, Rory has always kept his flat white and gloriously possession free – at least until now. Lately ghosts from Bevan have begun taking up residence here. These days there's scarcely room to move amongst the plaster busts, stuffed birds and varying Dutch watercolours. On the table by the sofa sits the vase Rory sold for three hundred pounds and in the corner stands the card table that a private dealer from Cheltenham bought only last month. Those moose antlers, hanging on the wall and currently making themselves useful as a tie rack, recently fetched four hundred pounds at Sotheby's. Except they didn't, any of them. It's a game Rory and Alistair play. A humiliation-free method of inter-family money laundering. See, this is what happens with our parents, you nail your foot to the ground, then spend the next twenty years trying to gnaw it off again.

Rory gives the bin a considered kick. It's not beyond the realms of possibility that the chief of the Zulus once urinated in it during a full moon and it's an irreplaceable African artefact that by rights should be attracting millions of visitors in the British Museum. 'Who would have believed it,' Rory will be able to say to the newspapers, 'and to think, we just kept rubbish in it.'

maggie

'Now let's see,' Dwight said, 'An earl is more important than a marquess, but a lord is more important than a sir . . .'

It was early evening and we were propping up the hotel bar having a drink. Dwight, my sound recordist, was a spry little man from Brooklyn prone to name dropping, preppy clothes and the occasional aggressive outburst. He was reading the copy of *Burke's Peerage* I'd purloined from Massey and acting like he was thrilled to be this close to a title, even if it was only on the printed page.

'Look. It's like poker,' I told him.

'How's that?' The barman, with whom I'd been flirting madly, was one of those Australian boys with a cherubic smile who was probably happier tossing sheep than shaking cocktails. He poured another shot of Jack Daniel's into my glass.

'Well see, a marchioness beats a viscount, which beats a sir. A full house of lords over earls is better than a couple of honourables – providing of course they aren't a pair of queens. A straight flush is better than a hot flush, but a royal flush,' I downed the bourbon in one, 'a royal flush scoops the board every time.'

The barman shook his head admiringly. 'I've never been able to get the hang of those.'

'Oh it's one of the few skills I'm really proud of.'

'Let's not forget baton twirling,' said Wolf. He emptied a bunch of photos out of a brown envelope. 'For you. Arrived Fed-Ex,' he raised one shaggy eyebrow, 'executive suggestions.'

I flicked through them quickly. English tourist scenes, even including one of the changing of the guard. 'Hmm, I think I might just manage to recognize the queen without a visual aid.' I dropped them into the bin behind the bar.

'Interested in the royal family are you?' The barman slid over a dish of monkey nuts.

'Why?' I asked, 'you friendly with them?'

'If I was, would I be working my hairy arse off in a bar?'

'I don't know. You could be their token peasant friend.'

'Poor Queenie,' the barman said. 'A nice lady with a bum job.'

'Yeah, poor Queenie,' Wolf said. 'Try to think of her as a downtrodden little woman who needs rescuing from her dysfunctional family . . .'

'I'll try,' I grinned, 'but it won't be easy.'

'Bishops, marquesses' younger sons, earls' elder sons, viscounts of England, Scotland then Great Britain . . . this is amazing,' Dwight said. 'It says here, one family can have up to ten different titles . . . ten!'

'Disgraceful, where's the guillotine when you need it.'

I swivelled my stool. It took me a second to realize that the man who'd spoken was Rory from Stately Locations. He looked different. He was dressed for a start. Black pants, grey turtleneck and heavy-soled boots. He had a deep frown line in the middle of his forehead which didn't dissolve when he smiled.

'Would you a like another whisky?' he asked.

'Bourbon? Sure, great, thanks.'

In his office I'd put him around late thirties. But there something really boyish about him. When he moved to the bar stool, I noticed his limbs were so loose they seemed attached to one another by holes and string.

I introduced the crew. 'Wolf, Dwight, this is Rory . . .?'

'Jones,' he said.

The three of them shook hands and I watched Rory Jones, like everybody else who's ever come across Wolf, trying to deconstruct his nationalities feature by feature. Wolf, a Japanese, Jewish American, is positively bizarre looking. Every feature he has is contradicted by another – a long ponytail at the back, a bald forehead at the front, the nose and the heavy skin of his Jewish father but the delicate almond eyes of his mother.

'Drink?' Wolf asked Rory.

'I don't, thanks.'

I was going to be facetious and say – what, never? Then I realized that 'don't', coupled with 'drink' always did mean never.

'So are we all set?' I said instead.

He undid a bulging envelope. 'We're all set. The good news is that the Duke of Roxmere has changed his mind. He's opening his house to the public next spring so this is a good time to get him. Also, if things go well, it will be easier for me to get you in elsewhere.'

'Fantastic.' This was a real scoop.

Researchers at *Newsline* had come up with the following: Roxmere family came from one of the most obscurantist sections of the English nobility. He was a diehard conservative who'd written several papers lamenting the loss of power and prestige of the aristocracy. He believed that the Empire's gravest error was to place political power in the hands of the lower classes. Thinking about Jay's sound bite, he seemed like a great candidate for snobbery.

Rory unpinned the envelope. 'Start with this. Map. Explanation of the house. History of the house. History of the family. Plenty of pomp and circumstance for you at Roxmere, dozens of servants, hundreds of staircases, wonderful pictures and . . . well, anyway, they're expecting us for lunch tomorrow.'

'Us?' I caught Wolf's eye. 'Oh no, there must be some mistake.'

'No mistake,' Rory said cheerfully. 'That's our job, read our brochure. We accompany people.'

'Well,' I said doubtfully, 'we work alone.'

He looked at me carefully. 'I don't think you quite understand. My clients are deeply distrustful of . . . er . . . *journalists*.'

'No problem,' Wolf said. 'Maggie's entirely used to that.'

'Plus the language in these places can be a little . . . oblique.'

'Oh I'm sure I can manage without an interpreter.'

'The point is,' Rory went on, 'it's a lot easier than you might imagine to put your foot in it.'

'So you're suggesting we "*Americans*" should be on best behaviour.' I was kidding, trying to keep things light.

'I'm simply suggesting that these people can require a little subtle *handling*.'

'You have my word. I won't snap my bubblegum between courses.'

His frown line only deepened. 'I think you're missing the point.'

I wasn't missing the point at all. The last thing we needed was somebody breathing over our shoulder.

'You're right,' I said. 'I'm sorry.'

'Fine,' he relaxed.

'Maybe it would be better for both of us if we found someone else to work with.'

I was startled by the flash of real anger behind his eyes. For a moment I thought he was going to tell us to go to hell, but I'd seen his offices; I had no idea what the English paid to film shampoo commercials in manor houses but I imagined it wasn't all that much.

He backed down. I could tell he didn't like it one bit but he covered it well. He secured the envelope with its metal pin. 'I'm sure you'll be fine,' he said. 'Good luck.' He shook hands with Dwight and Wolf. Then he put the envelope on the bar and walked out.

At the door he turned on his heel. 'Just one small word of advice.' The smile was back, lurking behind his eyes and for some reason it made me nervous, 'Be nice to all pets and for God's sake . . . don't be late for meals.'

'You look like you slept in the back of a truck,' Dwight said to me the following morning.

'Uhuh?'

'Want me to drive?'

'No thanks.'

'Because you know, if you're tired I'm very happy to drive.' He peered anxiously at the verge of the road. Dwight is a terrible passenger, always sucking in nervous intakes of breath and ostentatiously folding away side mirrors, but then I'm not much better myself. I'm visually dyslexic, I pretend to like to drive, but the real story is I have the greatest trouble reading maps. Not just maps either, architectural plans, Lego instructions. It's the reason I never did ballet. I always pirouetted anti-clockwise.

'I'm good thanks.' Really though I was tired. Unable to sleep, I'd spent half the night talking to Jay. 'I'm going to send you a screen saver with little computerized sheep leaping fences,' he yawned.

'Yeah right, you can't even work a computer.'

'I'll have one of the young people in my office see to it,' he said loftily.

'Sometimes a person can be tired without even knowing,' Dwight ventured.

I hit the brake. 'Dwight, Jesus, if you feel more comfortable driving, just say so.'

'I would feel more comfortable driving,' he said meekly.

I pulled the van over and we changed places without another word.

'Who would you rather sleep with, Wolf?' asked Dwight, 'Ophrah or Joan Rivers?'

'Joan,' Wolf said, 'Oprah would be too preachy.'

'Hillary Clinton or Cherie Blair?'

'Cherry who?'

Dwight's teeth were small and very stubby and he ran his tongue over them now as he looked at Wolf suspiciously. He had always been confused by Wolf's stir-fry genealogy, figuring it made him frighteningly unpredictable.

'The British prime minister's wife.'

'Is she cute?' Wolf had graduated summa cum laude from Yale with degrees in political studies and socio economics. He knew exactly who Cherie Blair was. Wolf was rarely mean to anyone but he was mean to Dwight, referring to him as Smallboy behind his back.

'No, but Hillary's no peach either.'

'Oh please, she's a babe,' Wolf said. 'What's more she's the First Babe.'

I wound down the window of our rented van. The English countryside smelt of wet tarmac. 'Lunch was what time?'

'One o'clock sharp,' Wolf said.

'Time now?' I turned the map the other way round.

'One o'clock sharp.'

'What!' Dwight exclaimed. A passing signpost read Stourton on the Water.

'Godammit, Maggie. We've been through here. We've been going round in circles.'

For some reason, definitely one other than sartorial, Dwight had chosen to wear a necktie in the style of an English Rake. He tugged distractedly at the jaunty piece of silk as though it were choking him. 'I told you we should have left earlier. I told you.' His baby face scrunched up.

I looked at him apprehensively. The last thing I needed was Dwight going off at the deep end.

When I first worked for *Newsline*, Wolf and I had been researching a story about funding for schools. In a small town in Mississippi we witnessed a peculiar episode. We were in a hardware store buying batteries, standing in the queue behind some guy at the checkout. When he pushed a packet of shoelaces over the counter, the lady with 'Honey' pinned to her bosom said, 'That'll be thirty-nine cents and do you have a Slavens Value card, sir?' whereupon this man began shouting at the top of his lungs, 'You fuck ass overweight nigger scumbag, your fat black face makes me want to PUKE,' before calmly handing over his dollar and strolling out of the store. Wolf and I stared after him. It wasn't so much his behaviour that stunned us but the lack of reaction from everyone else. I mean this was the land of fried catfish and baby alligators, a town where the ghost of the Ku Klux Klan had not entirely been exorcized. Apart from us, and you couldn't really count Wolf, he was the only other white person we'd seen. Honey just shrugged. He was a local she told us. He was sick and couldn't help himself. 'He jest opens that mouth of his,' she said, shaking her head solemnly, 'and out pours all the filth o'the world.'

Turned out he had Tourette's syndrome and Wolf and I figured that in any situation that involved transport, punctuality or paperwork, Dwight displayed minor symptoms of this same disease. Everyone in *Newsline* had a story about him. He was once arrested on landing because he'd kept up a tireless commentary throughout a flight about the plane crashing. Another time he'd been caught hyperventilating by the colour copy machine because he couldn't find his passport. The first assignment I flew with him he'd nearly come to blows with an air stewardess.

'What do you mean the hand baggage allowance is only twelve kilograms,' he'd demanded at check in.

'Civil Aviation Authority tests have shown, sir, that if a bag falls from the overhead locker and it's under twelve kilos, then it's safe.'

'Oh yeah, what's the baggage allowance in premium class then?'

'Fifteen kilos, sir,' said the poor girl, beginning to sweat.

'You're telling me it takes twelve kilos to hurt a man in coach but fifteen kilos to hurt a premium class passenger?' he'd yelled, 'What – they got better quality heads or something?'

He jest opens that mouth o' his and out pours all the filth o' the world. I wanted to apologize to her.

On the plus side, he was one of the best sound recordists in the business and indispensable for paperwork. He had a traffic cop approach to minutiae, in that once he started writing a ticket, he had to finish it. Didn't matter what it was: labelling of films, the spelling of interviewees' names, routes, maps, plane tickets, gas receipts. Dwight was meticulous.

Besides it was my fault. I should have rung Stately Locations for directions, but Rory Jones's parting shot had been issued as a challenge, not friendly advice, and like a moth I was now sizzling on the burning light bulb. Not only were we late for lunch, we were also lost. We'd hit this town a full hour earlier and it wasn't even much of a

town, more like a piece of hived-off countryside criss-
crossed by electricity pylons, gas stations, bypasses, round-
abouts, the design of which all seemed pretty haphazard.
Even the telephone boxes looked like they'd been acciden-
tally dropped from an aircraft and lodged randomly in the
mud. It was thoroughly depressing. A man in a cloth cap
was sitting at the bus stop. He looked like he was prepared
to wait for several years.

'Pardon me,' Dwight quickly wound down his window,
'the quickest way to Bedlington?'

'Well now,' the old man scratched his head, 'it's a good
question. Let me see . . .' the regional accent curling his
tongue made him barely decipherable. 'You go straight on
about a quarter of a mile until you reach the field of corn.
There's a turning just after the field, hidden by a bank on
the right-hand side, mind you don't take it. Rather, take the
fork after Frogsfarm, past the King and Custard, over
the humped-back bridge, sharp right at the scarecrow,
through a small hamlet then . . .'

Fidgeting like a live prawn on a griddle, Dwight ran out
of patience. Muttering profanities, he rolled up the window
and shot off leaving the local staring after us.

Dwight pulled up the van in the next turning.

'You drive, I'll map read,' he said and again we changed
places.

In the back seat, Wolf lit a joint.

An hour later an enormous set of gates flashed by.

'Back, back!' Dwight yelled.

I rammed the gears into reverse, charged through the

gates and there, through the drizzle, was Jane Austen's England. Rich, lush countryside, deer wandering through immaculate parklands, which rolled down soft green banks towards a river. In the distance, a house loomed, terrifyingly grand.

'Whoah,' breathed Wolf. 'Magnificent.'

I stared through the windscreen. I knew houses like this existed but this was something else. It wasn't a house, more like twenty houses built one on top of another.

'Come on,' said Dwight feverishly. 'Come on.'

DANGER. CATTLE GRIDS. DEAD SLOW.

The significance of this sign entered my consciousness way too late. The car hit the grids doing fifty. Dwight's head cracked against the roof, Wolf's arm smashed against my shoulder, but as we hurtled up the other side of the grids I was aware of something else – a wild flash of colour, the sickening thud of a body. I yanked at the handbrake. The van went into a circular skid then came to a halt on the soft verge.

Dwight was swearing, Wolf groaning, I was white with fear. There was blood on the windscreen. I felt faint as the reality sank in. I'd injured, or worse killed, a human being. Possibly even a child. Robotically I reached for the key and cut the engine. My hands trembled as I wrenched open the door. I walked unsteadily round to the front of the car but what I'd hit was not, thank God, a human, but a peacock. A beautiful, magnificently multicoloured peacock.

'Oh, dear God,' I said, flooded with relief.

The peacock lay on the road, tail fanned out defensively, emitting weird sounds from its throat.

'This is really extremely bad karma, Maggie,' Wolf said. He peered at the bird. 'Is it dead?'

'Of course it's not dead.' Dwight rubbed his forehead where a small egg was forming. 'Who do you think's making all that noise.'

'I thought that was Maggie,' Wolf said.

One of the peacock's legs was broken. It used the other to push itself away from us. A dark stain of blood discoloured the green of its feathers and seeped onto the road.

'Poor thing, look,' I knelt down. 'It's in pain, we've got to help it. Dwight, pick it up.'

'Are you kidding?' Dwight said. 'What if it bites? You pick it up.' He peered closer.

'How can it bite? I've practically killed the poor thing.'

'It's got a mean look to it.'

'I'll do it,' Wolf bent down and clumsily gathered the peacock in his arms. Quick as a flash the bird struck.

'Jesus!' Wolf jumped back clutching his mouth. Blood dripped down his chin.

'I know what we're supposed to do,' Dwight said. 'We're supposed to put it out of its misery.'

'Gee, let's give it a Tylenol' Wolf said.

'No, we're supposed to put it down. I read it somewhere. It's the kind thing to do.'

'Are you crazy?' I said. 'You want to *murder* it?' What was the deal with peacocks? Were they wild? Vermin? Good luck, bad omens, family pets? I could only pray this one didn't have a name and a sobbing child attached to it.

'We could wring its neck.' The peacock blinked its eye accusingly at Dwight.

'Great, and what if someone sees us?' I said.

'Who's gonna see us in a place like this?'

Wolf's lip was beginning to swell. He looked around the deserted parklands. 'Sherlock fucking Holmes,' he said sourly, 'that's who.'

We stood at the foot of the steps. From the top, a group of people were making their way down to us. An ancient man in a butler's uniform. Two elderly women, one in a smart floral outfit, the other in trousers and a sweater. A few steps behind them walked a priest.

There are rules in this business. My God they're pretty basic but you need to follow them if you want people to talk to you, because whatever preconceptions you might have of them, you can bet they'll have a worse one of you. So let's be clear: first impressions are paramount.

The group reached us. Like two warring parties on a tentative and possibly doomed peace mission we stood before each other. I had a sudden flash of who we were. We were the enemy. We were the Americans; the miners, ranchers, the soldiers who'd come to encroach upon the native's ground and steal their heritage, we were invading the Roxmeres' privacy and questioning their right to their land. My clothes were spotted with blood, Wolf, with his dishevelled ponytail and swollen lip resembled a demented Sioux tracker, Dwight with his absurd necktie looked like a private from F Troop.

The butler turned and signalled. At the top of the stone steps, silhouetted against the sky, flanks of servants appeared. We were badly outnumbered. Hell, if I'd had a white flag this would have been the time to wave it. The servants swarmed down the steps, formed a circle around the van and began unloading suitcases and equipment.

'What are these people called again?' Wolf muttered.

'Roxmere,' I hissed.

'Title?'

'Leave it to me,' Dwight said, and before I could stop him advanced unctuously on the floral lady, taking her hand and pressing his lips to her liver-spotted skin.

'Profound apologies Your . . . er . . .' he cast around wildly, '. . . your Liege.'

'Oh dear me no.' The floral lady squirmed uncomfortably. She stepped aside. 'This is Her Grace, the Duchess of Roxmere.'

The second lady stared incredulously at the peacock in my arms.

There was little hope for a treaty – only surrender. I held out the peacock. As a peace-offering it was surely ill-conceived.

'It just ran straight out in front of me,' I heard myself saying, 'there was no way I could have stopped in time.'

The Duchess looked from me to the peacock then back again. *Enough of these obsequious and false avowals of friendship.*

'In fact, not that I want to cast the first stone or anything, but I don't think it can have been looking,' I added weakly. Behind me, Wolf groaned as if to say, *Duchess, I am ashamed to have sworn allegiance to these Americans.*

To add to our woes, a grizzled little dog had appeared

from nowhere and began leaping at the terrified peacock in frenzied excitement.

'I feel awful,' I shouted at the Duchess over the chaos. 'I really truly am very sorry.'

I will punish those who have washed their hands in innocent blood said She Who Wears Rubber Boots, or maybe she just said, 'Take care of it would you, Father John,' because I found myself putting the peacock gently into the priest's extended arms, 'but you know,' I babbled, 'with the proper care and assistance – a long period of convalescence, I'm quite sure it will make nothing less than an absolute and complete recovery.'

At which point the priest snapped the bird's neck.

Jesus Christ was not only the Son of God. He was also of a very good family on his mother's side.

— Seventeenth-century French bishop

daniel

Rory parks the Rover on a bay in Irving Street, behind Leicester Square. The parking meter is out of order earning it a good kicking followed by a stream of abuse while Rory scrounges around the car for a pen and scrap of paper to leave a note. By the time he presses the entry buzzer to the Beefsteak club he is steaming with irritation.

He gives his name to the doorman and moments later the Maître d', a large gentleman experiencing no small difficulty fitting into a pair of velvet britches, hurries towards him.

'Good afternoon, sir.'

'Afternoon, George.'

'Thank you for coming, sir,' he says leading Rory through to the club's inner sanctum. Rory neither knows this man well, nor is a member of this establishment, but all staff who work at the Beefsteak club are called George so as not to humiliate the memory-impaired peers who do belong here. That something as archaic as a gentleman's club still exists is anathema to most people including my brother. Personally I like to think of them more as a harmless form of petting zoo where remnants of our species are kept alive by a soothing mixture of familiarity, tradition and stodgy food – and frankly, if a group of old codgers find it comforting to sit around reading *The Field*, boring each other senseless with anecdotes, repeated ad nauseam, better they should do so in a controlled environment.

'He's in here, sir,' George says pushing open a heavy pair of doors, 'But I have to warn you that his father's only just left.' He withdraws discreetly.

Like its occupants, the air in this room belongs to 1920. No amount of spit and polish can exorcize its staleness. Rory passes an old man slumped into an easy chair smoking a cigar and reading the *Racing Post*. On his feet are a pair of velvet slippers embroidered with Mallard ducks in flight. Rory can barely hold his exasperation in check. What the hell was Benj doing here forty years too soon?

Anger fades as he rounds the corner. Benj sits in the seat below the bay window, a pyramid of cigarette ash in front of him. He's been crying, that much is obvious. His eyes are red and the sadness in them goes deep, tunnelling back to his childhood, to the interminable days of loneliness. Rory doesn't know how to mend the gaping holes in Benj's life but he's damned if he's going to allow him to fill them with alcohol. Benj glances up from the tumbler of neat gin in front of him. He looks shell-shocked. His eyes drop from Rory's face to the table. They both look at the glass. Then before Rory can stop him, Benj snatches up the tumbler and gulps down the clear liquid within.

maggie

My clothes had been unpacked for me and laid out in the Chrysanthemum bedroom, even my underwear had been folded neatly and put into drawers. It was all a little unnerving. I walked round barely daring to touch the fine fabrics and beautiful old furniture. The curtains were made of a flowery chintz (chrysanthemums?) and the four-poster bed was dressed, top, bottom and sides, with ruched skirts made of the same print. I tried to imagine sleeping in it with Jay but decided it would be like having sex inside a giant Kleenex box.

In the en-suite bathroom an old-fashioned set of hair-brush, comb, and clothes brush, all with ivory handles, was laid out on a glass shelf. On a table next to them a hairdryer looked like it might be on loan from a museum exhibition of twentieth-century inventions. Through the window, on the lawn outside, a skinny little girl was playing with her rabbit. There was something so self-contained about her that I fetched my camera off the bed. She had a ritual going: she would pick up the rabbit, stroke it, then let it go. The rabbit would hop two paces, then turn round as if to check, this far OK with you? Whereupon the little girl would pick it up stroke it and release it in a different direction. I wondered who she belonged to.

Along the corridor, in his appointed bedroom, Dwight was preening himself in front of a large gilt mirror. 'The Right Honourable Dwight,' he intoned, 'Dwight, peer of the realm, Viscount Dwight . . . Dwight . . .' he puffed out his chest and saluted . . . 'Heir . . . to the throne.' He jumped as I opened the door. His bedroom was even more extravagant than mine with flocked wallpaper and a wonderful bed whose walnut headboard was intricately carved with fruit and birds. At the foot of the bed a lacquer box stood open on a table. Set into its velvet was a seal, a stick of red wax and an ink pad. Dwight touched the pad gingerly and held up a blue finger to show me.

'Excuse me, sir, madam?' As the butler appeared, Dwight closed the inkpad guiltily pretending to examine the wallpaper instead. 'Laura Ashley?' he ventured, running a hand over its elaborate surface.

'Eighteenth-century Chinese, sir,' the butler corrected gently, 'and of course, quite priceless.'

Downstairs, in a small anteroom, a reserved man of around fifty was waiting to greet us. Dwight, apparently recovered from his earlier gaffe stepped forwards without hesitation. 'Ah, Your Grace,' he said smoothly, 'a very good afternoon to you.'

The man looked faintly embarrassed. 'I'm His Grace's agent Glenville,' he returned Dwight's enthusiastic handshake limply. 'His Grace has asked me to put myself at your disposal.'

Behind me Wolf sighed.

'See, the way we work,' I told Glenville, 'there's no preparation, no set-up, it's all purely observational, behavioural, fly-on-the-wall if you like.' We were moving through one imposing room to another. All around us servants busied themselves with chores. In the State dining room, a line of men stood shoeless on a long table, polishing its surface, feet bound in soft chamois leather. In the Green drawing room another man at the top of a ladder was painstakingly cleaning dust from the cut crystal of a chandelier with a toothbrush.

Truth is, it was frustrating. Visually these were great scenes but Glenville wouldn't allow us to film. One excuse followed another. There was a problem with the insurance, the lighting might damage ancient tapestries, His Grace had not sanctioned that the staff be questioned. Finally Wolf was allowed to set up the camera in a never-ending corridor of family portraits. Glenville, all blushes and unnatural hand movements, began narrating in a stiff museum guide voice. 'The first Duke of Roxmere married the eldest daughter of the Beaufort family whose ancestors of course were descended from the—'

We needn't have wasted the film. It was hopelessly dull footage but I didn't want to risk offending him.

'Am I going too fast for you?' Glenville said.

God forbid. 'No, no, you're doing great.' Then I noticed something. To our left was a door to the wing of the house we'd been informed was private. 'Are you getting this, Wolf?' I shot him a look with a subliminal order attached.

'Now you mention it, I could use re-shooting the portraits from the beginning,' he said, eyes skimming over the no entry sign.

We had only a day and a half at Roxmere – fine if you're shooting a documentary, say, and have set up shots on a previous visit but with *Newsline* you shoot and scout simultaneously so you can't afford to get stuck with dead wood in front of the camera. As the only member of the crew without a proper job, as Wolf was fond of telling me, it fell to me to charm, waylay and flatter the dead wood so that those real villains, sound and visuals, could go about their work of finding something interesting to film.

I managed to get Glenville all the way to the Duke's library before he noticed the crew were still absent without leave. He looked anxiously to the door. 'I fear your colleagues may have got lost.'

I was happily sure of it.

'They're probably sneaking a beer break,' I said and Glenville looked reassured. The Duke's private library was a small square room lined in bookshelves. Glenville moved aside a pair of library steps and took down a slim volume.

'This might interest you. Dates back to the Magna Carta. Been in the family for generations.'

The door opened behind us and the butler walked in carrying the squirming terrier. 'Message for you, sir.' He released the dog which scampered off to its basket under a low table.

Glenville folded the note. 'I'll be back shortly, if you don't mind waiting here. Though if I could possibly draw your attention to . . .' He gestured to a discreet no smoking sign propped against the mantelpiece.

'And could I please impress on madam the importance of not, under any circumstances, letting the dog out,' the butler added. 'Little Timmy does tend to hunt.'

The dog glared from its basket, resentful of my role as temporary jailer, but it was no bad prison even for a dog. On a writing desk stood an eclectic array of objects: iron statues of political figures; a freakish miniature chihuahua in a bell jar; a dried hand on a stand, property of, its plaque informed, the Marquis de Sade. The dog soon settled into a routine of rasping snores and atomic smells. I turned my attention back to the bookcase. A volume of *A Midsummer Night's Dream* caught my eye. I took it down. Illustrated by Arthur Rackham, each plate was covered in delicate tissue paper. I carried it to a chair and opening the window for my cigarette smoke, settled down, soon too engrossed in goblins and fairies to worry about what the boys were up to.

Not that they lost much time in telling me later. After splitting off, Dwight and Wolf had found themselves in a vast ballroom. Though empty of furniture, Chinese urns, over-sized candlesticks and decorative dragon vases had been arranged slalom-style on the floor and the skinny girl I'd seen earlier was Rollerblading round them, a look of determination on her pale features. When I studied the footage later, I noticed that there was something else Wolf had caught on film, an expression of a freedom but a freedom tinged with wistfulness – almost as if she suspected fate was hunched right around the corner waiting to kick the wings from her heels.

She turned and glided towards the camera. 'I'm Artemis,' she said. 'Who are you?'

The crew introduced themselves.

'You don't look like a Wolf, do you eat girls?'

'Only ones dressed in red,' Wolf said.

She pointed her chin thoughtfully at her red skirt then back towards camera. 'Methinks you're an NQOSD.' She took a crushed packet of cigarettes from her pocket and placed one languidly in her mouth.

'A what?' Wolf said.

'Not Quite Our Sort Dear,' she cocked her head to one side. 'Or maybe you're an LMCM.'

'Is that a good thing?'

'Good heavens, no. It means Lower Middle-Class Monster.'

'How can you be lower and middle at the same time?'

The little girl looked thoughtful, then, puzzled herself, did a figure of eight backwards and pirouetted off still holding the unlit cigarette.

daniel

'*Learn to cook. Catch a crook. Win a war then write a book about it . . . I could paint a Mona Lisa . . .*' Benj sings tunelessly as Rory, reeling under his weight, pushes him up the staircase. He roots around in the hem of Benj's overcoat. Benj's keys are attached to a plastic model of Kitchener's head which barks, 'YOUR FRONT DOOR NEEDS YOU' as Rory inserts them into the lock.

'*I could be another Caesar. Compose an oratorio that was sublime . . .*'

'Alternately you could just try turning up for a full day's work for a change,' Rory says sarcastically.

'*The world's not shut, on my genius butt . . . I just don't have . . . the time.*'

'Work,' Rory struggles to turn the key, 'surely you remember – that strenuous activity where you go to the office . . . sometimes for as long as five whole days consecutively?'

'Nope.' Benj tries to focus, 'Sorry, doesn't ring a bell.'

Rory kicks the door open.

Pimlico is a dead-end residential spot of London at the best of times but Benj's flat, inherited from a great-aunt, is in one of those Victorian mansion blocks that old people invest in when they get fussed about being mugged at night. The small windows make it dark enough but the addition of floor-to-ceiling wood panelling transforms it to suicidally depressing.

Rory brews up strong coffee and forces it down Benj's throat. Shortly afterwards Benj makes a dash for the bathroom. On the ledge of the bath five Action Men in camouflage gear sit watching him in affable silence as he vomits. Rory watches him from the safer distance of the doorway. Rory feels like an alcoholic by proxy, Alistair and Audrey, myself, now Benj. *We're the generation that can kick it.* Today he's less sure. He wants to shake Benj till his nose bleeds. Go on! Puke your guts out, hope it hurts, hope it lasts for hours. In this moment he hates Benj. Selfish little prick. Why is it his responsibility anyway? He toys with walking away, but he won't — not just because Benj is family and Rory loves him but because in the complicated debit and credit system he uses for measuring his own guilt, Rory still believes he owes big time.

maggie

While the boys were filming Artemis, I continued reading until the clock on the table chimed loudly. I closed the book quickly. Where the hell were Dwight and Wolf? Then my eyes dropped to the basket under the table. Empty. 'Little Timmy' was gone. But how? The door was still shut.

I ran to the open window. Cloud had settled low over the valley. It was dusk but across the lawn and next to an elaborate Victorian monument, I could just make out a bush shaking violently. I stuck my fingers in my mouth and gave it all I had. My screeching whistle brought the dog crawling out from under the bush. It streaked towards the window but before I could snatch it up, veered sharply away and disappeared.

Moments later there was a scratching against the door. I wrenched it open. The terrier stood on the threshold wagging its tail. In its mouth was a muddy object which it dropped at my feet.

Gross. A dead rabbit. I peered closer then froze. Around the rabbit's neck and under layers of drying blood was a pink collar with a silver heart-shaped tag.

'Oh no,' I said faintly. 'Please, God, no.'

*

'What the hell?' Wolf said, walking into my bathroom.

'Don't say a *word*.' I squeezed another dollop of the shampoo onto the bloodied fur.

'Jesus, Maggie are you insane? What are you some kind of animal psycho?'

'I was supposed to stop the dog hunting, but it escaped.' I scrubbed at the fur with the ivory-handled nail-brush. 'I panicked.'

'So what? It's not like you chased the bunny and killed it yourself,' he said.

I switched on the hairdryer.

'Unless you did.'

'Did what?' I shouted.

'Chase it and kill it yourself.'

'For pity's sake, Wolf, this isn't a joke.' I switched the hairdryer off. 'You know we were specifically told to be nice to the pets.' I thrust the bunny into his hands and fixed the collar around its neck. 'There,' I brushed the fur flat with the hairbrush.

'Looks much better now.'

Then I caught his eye and we both collapsed in helpless giggles. Wolf recovered first.

'So where's the rabbit hutch?'

'Oh god.' I wiped tears from my eyes. 'The what?'

'It's apartment . . . you know, its place of residence before it was murdered?'

'I don't know.'

'Well you can't just leave it lying around.'

'Maybe they'll think it died of a heart attack.'

'Then let itself out of its cage and came up to the house

for tea? I don't think so. C'mon', he grabbed my hand, 'let's get moving.'

The hutch consisted of two cages, one empty, the other locked. Inside the locked cage a brown and white rabbit hopped around, pathetically grateful at its companions return. I propped the dead bunny against the straw. 'Kind of cute, no?' I said.

'Tail's missing, Maggie.'

I turned the rabbit and positioned its back against the cage. 'There, looks quite life-like, don't you think?'

'Notwithstanding rigor mortis,' Wolf said supportively.

'Truly beautiful place you have here.' Next to the Duchess, Dwight perched on the edge of his upholstered stool in the drawing room and sipped his tea, little finger crooked expertly. 'Did I mention that I love chintz?' he continued, 'Joan, my wife, also loves chintz, we have drapes very similar to these ones in Brooklyn. My mother was a big floral fan, quite the anglophile, would you believe. I myself was nearly named after one of your kings.'

'Tell me, my dear,' the priest said to me, 'did you see that splendid winter flowering cherry in the garden?'

I couldn't answer. Rooted to my own chair. Somewhere in the house a child was sobbing.

'As I was saying,' Dwight persevered with our hostess, 'there's a department store right round the corner from us, sells beautiful florals – could be they do mail order.' He leant forward conspiratorially. 'You know something, Duchess? I think you and I have the same taste.' He winked.

The Duchess's social smile barely shifted. She rang the small bell on the tea trolley summoning the old butler. 'What *is* Artemis doing, Simmonds?'

'She's a little upset, Your Grace.'

I could hardly bring myself to look at Wolf.

'Do tell her to pull herself together and come into tea.'

Artemis sloped in and sat on the fireguard snivelling furiously.

'Artemis?'

The girl turned her back on her mother. Her thin chest heaved with sobs.

'What *is* the matter with her, Simmonds?' The Duchess looked helplessly at the girl. I felt sick. I'd never had a proper pet, but boy, do I remember wanting one. The rabbit had been this child's only friend, the one bit of warmth and affection she'd known –

'I do believe, Your Grace,' said Simmonds, 'that Master Beckham and his wife Miss Posh are rumoured to be parting company.'

Artemis burst into fresh wails.

'Artemis, darling,' the Duchess tried valiantly, 'it is awfully sad, of course, but I do believe . . . er . . . Oasis will be a much stronger group because of it.' Artemis threw her a withering look and retreated to the fireplace.

As I allowed myself to breathe again the door opened and a tall patrician man with a hooked nose and defined cheekbones padded into the room wearing scarlet knee-high socks.

'Ah, Hereward, here you—'

'Quite extraordinary,' the Duke interrupted his wife. 'My dear I must tell you. Dear Flopsy, who as you know expired the day before yesterday and was laid to rest,' he glanced at Artemis, 'with all due ceremony of course, has now been found back in her hutch and, what's more,' the Duke continued agitatedly, 'she's clean as a bloody whistle. *Clean as a bloody whistle!*'

Into the very long silence that followed somebody eventually spoke.

'A rabbit resurrection,' said the vicar. 'Heavens above, how very unusual.'

daniel

In the sitting room, Benj struggles to lever himself onto the sofa, but misjudging the distance lands flat on his back instead.

'I am a drunk,' he says mournfully.

'I had noticed.' Rory lies on the floor next to Benj and both stare vacantly up at the ceiling.

'You know something, Rory,' Benj says eventually. 'You've simply got to get a grip.'

'I know.'

'Because whilst I, at least, am a happy and on the whole amusing drunk, you, my friend, have become a boring frustrated son of a bitch.'

'You're right.' Rory sighs. Above him is a glass chandelier that Benj inherited along with the flat. Were it to fall right now, Rory wonders, would he be quick enough to roll to safety? Just how good were his reflexes these days? He moves out of range.

'For goodness sake get a job you like,' Benj says.

'Had one, if you remember.'

'Well get it back.'

'And my parents?'

'They can look after themselves, they're *grown-ups* for goodness sake.'

'As you very well know,' Rory says grimly, 'they are not.'

Benj grunts at this.

'You're lucky,' Rory says, 'your parents are cold, unemotional, uptight . . . reasonably normal in fact.'

'And they spoke to me for the first time ever when I was twelve.'

'Well, my mother has an extremely large quadruped.'

'You know,' Benj says, 'recently I asked my mother if I was breast-fed as a child.'

'And were you?'

'I don't know. She told me to mind my own business.'

Benj's childhood. So superficially perfect. So seriously sick. Benj's mother had not touched him as a boy, not even as a baby. I'd been shocked when he'd admitted it. 'I don't think it ever occurred to my mother to kiss me,' he'd said. 'She did hug me once – although she'd just tripped over the carpet divider, so that might have been an accident.' Benj's mother disliked physical contact of any kind. His father disliked emotional contact of any kind. It was a winning combination for an only child.

'I take it you haven't introduced your father to the notion of selling Bevan then,' Benj changes tack.

It's Rory's turn to grunt. Idly he scans Benj's bookshelves. All the C.S. Lewis books, three copies of *Sword in the Stone*, hardback editions of *Mungo* and *Zulu Dawn*. It strikes him that Benj has got lost trying to find a childhood that never even existed.

'He's simply got to be practical,' Benj says. 'Can't you make him understand?'

'Inflicting any kind of self-knowledge on my father at his age is tantamount to abuse of the elderly,' Rory says, 'and besides, Daniel would never have given up Bevan.'

This gets a sharp look from Benj. 'Well if you're opting for a life sentence at Bevan, at least make sure it's not solitary. Find a girl you like.'

'Had one.'

'Find another.'

'Aren't any.'

'Aren't any left you mean.'

'Don't think for a single second I'm going to take a lecture on women from you lying down.' Rory puts his hands under his head.

'Strikes me you've taken precious little lying down since Daniel died.'

'Coming from you, Casanova.'

'True, but then at least I have a good excuse.'

'Which is?'

'Which is, women absolutely terrify me,' Benj says simply. He sits up and hunts in his pockets for cigarettes, retrieving the lighter from under the carpet. 'God, but we're a pair of fuck-ups aren't we.'

'Yes, that we are.' Rory sits up as well and leans against the sofa. 'Why are we by the way?' His mobile is ringing for the umpteenth time and finally he answers it. Alison, beside herself with joy at finding a legitimate excuse for calling him after work hours, has already left four messages.

As Rory listens to them, a resigned look on his face, Benj draws thoughtfully on his cigarette. 'Well in my case my father was a fuck-up, his father before him was a fuck-up, my grandfather's father was also a bit of a fuck-up. You know, you just inherit it, along with the death duties and the ugly furniture.'

maggie

When I opened the door of the Chrysanthemum bedroom, Rory Jones was standing outside. I shouldn't have been surprised. I knew why he'd come. He looked at me, clearly irritated, and I wondered whether I should scamper off to a basket under the table like little Timmy.

'Skirt at the dry-cleaners?' I walked over to the fireplace.

'I only wear it for best.'

I could feel his eyes on my back and turned to face him. 'Look it probably sounds a little worse than it was.'

'Oh?' His eyebrows shot up. 'How exactly might it have been worse? I know I told you to be nice to the pets but surely the shampoo and set was just a tad over the top?' His tone was bitingly sarcastic. 'From now on I really can't have you sniffing around any more houses, unaccompanied, as it were.'

'Like we're not housebroken or something,' I said lightly. The fact was my ass was in a sling. Without him I would have to either abort or start fresh and I guess we both knew it.

'Here's the situation,' he said. 'We've banked your cheque. I think you'll find it's non-refundable. So, given the circumstances, you'll have to let me know if you wish to continue or not. Of course you don't have to decide till morning.' He opened the door. 'Assuming you can manage till morning that is.' His tone was angry but I could swear he was laughing at me.

'Believe me,' I said politely, though it was all I could do not to level him with a punch, 'I can manage.'

I tried Jay's number again on my cellphone then snapped it shut. 'What is the point of a boyfriend if you can never get hold of him?'

'It's a time consuming job saving the world.' Wolf was lying on his bed smoking a joint.

'Well, you know something, at least it's a worthwhile one.'

'Mr Jones really got under your skin, huh?'

I grunted. OK fine, it was a great moment of payback so I shouldn't have begrudged it, but God knows he needn't have looked quite so smug.

I flopped on the bed and rested my head on Wolf's legs. 'What are we doing here Wolf?' Nothing about this story was gelling and I had only myself to blame. I felt overtired, felt like I could do with a good cry, sex, a holiday. More than anything I could have done with seeing Jay.

The last time I'd been on 'holiday' was when I'd joined Jay in Sierra Leone. It was a mistake for both of us. I had wanted to understand what his life was about, and when I got there I understood. It was about sanitation, clean water, funding. It was about lobbying a sluggish UN. It was an endless, thankless task and I was in the way – just one person more for him to organize. 'This is not your reality,' he'd said more than once. But the point was, it was *his* reality and I didn't belong in it.

'You know exactly what you're doing,' Wolf said. 'You just blew it, that's all.'

I grinned. 'You could at least make a minimal effort to cheer me up.'

He passed me the joint, and we smoked it in silence. 'Remember in Anchorage,' he said finally, 'when we were doing the stolen land story, that time when you tried to get in with the tribe elder and you agreed that me and Dwight would do that ice bonding thing and we had to squat in a deep hole naked with the Inuit guy with the mackerel breath and Dwight ended up losing feeling in the tip of his—'

'I remember.'

'That almost seems like fun now.'

I put my head on his chest and he combed my hair through with his fingers. I really loved him a lot.

'Are you happy?' he asked.

'I think so.' I was startled by the question. 'Are you?'

'How can you tell?'

'I don't know, but I can tell you what keeps me awake at night,' I said. 'What if you believe you're driving on a main road, one that takes you to a capital city, let's say, but you're wrong – all along you're on a parallel road but it's smaller, less interesting, it's going nowhere and the worst thing is – these two roads never converge?'

He thought for a while. 'At least there'd be no tolls to pay.'

I laughed and took another hit of the joint. Wolf always

had the strongest grass. You could chart his progress round a party by the line of monosyllabic glassy-eyed victims in his wake. 'One more before I go back to my room,' I squeaked in a helium Micky Mouse voice. 'How do I get back to my room anyway?'

I woke needing a pee. My left arm was numb. Wolf was asleep. His hair, loosed from its ponytail, was spread over one cheek. He looked like the bearded lady, on leave from the circus.

The corridor was dark. I tripped over the carpet then turned my ankle negotiating the steps to the bathroom. As I opened the door something brushed against my face – I yelped, thinking it was a spider but it was only the string from the light. I pulled it but no light came on, instead a bar heater above the mirror glowed red. It gave off just enough light to confirm that there was no toilet in this bathroom, just a bath and a sink. It took another ten minutes not to find where the toilet was located and arrive back where I started. If I hadn't been quite so stoned, I might have chanced the journey to my own bathroom, more than a thousand stubbed toes away – instead I eyed the sink. Oh well . . . I'd certainly peed in stranger places than this . . .

Dwight told me afterwards it sounded like a bomb exploding. He'd shot upright in bed. The blackness in his room was thick as tar and just as impenetrable but the noise had been too loud to ignore. He searched in vain for the switch on his table lamp, then, pulling back the covers, took a tentative step into the abyss. Hands extended to feel his way around the room, he found a cold surface to lean on. His hands pressed on something damp and soft. A face towel. That meant he was at the basin, which meant a ninety degree turn to the door. He took one giant step forwards and slammed into the wall. Befuddled and now in pain he felt with his hands round the wall until he found the light switch. His eyes had difficulty adjusting, because even when he'd switched it on his hands looked so dark. He shook his head stupidly. Then something caught his eye. The lid of the antique ink pad was up. He looked at his fingers, took a horrified step back. Around the room, indelibly printed onto the priceless eighteenth-century Chinese wallpaper, were the inky blue imprints of his hands.

Comedy cut to the bathroom. As silly accidents go I have long since cornered the market. Once, at school, I took a basketball so cleanly to the centre of my forehead it knocked me onto the floor and cracked open the back of my head. The double egg forced me to sleep on my side for a month. In Mexico, Wolf turned our jeep, a goat lethargically crossing the dirt road mistaken for a child. That time it was a telephone pole that cracked my head open. I have sliced my calf on a picture hook, got a black eye from a flying lens cap, a fractured ankle tripping over a *Dictionary of Erotica* at university but I had never heard of anyone being clobbered whilst actually peeing. At first I thought I had slipped off the sink and fallen to the floor, then I realized the sink had slipped off the wall and fallen onto me. I lay semi-naked covered in rubble, T-shirt hiked up, wondering whether things were broken; important things like my head for instance, because the whole thing seemed so funny, but then the lights snapped on, the dust cleared and Rory Jones stepped into the doorway.

The stately homes of England, how beautiful they stand,
To prove the upper classes have still the upper hand.
. . .
The stately homes of England we proudly represent,
We only keep them up for Americans to rent.

— Noel Coward

maggie

I got hooked on watching people at Rock'n'Roll concerts.

You could say that my dad, Mike, was one of the founders of modern rock'n'roll stage lighting. He was a bona fide hippy and proud of it – he still has a *Sergeant Pepper* outfit somewhere in the back of his closet. He avoided being drafted by claiming to be homosexual, a good wheeze at the time you might think, but he's spent a disproportionate amount of effort since trying to access his papers through the Freedom of Information Act to see whether this boyhood lie is still following him around. Every time his credit card is turned down, his bags searched at the airport, his mail is late – it's always the same, truth is he's a little paranoid.

Dad was at the Thanksgiving dinner when Arlo Guthrie wrote 'Alice's Restaurant' and was famous, before he married my mother, for his sexual exploits with various female rock divas who wished to be well lit.

My parents met in Haight Ashbury where my mother was making a documentary called *Love is Dead* about the decline and fall of the hippies and Dad was mounting the farewell concert of Jefferson Airplane. He was beautiful, laid back and stoned, but Mom was fierce. She prised him away from Grace Slick and marched him back to New York.

They were all set to make love not war and sure as hell not babies. My mother could organize a protest of 400 people standing on her head, but she couldn't organize a plumber or decent contraception. Even after the shock of my arrival, parental duties were fulfilled as an afterthought. I got new pants when old ones had shrunk to my knees. I had to walk around barefoot before either of them noticed I needed a larger shoe size and theirs were always the two empty seats at the school play. It wasn't that they were mean, they just never signed on for the whole stroller-pushing PTA parent thing. They never let me need them as a child and they don't need me now and I guess I'm the stronger for it. Still, it meant we never established much of a sense of family. Instead my life was slotted into their agenda. I didn't mind. I was happy trailing my mother's causes, and if Mom was away and Dad had a concert out of the city, he'd just pluck me out of school and take me right along with him.

Concerts were a blast. 'Just stay still and watch,' my father would instruct — which I would until, out of the blue, some huge man would hoist me up saying, 'This is no place for a little prawn like you,' and whip electrical cables onto the spot where'd I'd been sitting before stashing me like Raggedy Anne in a new place from where the whole scene would shift and change. Minutes later somebody else would come along. 'You shouldn't be here,' and again I'd be relocated. I became brilliant at being where I shouldn't. I was thinking about this the morning we set off. Being brilliant at being in the wrong place. It's a strange skill to have.

It was a windy morning. People struggled with umbrellas. At a pedestrian crossing a woman's headscarf whipped over her face just as she stepped out. Startled, she withdrew to the kerb as the traffic roared by.

A wedding party poured out from a Greek Orthodox church. Children in old men's suits and women in young girl's dresses. The bride's veil blew around her, engulfing her in a cloud of swirling net. In vain, guests tried to untangle her but she eventually cast off the veil, laughing as it sailed up to the sky, while children hopped and jumped to catch it.

'I'm sorry, did you say something?' I said.

'I said, you're not going to sulk the whole week, are you?' Rory Jones repeated. We were driving through the outskirts of London in his car, an old Rover. Wolf and Dwight were following us in the van. I could have ridden with them but I'd opted to ride with Rory out of – what? Who knows. It had to be either masochism or some kind of reverse pride.

His comment was especially annoying as I hadn't been sulking at all, I was thinking how much I liked the expression on the Greek bride's face as she watched her veil spinning into orbit, like she was symbolically freeing herself from the prison of single life. It was a nice moment. One I would have liked to have had on film, but Rory had caught me with my pants down – quite literally. The joke was on me and he'd lost no opportunity to rub salt in the wound.

In the Stately Locations office that morning, he'd rung our next appointment to confirm.

'No, no need to have second thoughts, Lady Harcourt,' he'd said. 'Not *all* American women are brash, vulgar and distasteful,' he caught my eye and grinned. 'No, no, I'm quite sure you'll like her . . . yes, yes, very polite, charming, yes, yes, marvellous with animals.' He'd put his hand over the receiver. 'You do *do* charming don't you?'

To hell with him anyway. Maybe having him come along might not be a disaster after all. It passed responsibility for his clients directly to him – and he'd better be up for the ride because from now on, the way I figured it, these clients, whoever they were, were firmly in my sight line.

'The thing is,' he said, 'if you don't talk, I'll have to. I mean, after all, it's a question of manners.'

I continued flicking through the itinerary, around ten houses in all.

'It's my English upbringing,' Rory said. 'No matter how obstreperous or dull the person sitting next to you is, you must engage them in conversation.'

I doodled a hangman onto the back of the envelope. A man with a coronet hanging by the neck.

'Funny business to be in for someone who's not interested in people,' he added.

'I'm interested in people.' Goaded, I took out a cigarette and lit it. 'Talking to people is my job.' My matches had a picture of Roosevelt on the front and had arrived by FedEx that morning at the hotel. Jay collected presidential matches, thought they were very kitsch. It amused him to send them to me from time to time. The idea of the FedEx office trying to find a small enough box to pack them in amused him even more.

'What the hell is it?' the FedEx man would ask as he signed over the miniature package.

'I'm afraid it's the president's head,' I would reply solemnly.

Jay also collected president stories. Apropos nothing he might say, 'you know Lyndon Johnson once replied to something Jimmy Greenfield said with, "You dare to ask the leader of the Western world a chicken-shit question like that?" '

'Who's Jimmy Greenfield?' I'd say and get his 'oh-the-cultural-desert-that-is-youth' look for my trouble.

Rory was eyeing me from the driver's seat.

'What?'

'You know that thing in movies?' he said. 'When two people meet for the first time, spot each other across a crowded room and fall instantly, passionately, hopelessly in love?'

I looked at him.

'Well,' he said, 'I'd say quite the opposite thing has happened here wouldn't you?'

I stared out the window. Damned if I was going to let him see me smile.

'Nice day.'

'Beautiful,' he agreed, ignoring the sarcasm.

'It's true what they say. It really does rain *all the time* in this country.' I gave up fiddling with the car's dials.

'It's only been a couple of days.' Rory said, 'I'm sure it's been known to rain two days running in New York.'

'Yeah, but it's different rain.'

'How's that?'

'Less wet for a start.' I sipped my gas station coffee in its plastic cup. The world outside the window was grey, the sky dulled by cloud so thick you could have spread it on a bagel. Black crows circled in the boughs of leafless trees. 'Jesus,' I shuddered. 'I mean, no wonder you Brits are so repressed.'

'Ah, here we go – and this based on what? Your extensive experience of . . . ah yes . . . one family?'

'Come on, anybody would have felt uncomfortable in that place, I mean, even the butler knew more about that little girl than her mother. The woman didn't have a trace of warmth.'

'She was being polite.'

'She was totally inhibited.'

'I'd say reserved.'

'Try archaic.'

'A little old fashioned.'

'Uptight.'

'Shy.'

'They're just privileged with no purpose.'

'Oh yawn,' said Rory, 'that old aristocracy versus meritocracy chestnut. Your problem is you're incapable of seeing past the house and title—'

'Oh right, like you people aren't a little over preoccupied with blue blood and class?'

'As if *your* people don't have an overriding need to believe in Camelot.'

'Forget the Roxmeres, this isn't about one family – as a race you're cold, no passion.'

'The English don't consider it gentlemanly to have passion.'

'Oh – a little lame don't you think?'

'Well of course we have passion. It's just that we don't get quite all our emotions from those self-help books.'

'What emotions are you talking about? You send your kids to boarding school before they can walk.'

'Well, better the world of beatings and buggery than having them settle junior high school disputes with Uzis.'

I opened my mouth to say something then clamped it shut again.

'Oh my God,' he said, 'you're laughing, it's a miracle, alert the national press.' He paused. 'Why are you laughing by the way?'

'I don't know, you sounded just like my mother.' My mother, like everyone else in America, had long been obsessed with high-school shootings and was on the committee of Women Against Guns.

'Right wing blames it on the media, left wing blames it on the availability of guns.' I'd heard it a million times, 'be careful who you diss in school, honey,' she used to tell me, and by the way this was the full extent of her teenage advice, 'cos if they know anyone who even looks eighteen they can go down to their local Woolworths, buy a shotgun and blow you away.'

'So the question is,' Rory said, 'will your broadly objective views on the English be serving as the basis for your film?'

'Hey,' I said loftily, 'I'm just making polite conversation. I film what I see.'

'Oh and what's that?'

'What's what?'

'Well you're not exactly the "oh-gee-that-accent-makes-me-go-weak-at-the-knees, wasn't-princess-Di-a-saint" type of big-haired gushing American that we at Stately Locations have come to love and cherish.'

'Why have you got it in for journalists so badly?'

'Because they're unscrupulous and intrusive and they ride roughshod over people's feelings.'

I eyed him. 'Funny business to be in for someone who doesn't like talking to the press.'

He broke into a grin. 'Touché . . . It's a long story.'

'Which you're not going to tell me sometime?'

'Correct.'

'Even if I ask really nicely?'

'Are you always this nosy?'

'Being nosy is my job.'

'You must get a lot of doors slammed in your face.'

'Yeah, but the trick is to be on the right side of the door.'

'And you achieve this how?'

'My charm, naturally.'

'Of course,' he said. 'Your charm. How very unobservant of me.'

See here's the thing. You pick and choose who you work with on most assignments and you're careful, because the relationship between a crew can get precarious at the best

of times. How much you all need each others' skill is
carefully balanced. But people like Rory, the accidental TV
tourist, can be a liability. You need them, so you put up
with them. Once in a while you get the clever ones who
think you might need more than a guide, a driver, an
interpreter, whoever it is they've signed on as, and in those
situations the only thing you can do is keep as far away as
possible, stay professional and on the whole they're pretty
easy to ignore. Or not, as it turned out . . .

The Harcourts lived in a breathtakingly pretty Georgian
house south of the Wiltshire Downs. The moment they
invited us in, had the tea fetched and eagerly began telling
us the history of the place: grade II listed, twelve bedrooms,
epitomizing the era's architectural details, pedimented col-
umned entrance porch, well-stocked lake and flight ponds
etc. etc. etc., I knew that the sooner we left the better.
There was nothing wrong with them as such. The Harcourts
failed us by being essentially nice decent people, and nice
decent people just don't make good television. I took the
opportunity to waylay Rory's suspicions by behaving beautifully. Rory took the opportunity to rub my nose in it by
telling endless scatological anecdotes. 'Did you know the
King of France used to go to the loo every morning and
he would have all his ministers around him to discuss the
doings of the country. I mean how many people can hold
meetings in the middle of having a crap?' then even going
so far as to present me, in the evening, with a map he'd
drawn of the house's interior, with arrows marking the

route from the living room to my bedroom and with every toilet highlighted by red stars.

We pleaded schedule nightmares to the Harcourts and planned to leave the next morning.

'So what do you do when you're not working?' Rory Jones asked me over breakfast. We were standing in front of a sideboard laden with silver dishes. There were tomato halves (fried), pork sausages (fried), bacon (fried), mushrooms (fried), triangles of bread (fried) and eggs (scrambled).

'Oh, you know,' I said airily, 'see friends, read, eat out . . . uh . . . see friends.'

'You said that already.'

'What already?'

'You said "see friends" twice.'

'Oh. Well the first ones are different to the second ones,' I said, defensively. Then I thought about the day I was offered the job on *Newsline*. I'd wanted to celebrate with someone but I hadn't known who to call. Eventually I got hold of Marnie, my oldest girlfriend and probably the sweetest person I know.

'Yay, Maggie,' she'd said, 'triple yay, the fruits of your labour – or labours of your fruit, can't remember which – are finally being realized. You are a goddess, of course you should come over, we'll crack some champagne.'

When she opened the door she was holding a tiny baby on one hip. I just stared and stared. I hadn't even known she was married.

'I know what you think I am,' I said to Rory.

'What?' He bit into the fried bread. Grease dripped down his chin.

'You're thinking work-obsessed, politically correct, lefty liberal New York neurotic feminist.'

'Oh no,' he slapped his hand to his cheek in pantomime horror, 'you're not a feminist are you?'

You don't know the half of it, I wanted to say. At my college, Welsley, people didn't burn their bras and dance around the Maypole because they considered the Maypole to be a phallic symbol, so instead they dug a hole and danced around the May*hole* . . .

Later in the car he asked, 'So what about boyfriends?'

'What about them?'

'Do you have one?'

'I hate the word boyfriend.' My hand closed over the cellphone in my pocket.

'I see.' He swung the car into the fast lane of the highway, 'What about dogs?'

'What about them?'

'Do you have one?'

'No.'

'Cat?'

'No.'

'What about a gerbil?'

'Nope.'

'Canary? Potted plant?'

'I'm not sure I want to stop long enough to have anything land on me.'

'OK, fine, commendably independent but where do you have to be at Christmas?'

'Nowhere, thank God.' Then I saw he was looking horrified. 'Your point being?'

'My point being – are you attached to anything apart from that damned mobile phone?'

I switched the cell off. Jay had once surprised me by claiming he didn't know how I felt about him. I admitted I had never dared let my guard down in case he took aim and fired.

'What are you so worried I'd hit?'

I told him he'd probably be aiming for my head, but being a senior citizen, might miss and shoot me in the heart by mistake.

'Think Charlton Heston,' he'd said dryly.

Rory was still waiting for an answer.

'I just did a story on child prostitution in Brazil.'

'Uh huh, that's nice.'

'Oh I suppose it's a new concept for you to care about people you don't know,' I said hotly.

'Perhaps it's a new concept for you to actually know people you care about,' Rory retorted.

'Ouch,' I said.

The problem was that Rory was not easy to ignore. He was totally obnoxious and delighted in winding me up. Everywhere we turned, there he was, self-importantly pointing out No Entry signs, frowning if I dared ask a question he considered out of line.

'Why don't you just stop telling me how to do my job,' I had a meltdown after one particularly bad day.

'Well you're like a badly behaved dog,' he said, 'I don't want you going off like a loose cannon.'

'If that isn't a mixed metaphor, I don't know what is.'

'Getting off the leash then. Is that better?'

'I don't like being put in a box, if you put me in a box . . .'

'Kennel.'

'What?'

'Kennel would work better with my dog metaphor,' he said apologetically.

'Fine . . . if you try to put me in a *kennel*, I will try to get out.'

So we established an uneasy pattern. Rory would deliver us, either stay the whole visit or long enough to gauge whether we were going to make trouble, and if not, would tuck us into the bosom of the aristocracy before driving back to London. He puzzled me. He seemed almost openly contemptuous of what we were doing and I didn't understand why he was in a job he found so distasteful.

'Did you leave the maid a tip?' Dwight asked pulling his shirt cuff down under the new tweed jacket he was wearing. We were loading up the van, on the move again after a two-day shoot at a house in Oxfordshire.

'A few dollars,' Wolf said. He caught the look on Dwight's face. 'What? How much was I supposed to leave?'

'Rory said at least twenty pounds.'

'I wanted to tip her not fuck her,' Wolf said mildly.

Dwight's face turned pink. He flipped open his holdall.

'Hey,' I intervened quickly, 'let's take a look at the map, Dwight.' I put my hand on his arm, 'Where to next?'

Dwight pulled out his maps and methodically began checking houses against locations. 'Let's see . . . if it's Tuesday it must be . . .' he flicked through the Stately Locations list of houses, 'Bevan,' he read and looked up for confirmation.

'You must be looking at an old list,' Rory appeared over Dwight's shoulder and took the file from his hands. He tore out the sheet with the photograph of Bevan.

'Bevan is out of bounds.'

Our England is a garden, and such gardens are not made
By singing:– 'Oh how beautiful!' and sitting in the shade
While better men than we go out and start their working lives
At grubbing weeds from gravel paths with broken dinner knives.

– Rudyard Kipling

daniel

Audrey hangs the telephone back on the kitchen wall.

'What's more she's going to pay us!'

Alistair looks up from his plate. '*Cash* money?'

'Cash money,' Audrey repeats in a daze, 'two thousand pounds.'

She sounds incredulous, as well she might. The last time either of my parents saw a windfall this large was when they put five pounds to win on Sore in the Saddle, a 300–1 outsider running in the Grand National.

'Not Sore in the Saddle,' Alistair said when Audrey returned from the betting shop in Skimpton. 'Sawsally, you silly fool.' He examined the betting slip. 'If this Sore in the Saddle is 300–1, it's more likely a goat than a horse.' When the goat had romped in first, Alistair bought shares in a company that intended to reproduce old master paintings in Braille.

'Bound to make a fortune,' he remarked at the time.

'Just wait and see. Robert will be awfully pleased with us, you know.'

'Can't count on it, he's so bloody bolshy these days. Anyway, what do they want with us?' Alistair says, having just identified the flaw in this otherwise perfect plan. 'What are they filming?'

'You know . . . old houses . . . English grandeur . . .' Audrey says vaguely.

'There's nothing grand left here.'

'Never mind, we could always show them the cellar. Pretend it was used for medieval torture.'

'We'll lock them in the cellar if they're tiresome.'

'They'll expect servants.'

'We could always dress Grandpa up as a butler.'

'Oh don't be so silly,' Audrey says fondly. 'Besides, he's at the chess club for the day.'

Few people who stayed at Bevan realized that there were no staff. They assumed that in a house this size, despite the ruined wing, there would be at least one or two people and Audrey and Alistair never disillusioned them. Instead they did everything themselves and when guests left a little something, they simply pocketed it. Being tipped by friends and relations, most substantially better off than they were, had been something of an eye-opener.

'What'll we feed them?' asks Alistair.

'I'll think of something.'

'Talking of which, what is this, darling?' Alistair says curiously. The slab of meat on his plate is the standard grey that all meat becomes following my mother's infallible recipe for 'safe' cooking.

Once upon a time there'd been a cook at Bevan. Mrs Preston used to dish up proper old-fashioned English fare. Suet pudding; jugged hare; chicken croquettes; treacle tart; rice pudding, always with a thick skin; summer pudding; roast beef with Yorkshire pudding, soft in the centre, its edges curling and crispy. When Mrs Preston finally died, eighty-two and no change out of nineteen stone, Audrey, who'd scarcely boiled an egg in her entire life, decided she'd have to make do. Alistair shot for the pot, Audrey made the pies and thus began her fateful love affair with the deep freeze.

In the beginning, Rory and I tried bringing down emergency rations. Fresh bread, the smelliest of cheeses, cod's roe, smoked fish. Instead of feeding us, these things fulfilled my mother's seeming pact with God to keep a well-stocked freezer. In went the fresh food, out came the frozen pie, that dreadful, dreaded, stringy mystery-meat dish.

Audrey takes another bite, giving the matter some consideration. 'Found it at the bottom of the deep freeze,' she says. 'We could have the leftovers tomorrow. We'll just say it's grouse or pigeon, they'll never know the difference.'

'Is it not grouse or pigeon?' asks Alistair.

'No,' says Audrey, 'I think it's badger.'

Oh . . . Oh . . . Aaaaaaaargh. I bloody well knew it.

'Frightfully good,' is all my father says.

maggie

Maybe it was the way he'd said it, maybe it was the expression on Rory's face — too set, too considered — or maybe the reason why this house had become compulsory viewing was because we'd been warned off. For the second time that trip. Bevan. The name had come up again and again. The only reason I'd added it to the original *Newsline* list was because the morning I arrived at the Cadogan Hotel, I'd found myself eavesdropping on two old ladies who were breakfasting at the table next to mine.

I'd noticed them because they looked like sisters, one with white hair coiled up in bun, the other's neatly waved over her ears but dressed identically in pleated skirts, shirts, cardigans and pearls.

'Always was of course. Even as a little boy.'

'Do you remember at picnics, his mother, old Lady Bevan—'

'The one with the dreadful Catholic hair?' One kept interrupting the other.

'That's right, she always made the butler sit twenty feet away with jam smeared on his head to keep the wasps off the food.'

'Wasn't she the one that kept a lion?'

'Indeed, bit the arm off the customs official at Heathrow.'

They were both amazed when I confessed I had never heard of Bevan. 'Oh my dear, but you must have. It's one of the great English houses.'

Judging from it's two-mile-long drive, however, there was no way you'd know it. The road was in a terrible state of neglect, the surface all torn up and pockmarked by giant craters of muddy water. In contrast, young trees on either side were painstakingly fenced out in small wooden crates and in the parklands beyond, a tractor stood stationary while activity in the form of several figures with chainsaws hummed around it.

'So how did you swing this by Rory?' Wolf asked.

'I didn't. I told him we were taking a "personal day". I don't think he knew what that was,' I grinned, 'but I must admit, he looked pretty embarrassed.'

'Aren't these the people that are supposed to be in the nut house?' Dwight said.

'Yeah. What was the deal with that anyway?' Wolf added.

'Beats me.' The drive had looped on itself and I could now see what was going on next to the tractor. An immense bonfire was in the process of being built. Shaped like a witch's hat it was already a good 12 feet high. Alongside it, several men were laying into a fallen tree with saws and axes then heaving branches up to another guy on the bonfire's summit.

'Beats me too . . .' Dwight stomped on the brake as sheep wandered across the road. More sheep were dotted around and a buffalo was grazing amongst the trees. Jesus, a *what*? I did an enormous double take.

'Because they sounded perfectly normal on the phone,' Dwight finished.

daniel

Upstairs in the first-floor corridor, Alistair rifles through Nanny's handbag. He gives it a quick sniff.

'What *are* you doing?' Audrey hisses.

'Smelling it.'

'What on earth for?'

'I don't know,' says Alistair much struck. 'Comfort I suppose.'

'Well be quick,' Audrey beseeches him, 'or we'll be caught.'

'Check the door then.'

Audrey peers through the keyhole of Nanny's bedroom as Alistair extracts a clip purse from her bag. 'One bottle of whisky, or should we risk enough for two?'

Audrey glances plaintively at the bulging purse. 'Why is Nanny so much better off than we are?'

'Because in fifty odd years,' Alistair folds the twenty-pound note into his pocket, 'Nanny has only ever spent her wages on Basildon Bond writing paper and blue hats from the Army and Navy store. She's probably amassed a small fortune by now.'

'Do you think she keeps accounts?' Audrey says. And

she might well be worried. When Nanny discovered Rory and I had stolen a pack of Wrigley's gum from the milkman's float there'd been hell to pay. I think our poor mother was more traumatized than we were by the dire threats of Borstal that followed. She has a sudden flash of us standing, knees grimy, heads hanging, and at the memory her eyes cloud.

'Shhh,' says Alistair.

'What?'

'Hear that?'

'What?'

'Car.'

'No.'

'Yes, listen.'

'What?'

'*Will* you be quiet,' he says creeping to the window. 'It's *them*. They're *here*.'

Out of habit Audrey breathes the smoke out of the window. Alistair made her give up when they were first married and she never lost the habit of hiding it from him. She can hear him below. 'Well done, well done, directions all right?' She leans out of the window. Good God, look at the equipment they were carrying. The girl was in front with the two men behind. One of the men was Chinese or Japanese, but enormous! A Buddha! The girl was younger than she'd imagined. Dark, pretty, but dressed in the sort of ubiquitous army gear of the young. She herself had never taken much care with her appearance. You couldn't very well grow up vain in Ireland. In the sixties when she moved to London, she felt horribly out of place. Her legs were too stocky for miniskirts. When she'd cut her hair short she hadn't looked gamine or pixieish at all – in fact, not long after it had grown out, Alistair told her she'd looked like Henry VIII.

She grinds out the butt on the window sill noticing that the rhododendron bushes need cutting back – and wonders how she will ever manage without Bindey, finally retired aged eighty-nine. Damn, the telephone wire has come loose. She stretches out her hand, gets a finger to the black cabling and prods it back into a crack in the brickwork. But she's leant out too far. Her hand slips, she loses balance and in an instant I see she will fall.

It's only a half landing, but I'm terrified it will break her hip. Instead her beloved rhododendrons envelop her in their prickly centre. 'Bugger,' she says with feeling. She touches the long tear in her stockings. 'Bloody bugger.'

'Ah, here's Audrey now,' says my father, rounding the corner just in time to see his wife pick her way out of a bush pulling twigs from her hair. Audrey strides purposefully towards the group trying not to limp. 'Well done, well done,' she says with a beatific smile, 'Directions all right?'

Alistair thinks they're very odd. He's never clapped eyes on a group of people less well equipped for the English countryside. Only the shortish one has brought his own boots but is, bizarrely, dressed straight out of the pages of a Jeeves novel. The girl is wearing gym shoes and a thin coat whilst the Buddha sports a pair of sandals with socks. They seem nice enough, however, so he gives them a tour during which they film the wine cellar, significant only for its lack of wine, the May bedroom, significant for the suicide of a jilted chambermaid who hung herself with my great great-grandmothers pearls. Then they film the dairy where there are no longer cows to milk just as there are no horses to ride in the stableyard.

My father relates the full history of the house for the camera and is gratified that Miss Monroe shows so much interest in his endeavours to keep it afloat.

'But what were you hoping to do with these?' She plucks a smooth pebble from a tray by the stone-polishing machine.

'Make them into toys,' Alistair says vaguely, 'arts and crafts, pebble dogs, birds, that sort of thing . . . made a whole family of rooks once but nobody was interested. People used to eat rook pie around here. They'd shoot the young peeping over the edge of their nests with an air gun. Thought to be a great country delicacy at one time . . . caught some young boys at it the other day as it happened, gave them a frightful rocket.'

At one point he asks whether she has met his son Robert, and I look forward to a potentially interesting moment. Though it can't be legitimately classed as six degrees of separation it is a spectacularly fine piece of irony that she's here, quite oblivious of the connection, and at some point the shit must inevitably hit the fan, as it were, but not right now – because when the question is asked, the entire crew is distracted, quite understandably, by their attempts to frame the buffalo in shot and Maggie treats the question in much the same way as being asked by a London cabby whether she'd ever come across his first cousin who lived in Delaware.

They're now in the old laboratory where my father is showing them the Heath Robinson contraption of pipes, funnels, bowls, milk and muslins he has erected. The Americans stare into a vat of some indescribably repellent gunk, which sits underneath to catch the drips.

'From the buffalo milk,' Alistair explains. 'Oddly enough *this* milk, when left to curdle, turns into an interesting cottage cheese texture which when mixed with . . .?' He turns to Miss Monroe.

'Chives?' she hazards gamely.

'No, no . . .'

'Pepper? Honey?'

'No, no, you're entirely on quite the wrong track. Sand! Here try some,' he passes Maggie a spoonful which she sniffs suspiciously.

'Go on,' he says, 'be brave.'

'Sand,' she repeats faintly, raising the spoon to her lips. 'And you eat this on . . .?'

'Don't be silly.' he snatches the plastic spoon from her, 'you can't eat sand, good Lord, *the milk* is against every EEC health regulation ever dreamt up.' He smears the contents of the spoon on his cheek with one finger. 'It's for face packs! You see the mozzarella was not a great success,' he confides and is deep into a colourful description of the creature's medical problems when Maggie interrupts him.

'But surely mozzarella doesn't come from the American buffalo?'

'Quite right, good for you. Water buffalo's the one you really want.' He lowers his voice conspiratorially 'got one of those on order as a matter of fact.'

But Maggie is now wearing an expression of exhausted confusion as if she'd been asked to memorize the 3,000 components of a nuclear warhead.

'Something wrong?' asks my father.

'No, not at all,' she says puzzled, 'it's just that I was wondering . . . well . . . are you sure it's a water buffalo? Isn't it an Italian buffalo you need?'

maggie

Another reason I love living in New York is the fact that it's a functional city. Obviously not in the psychological sense – I mean as a collection of people we're as psychotically challenged as anyone else – but in a practical sense, New York functions like nowhere else on earth. Everybody *does* something, provides some service, everyone, everything, has a purpose. The Bowery, for example, where I live, is not just a residential area, it's also the stainless steel headquarters of the city. For five blocks square all you can buy anywhere is kitchen equipment. Industrial stuff mostly: stoves, hoods, griddles, broilers as big as my sofa all hoisted onto the sidewalks by the guys who run the shops. In winter you see them standing outside clapping their hands for warmth and chatting to locals, blowing hot air out of their mouths. From my window their breath looks like cooking steam. I keep telling them they should cook on their stoves, sell a little chicken noodle soup to warm the souls of passers-by.

Outside stainless steel, you get plumbing. Sprayed on shop fronts are enticing offers. Ball caps! Filigree end scrolls! 45-inch elbows! The exclamation marks making them sound

like new and exciting sex toys. Lighting lives beyond the
plumbing and then you get to the thrift shops of SoHo –
it's as I said – everything has a purpose whether it's buying,
selling or recycling. One man's trash is another man's trea-
sure. Nothing stays around long enough to gather dust.

This was not the case with Bevan. The house was extraordinary and tragic and unlike any place I had ever come
across. Rooms led one to the other through panelled doors,
each a degree colder than the previous; each in a progress-
ively worse state of disrepair, boasting a different shade of
gloom, a more marked degree of fade. Most depressing
of all was the sheer quantity of useless *stuff* crammed high
on every surface, but whether this stuff was tokens of love
or just garbage, it was impossible to tell. Wolf slowly panned
the camera over surfaces as we passed through. Newspapers,
brittle and yellowing, piles of matchboxes, rusted hunting
knives, old bits of guns, shelves of dried-up magazines –
you had to struggle to get your head round it – if in another
part of the world human tissue was being cloned and emails
were flying through space, what were people doing living
this way in the twenty-first century? Why did they need this
house? Why not sell up? Was it fear or stubbornness or just
plain stupidity.

The Earl conducted the entire tour in his dirty boots,
insisting we did the same. So we tramped through leaving
our own streaks of mud and I imagined them melting into
the general brownness of the floor, gluing together the fray
of the carpet, hardening in holes left by woodworm. As the
house merged together into the murky colours of neglect I

began to feel wildly claustrophobic. I longed for the emptiness of my loft, for its clean, uncluttered space. I wanted to lie on the floorboards with nothing better to do than listen to the whirr of sewing machines immediately below in the Chinese sweatshop and wonder at the irony of the twenty-seven immigrants who spend their miserable days sweating, running up tracksuits in which others will run in order to sweat for pleasure.

Still, the Earl himself was pure *Newsline* Gold. Apart from who he was (cousin of the queen, peer of the realm, with one of the oldest family seats in Britain and God only knew how many titles) he surely epitomized the pointlessness of the aristocracy. He was a total anachronism, a twenty-first-century dinosaur, and I wanted to get him to admit it on camera.

'Well, since the House of Lords has lost most of its hereditary peers,' I asked, 'what relevance has the aristocracy in today's Britain?'

'Absolutely none.'

I was a little wrong-footed by such frankness.

'Er, so . . . what would you say was left of the so-called "playing fields of Eton".'

'Bugger all,' he replied in much the same tone of voice. Wolf caught my eye and winked. I floundered on. 'Um, well if that's true . . . what would you say your role was now?'

He took pity on me. 'If you're suggesting we have outlived our usefulness,' he said gently, 'I would have to agree with you, we are, in the words of the Duke of Devonshire, "a spent force".'

'Do you think that the hereditary peers should have been expelled from the House of Lords?'

'It was entirely undemocratic, so I understood, of course, but in a curious way the system worked very well.'

'You don't think people should be chosen for that position on merit.'

'Just because a man has risen to the top of his profession through drive and ambition does not necessarily make him a suitable public servant. Indeed there may well come a day when a man whose sense of public duty is motivated purely by his obligation to society will be sorely missed.'

I told him this sounded like a warning, and he agreed perhaps it was. When I quoted him Lloyd George's 'by what right are 10,000 people owners of the soil in this country and the rest of us trespassers in the land of our birth', he said, 'Oh but you see I'm not really the owner of the soil. I am a keeper of the soil, and in answer to your earlier question my "role" now is no more than guardian, curator of this house if you like. The only thing we're expected to do is keep things going for the next generation.'

'Expected by whom?'

'Good question,' he said.

I liked him. He made no attempt to wriggle out of tough questions and his wasn't the practised seductiveness people sometimes turned on for the camera. The Earl was totally genuine.

'Was there ever anything you wanted to do?' I asked him curiously.

He frowned and I realized he hadn't understood the question.

'You know, when you were young?'

'You mean what did I want to be when I grew up?'

I nodded. He thought for a while then he said, 'Yes. Not the eldest son.'

daniel

There is an image people have of alcoholic parents. It's an image that conjures up violence, wife beating, child abuse, self-destruction, family secrets, broken childhoods and it's not a pretty picture.

Benj's father is an alcoholic like this, effete, sneering, racist, sexist. When we were boys, home from school, he would hold court at the dining table demanding everyone's attention as his poisonous diatribe flowed against the world. He was certainly amusing, but amusing at everybody else's expense and the drunker he got the meaner he became. During those interminable meals, he would unaccountably cease from holding anecdotally forth, turn to Benj and rasp, 'Your turn to say something clever, Benjamin,' and a terrible silence would fall. If Benj failed to amuse the assembled company, his father would accuse him of being unspeakably dull and send him to eat in another room while guests and relations shifted uncomfortably in their chairs.

We were lucky. Our parents were not like that. We were also fortunate – or rather Alistair and Audrey were fortunate – in that they were entirely complicit in their drinking. If this had the result of closing them off from us, at least they were not closed off from each other. Our childhood was not overshadowed by cruelty or violence, it was instead governed by lack of focus, near misses, and yes, of course, there were family secrets. Our childhood was defined by omissions, places we didn't go, conversations we couldn't have, cousins we were no longer allowed to see.

But family secrets were not our biggest problem in those days. Our immediate task was to stuff our thumbs in the leaking dyke. Our most pressing concern was damage limitation – to keep the smouldering embers off the carpet, to lift my mother back into her chair, and always, always to prevent others from knowing. Then there was Alistair and Audrey's propensity for foot in mouth, their talent for causing embarrassment by simply being themselves. It wasn't just contained at home; it followed us to school. Cheques were bounced, forms were left unfilled. Rory and I, standing with our trunks at the school gates, forgotten and uncollected at the end of term. Our skill became the cover-up, the manufacturing of excuses. There are no places to hide from extreme behaviour. You deal with it by adopting extremes yourself.

Rory succeeded no better than I did in the impossible task of attracting our parents' attention and keeping it. What tools can you develop to turn the beam of somebody's spotlight onto you? 'Dad, I'm an alcoholic, a drug addict, Dad, perhaps you haven't noticed, but I'm actually black.' This is where our paths began to split. Rory retreated, I attacked. We embraced different religions. Rory drank the water, I took care of the wine. To me it's so simple. You drink, snort, take pills, it's only ever about trying to find a place where you can be happy – but here is the nub, I suppose, of Rory's resentment. Double abandonment. First by them, then by me. He does not forgive my parents for who I turned out to be; his tragedy is he can't accept that I would never dream of blaming them in the first place.

Something happens to a man when he realizes he has no choice, when he realizes he's lost a freedom he never had any rights to. Something drains out of him. It doesn't matter how big your Estate, how tall your trees, how smartly dressed your beaters – nothing can compensate a human being for feeling absolutely worthless. I often wondered who or what my father dreamed of becoming when he was young, but he once told me in an unguarded moment that the day he inherited Bevan it felt as though his life was over before it had begun. But Alistair was an optimist. He loved Bevan. To him it was an enchanted land beyond whose boundaries the outside world barely existed – and Bevan, when he inherited it, had not seemed like the impossible task it does today.

Alistair didn't care if the house wasn't grand, he didn't care if it wasn't warm – as long as it functioned, and it did. The decay was gentle but probably not on a dissimilar time schedule to his own. Then came the fire. It decimated the east wing and nobody was sure how it had started. Maybe it was faulty wiring, maybe Alistair had been sloshed before it began. Certainly he was a lot more sloshed after they'd finished clearing away those great piles of blackened ash and bricks.

A year after the fire, the estate was ravaged by Dutch elm disease. It was 1976. Britain lost more than twenty million trees, thousands of which were on our land. Elms are one of the most romantic of trees, their apple-core silhouettes responsible for much of this country's graceful landscape. Dead elm was primarily used for coffins but there was such a glut you had to pay to have them taken away. Alistair, along with every other poor sod, was swindled blind by the timber merchants who claimed there was no market for the wood. The drive at Bevan had been lined with elms. Four hundred full grown trees, 100 feet high, 200 years old. Alistair refused to cut them down, thought they might survive. He spent a small fortune injecting them, but it didn't work. When they died, Alistair cut them down himself, every single one. Ten years of bonfires, maybe fifteen. I can see Bindey, grasping one side of the double-handed saw. I can see my father shirtless, sweating, leaning on the axe. I can still remember his face as he watched those trees fall. Over two centuries of growth and majesty reduced to stumps and I think it was the first time I ever saw a grown man cry.

maggie

Nanny, as the Earl and his wife called her, was a tiny, white-haired woman of extreme old age. She sat in front of the television, feet resting on a petit point stool. She presented a neat figure in tartan skirt and green cable cardigan. A cameo brooch pinned to the neck of her blouse kept in place, not just the peter pan collar, but also the strands of wrinkled skin that stretched from her throat to her chin and swayed gently as she spoke.

'I do watch *Friends*, yes, dear,' she said. 'I don't always understand the jokes but I do like to see nice young people enjoying themselves.' She poured another cup of tea and held it out to Wolf.

The old lady's quarters were a virtual shrine to the royal family. Walls were decorated with framed tea towels of the queen mother, and the engagement of Charles and Diana. The mantelpiece was home to a dozen or so commemorative mugs and there were even pictures of the two little princes, Harry and William, in silver frames. The other thing about the room was that, unlike the rest of the house, it was warm – in fact not warm, *boiling*. Wolf poured with sweat as he angled the camera through the door to Nanny's bedroom, picking out the headboard of her single bed. A large old-fashioned watch was pinned to its oyster-coloured satin and a bottle of lemon barley water stood on the bedside table.

'And you've been Nanny to all the family?' I asked her. I was about to pass out with the heat but the old lady was unruffled.

'I was employed by Master Alistair's mother, aye,' Nanny, like the Earl, maintained perfect composure in front of the camera. My bet was this was because she couldn't see it. She was ninety-five years old and held an incredible scorn for old people, proudly telling us of her disgust at younger generations taking to their beds.

'Nothing makes Nanny happier than doling out meals on wheels to decrepit pensioners twenty years her junior,' said the Earl wryly.

'I've kept myself busy, dear, and that's why I'm so healthy today.'

She was shocked when I asked her if she was resentful always living in somebody else's house. 'I've been in service all my life,' she said. 'My father was a policeman. As a family, we have *always* been of use.' She prided herself on never turning out a bad child, dismissing the notion of bad genes as nonsense. 'Bad breeding is cured by good upbringing,' she announced emphatically, 'not that his lordship wasn't a rascal because he was, I can tell you, eighteen years I wiped his nose,' she glanced fondly in the Earl's direction, then rapped, 'Alistair, must I tell you again not to lean against the fireguard.' She turned back to camera without missing a beat. 'As I was saying, Alistair was my pet, then after he was married there were the boys and now . . . well and now there's just the baby left,' her face softened, 'but he himself needs quite some looking after,' she sniffed. '*Quite* a handful let me assure you.'

'How old is the baby?' I asked, totally confused.

'Thirty-eight and bright as a button too. Poor boy leads a terrible rackety life down in the city, never one to eat properly . . . much too thin, just like yourself.' She felt her hands towards the tea tray, 'if you're no' drinking tea, then will you take a glass of milk?'

'No thanks very much I don't like——'

'Now,' she said briskly, 'I don't approve of dieters or vomiters. Lady Diana, may God rest her poor soul, was a vomiter . . . but in my opinion it's a wicked waste of good food. Alistair?'

The Earl poured milk into the cup she was holding towards him, 'Nanny knows best,' he said with heavy irony. Removing a baby beaker which obscurely had been clipped to his jacket ever since we arrived, he added a dose of whatever was inside before handing it to me with a wink.

Brandy from the smell of it. The Earl had the look of an alcoholic. His skin was rough, his face heavy and jowled, but although he continually took swigs from the beaker, he never seemed to get all that drunk. Plus he was in good shape, striding ahead of us all afternoon, pointing his walking stick at trees he'd planted giving us both Latin and English names and describing them as if they were fine wines. 'Now that's a *Fraxinus excelsior* "Jaspidea", little like your common ash but goes a wonderful buffer yellow in the autumn, over there is a full-bodied *Fraxinus mariesii*, ravishing flowers, white, like feathery smoke . . . left of the oak is a rather perky little *Coculus trilobus* from the somewhat risqué-sounding family of Menispermaceae.' But as the day wore on his attention began to stray and I detected a faint slur to his words.

Downstairs in the drawing room, he poured us all shots of neat Scotch from a decanter. From his pocket he produced a straw which he stuck in his own glass. It was one of those curly plastic things Toys R Us sell as Christmas stocking fillers.

'Uh . . . what's the significance of the straw?' I couldn't help asking. I watched fascinated as the golden liquid rose through its bends like oil in a pipeline.

'This?' He picked it up. 'Simple really. Question of economy. Alcohol reaches your bloodstream quicker when drunk through a straw.'

I had no idea what he was talking about.

'A higher level of inebriation can be achieved through less alcohol,' he explained patiently. 'Saves money. As I said. A simple question of economy.'

'A simple question of economy,' Wolf pointed the camera at Dwight. 'Tell us, your Earlyship,' he mimicked my voice. 'Is it the drink or the bad genes that make you a candidate for the funny farm?'

'Survival of the weirdest, dear boy,' Dwight said in his best English accent, 'Although five hundred years of sleeping with my sister sure helped.'

'Are you boys taking the piss by any chance?' I murmured. We were through for the day, and reluctantly packing up. I would have happily stayed longer but Rory had been adamant about not messing around any more of his clients so we were committed to meeting him at Stately Locations early the next morning. I had my back to the crew, checking out titles on the shelf. Bevan's library was nothing like as distinguished as Roxmere's but there were some lovely old books. An illustrated complete works of Shakespeare, the imprint on its spine rubbed almost bare. A navy cloth-bound copy of Milton's *Paradise Lost*, which I pulled out.

'These people are awesome, Maggie,' Wolf said. 'We couldn't have invented better.'

'*From morn to noon he fell, from noon to dewy eve, a summer's day; and with the setting sun dropped from the zenith like a falling star.*' I closed the book and tried to ease it back into the shelf but it wouldn't fit. The books on either side had closed ranks as though relieved at the extra space, but it wasn't a question of width, something else was blocking it from behind. I stood on the chair to investigate. Another thinner book had slipped from the shelf above and wedged itself in the way. I prised it loose and wiped the dust from the cover with my sleeve. It was a volume of Nietzsche – its title, *The Birth of Tragedy* engraved in gold. A piece of paper fluttered out. I stooped down and picked it off the floor. In fact it was a photograph, a barely legible pencil mark on the back dating it as 1938. I turned it over and suddenly felt the hairs on my arm rise. The photograph was of a group of children with their nanny, a man and a large Alsatian dog standing in front of a mountain chalet. It could have been any family holiday snap: Italy, Switzerland maybe. It could have been a scene straight out of the *Sound of Music*. Except it wasn't – the man in the picture was Adolf Hitler.

I turned it over and over disbelievingly.

'What's wrong, Maggie?'

I handed it to Wolf and fumbled to the front of the Nietzsche book.

Wolf read over my shoulder.

'To my good English friend, Viscount Lytton-Jones, in memoriam of a most successful visit, Herman Goebbels.'

'Holy shit!' he said.

I stared at it, stunned. 'Holy shit is right.'

'Drive safely.' Alistair Bevan seized my hand and pumped it. I thanked him, worrying some gravel under the toe of my sneaker. 'It's been really interesting.' I looked at the house, looked at the open door of the van, at the Earl's wife smiling at us in her misshapen tweed skirt, friendly, trusting.

'You know what,' I said, 'I think I left my cell in the library.'

I'd just got the book tucked down my pants and my shirt over the top when the old lady walked in. 'Found it,' I said.

'Well done.' She answered politely, though I could swear she could barely see me, let alone the cell I was waving in the air.

I passed through the door she was holding open. 'Nanny?' I hesitated, '. . . I meant to ask earlier . . . who is Viscount Lytton-Jones?'

She was quiet for a minute and I held my breath. Uncovering the vague snobbishness and eccentricity of the aristocracy was one thing, uncovering a Nazi collaboration was something else entirely. 'He died tragically,' she said finally. When she raised her eyes there was something fierce in their watery blue depths. 'I wouldn't mention it if I were you. It still causes the family a great deal of pain.'

As soon as Wolf steered the van out through the gates he turned on me. 'Show and Tell, Maggie,' he said, and I eased the photograph from my pocket.

'And just what do you intend to do with that?'

I didn't know, but I knew what the photo meant. Alistair, Con, William, Dinah, Robert. The names of the five children were written in pencil on the back. Viscount Lytton-Jones was Alistair Bevan's father. There was a story there, even if he was dead. It was just a question of finding it.

My mother once said that as a documentarian it was her job to shine the light into those dark corners where injustice was taking place because if you don't know what's happening, it doesn't affect your life, and if things don't affect your life, you do nothing to change them. There were crimes being committed all over the world, there were dirty secrets in every corner . . .

Back at the Cadogan Hotel I called *Newsline*. Bevan, potentially, was a very dirty little secret indeed but Alan's direct line didn't get me through to him and it took forty minutes of back-to-back talking to robots, literally, before the system found him.

'You better have something really good up your sleeve,' he said.

'I do.'

'Keep me in the loop and make sure you get everything for your original brief.'

'I will.'

Wolf waited till I'd hung up.

'So what are you going to do?' he asked for the second time and when I didn't answer he handed the photograph back to me. 'Tread carefully, Maggie,' he said. 'Whatever this means, it's probably not their finest hour.'

daniel

Maggie and her crew do not turn up at Stately Locations at the appointed time following their 'personal' day so Rory leaves the address with Alison and treats Benj to brunch in Yo Sushi round the corner, where plates of food are plucked like startled commuters from a moving conveyor belt. When Benj blurs his eyes, he imagines the accompanying clear soup bowls are shot glasses of gin. To distract himself from this taboo image he asks Rory when he first discovered Alistair and Audrey drank.

Rory tells him it was the time he nearly drowned.

I remember our mother then. She was never beautiful as such, but very striking. Strong features, thick dark hair. 'She was a great swimmer,' Rory tells Benj. 'She could have swum for England.' She'd grown up in Ireland and learnt to swim in the loughs and the sea. At Bevan she used to swim in the lake most days even in cold weather, cutting across the water, from jetty to boathouse, sleek as an otter in her thick rubber swimming cap.

The water was damn cold in that lake. Pike nibbled your feet and slunk around the jetty where there were only a few painful steps before the ground disappeared to nothing and the water became ten degrees colder.

Rory had only just learnt to swim when I announced we would steal the boat to go fishing. It was mid August and a hot, hot summer. We'd had a picnic and both Ma and Pa were drinking from the coffee flask. Coffee was a big thing for our parents. They took it with them whenever they left the house, once even driving the 10 miles back to Bevan because the flask had been forgotten. After coffee they fell asleep lying side by side on the tartan picnic blanket.

The boathouse smelt musty as we tossed the anchor in the boat and jumped down after it. Rory balanced his feet on either side to steady the boat as I eased it through the reeds and bulrushes, out into the bright sunlight.

'There's a Babar story like this,' Rory reminds Benj. 'Celeste and Babar give birth to triplets, Alexander, Flora and Pom, then embark on a series of fantastically irresponsible outings which these days would have social services rushing to fill out foster home forms.' He picks a Californian roll apart with his chopsticks. 'First they allow Arthur, who's, what, three or fours years old, to take Pom for a walk, but Arthur, who's rightly pissed off to be presented with not one but three sibling rivals pushes the pram over the cliff. Next, Celeste, who's gone berserk from breast-feeding triplets, gives the new-born Flora a rattle to suck whereupon she chokes. Finally Babar and Celeste go for a picnic and drink themselves insensible, leaving the toddlers to play by the lake. I mean everybody knows you don't let small elephants play by water,' Rory says, '*everybody* knows,' he trails off.

'And sure enough,' Benj says quietly, 'Alexander sneaks out in the boat and falls in.'

Rory caught the fishing rod in the weeds and gave it a yank. I lost the oars and Rory fell backwards. He thinks of Alexander as he sinks through the water. It's deeper and much colder in the middle of the lake and Rory can't get himself horizontal. The blackness of the water pulls at his legs. The crocodile swims towards Alexander and Rory worries about the pike. If they were a foot long at the jetty then imagine how big they are out in the middle. He's a lot more scared of being bitten than drowning.

He splutters up and down, down and up but just as his vision blurs to milky he sees Audrey powering towards him, her short hair capless. How she'd spotted him all the way from the bank, I've no idea. Just in time Babar throws the boat anchor into the throat of the crocodile. Just in time Rory feels himself plucked from the lake like a bobbing apple from a water keg. Crouched in the still drifting boat, I never saw such determination and purpose in my mother and I never would again.

'On the bank she gave me mouth to mouth,' Rory said, 'and in her mouth I tasted coffee.' He'd smelt it too on her breath as she'd hauled him back to shore. It was *her* smell, cosy and familiar. It clung to her like a scent and neither of us had ever found it unpleasant. She smelt of it in the morning and it was even stronger in the evening when she kissed us goodnight.

The next morning, Rory walked into the library. Mrs Bindey was on her hands and knees picking broken glass off the carpet. He handed her the top to the crystal decanter which had rolled to the doorway. The whole room reeked of coffee and he said so. Mrs Bindey straightened up and stared at him.

That was the day he discovered what whisky was.

'In retrospect, Babar was a latent homosexual,' Rory says.

'He most certainly was not.' Benj is incensed at this outing of his hero.

'He had an unhealthy preoccupation with his spats.'

'He was happily married to Celeste.' Benj takes a plastic dog turd from his pocket, puts it on an empty chicken yakitori plate and returns it to the moving conveyer.

'It's not normal for elephants to be that pernickety about their footwear.'

'He was the king of the elephants, he doesn't go by normal elephant rules.'

'Celeste had Munchausen's syndrome, Arthur was a retard and as for the Old Lady . . .'

Benj laughs. 'My father's convinced I'm a latent homosexual.'

'Are you?' Rory asks idly. He can see the crew's van mounting the kerb of the pavement outside.

'I have no idea,' Benj says. 'Maybe one of these days I'll be lucky enough to find out.'

News is part of our communal experience. News is a public service. I believe that good journalism, good television can make our world a better, fairer place.

— Christiane Amanpour

maggie

Sir Harding Montague was a wiry, extremely articulate man who enunciated his words in a voice unsettlingly lacking in peaks or troughs. He reminded me forcibly of a toad and, like the South American version of the species, when you squeezed him poison leaked from every pore of his skin.

Waverley, his Estate, was a gothic miracle of a house in the county of Suffolk. *Newsline* researchers had turned it up before Christmas. It hadn't been on the Stately Locations books, but Sir Montague had jumped at the idea of 'expenses' and Rory had grudgingly orchestrated a deal.

Montague had quite a reputation. He was notorious for his affairs with other women while his wife had quietly and discreetly died from cancer. He'd held a government position under Edward Heath, but had been fired when caught, 'in flagrante', as Rory put it, with a senior minister's wife. Montague's own description of the lady who had cost him his career was, 'Labia like an elephant's trunk . . . had to be careful or it would snatch things off the table when you weren't looking.' This dazzling imagery had made Dwight choke. Montague was an appalling character; snobbish, mis-ogynistic, racist, and he took obvious delight in discomfiting us. 'I don't like that man,' Montague said, once he'd made sure Dwight was within earshot. 'I don't like his shoes.'

'Actually that makes two of us,' I agreed. Dwight's inexplicable transmogrification into an English gent was continuing unabated. For Montague's opening gambit – a show of Waverley's grounds, Dwight had worn a new pair of brown brogues, which Wolf gleefully later reported gave him terrible blisters.

The afternoon we arrived, we were able, by sheer good fortune, to film a fox hunt. It was everything we could have hoped for. The red coats, the sherry, the baleful howling of the hounds as they were given a whiff of fox. We even got the anti-hunt protesters, and Montague's hysterically funny dealings with them. Rory was totally against us filming and spent an hour on the telephone trying to talk Sir Montague out of it, but Montague clearly relished the controversy and Rory, having driven straight back to London soon after delivering us, was 200 miles away.

When he reappeared the following day he was still angry.

'The hunting issue is highly inflammatory, as you're well aware, so if you're going to include it you need to under-stand it.'

I had been about to make the same point myself, but the lecturing tone of his voice got to me. 'What was it one of your poets, Oscar Wilde or someone, called it? The unspeakable in pursuit of the uneatable? Yeah . . .' I said smugly, 'That was it.'

'Actually,' he said, 'it was Shaw—'

'Are you trying to say that you're pro fox hunting?'

'That's not the point—'

'Well I mean you either are or you aren't, right?'

'I'm pro fox hunting and I'm pro the fox.'

'My people might call that sitting on the fence.'

'I can tell you what I'm not pro,' he said, 'and that's the trumpeting lines of hideous sanctimonious do-gooders like yourself, ignoring the wishes of people in the country-side . . .'

'I suppose you're up for clubbing seals too.'

'. . . who feel they can dictate to their "intellectual" inferiors, ignoring the fact that everyone in a democracy has a free choice.'

'And why not eat a little dolphin in your tuna salad?'

'Before you start preaching to me,' he said furiously, 'perhaps you should be obliged, in between bites of your steak sandwich, to watch lambs and cows being butchered in an abattoir. Did you know that when cows smell the blood of their own species they start screaming in panic?'

He was insufferably pompous. 'Hey, I film what I see,' I yelled at his retreating back.

We didn't see him for the rest of the day, which was unusual, given his fondness for frowning and spluttering during interviews. We were talking to Montague in his dressing room where he had requested to be filmed, back-lit and coiled on his bed in a hilariously opulent velvet dressing gown.

'What would you say was the purpose of the aristocracy?' I pitched him the routine question.

'To be the elite of course, to maintain the hierarchies of wealth and rank, to set an example.'

'How to be illiberal and redundant?' I was hoping to goad him into a full-scale rant.

Sir Montague put out a claw-like finger and tapped my knee. 'Ah, you want to play the socialist agitator do you, pussykins? Incite the masses to riot and revolution? Well I'd like to suggest that you're motivated by nothing more glorious than social envy.'

I was happy to ignore the pussykins. Unlike the other two shoots we'd been on since Bevan, Montague was prime material and I didn't want to risk him drying up.

'You're suggesting that my motive for making this film is to, what?' I said. 'Exorcise my own inferiority as an American?'

'Of course. We have culture, you have *Star Trek*. Tradition is the law we live by – tradition in your country is that revolting little children's habit of begging for sweets at Halloween.'

'Yeah, and you Brits are damn lucky we saved your butts or you'd all be singing "Deutschland Deutschland über alles" right about now,' I shot back.

He gave a cackle of laughter. 'I think you'll find that some Brits are *still* singing "Deutschland Deutschland über alles".' he said.

'What do you mean?' I sobered up quickly.

Despite my bullish optimism on the phone to Alan, I'd got no further on the Bevan story. The evening we'd returned to London, I'd sat up half the night browsing the Internet, systematically entering names and subjects; World War Two, Fascism, the royal family. I'd stumbled across a few relevant pieces; a headline in a 1948 newspaper with an accompanying picture, 'Aristocratic sisters pose in front of marching Nazis.' A lot of information about the British Union of Fascists; endless articles on Edward and Mrs Simpson.

The boys had been no help at all.

'What do we actually know about the English royal family?' I'd asked over room-service burgers.

'Well, even I know they're *all* a bunch of Germans,' Wolf said. 'Look, it says here that Lord Mountbatten changed his name to Mountbatten from Battenburg.'

'Why?' said Dwight. 'Was he Jewish?'

'You know,' Wolf salted his fries, 'I bet poor Nietzsche got a really bad rap because Goebbels admired him so much.'

The truth was Wolf had lost interest. With the Viscount dead he didn't think there was a story to pursue and though I badly wanted to find one, I was beginning to think he was right. Even Simon Brannigan, my BBC contact, had been dubious. 'It was well-known that members of the aristocracy saw positive virtue in fascist regimes,' he said. 'Hitler had acquaintances in some very influential circles. The problem is families and friends have always closed ranks . . . there's tremendous class loyalty. There have never been names.'

I mean, it was frustrating. I had a name, but I couldn't give it to anyone nor could I find any threads of a story to tie up to it.

I looked at Montague. His remark had been completely unguarded and I wondered how far he'd let himself be pushed.

'Isn't it true,' I said carefully, 'that certain members of the aristocracy were involved with—' but that was as far as I got. His hand snaked out and grasped my wrist.

'My dear,' he said, 'there are several reasons why you would be particularly ill advised to follow this line of questioning further.' I was startled. His tone was measured but there had been steel in that grip.

I couldn't concentrate on the rest of the interview. As soon as we wrapped it up I switched on my laptop upstairs and read through every note I'd made. The morning after Bevan, I'd blown off our early start at Stately Locations and instead raced off to a historical bookshop in the Strand where I'd found books on the fascist Oswald Mosley, the BUF and the Mitford sisters. Now I took them out of my suitcase and searched through their indexes and bibliographies looking for inspiration. One of them, *British Fascism*, had been written by a historian, a Professor Lunn, who I now noticed from the blurb on the inside cover, lived in London. After Montague we were scheduled to shoot background footage of the House of Lords back in London so on whim I rang information and to my utter surprise Lunn's number was listed. My luck held out because when I dialled the number a soft, cultured voice picked up on the first ring.

'Professor Lunn?' I asked.

'For reasons that escape me,' Rory said walking into the room a few minutes later, 'Your company is required at dinner.'

I snapped my cell shut guiltily. 'Don't people knock on doors in your country?'

'Been doing your homework?'

'Just looking up the genetic factor that makes Englishmen

so obnoxious.' I shut down the computer and slid it forwards to cover the address Professor Lunn had dictated.

'Well, tomorrow's project is to find ten more things about the English you really dislike,' he said grimly, 'and don't worry, you can be sure I'll be working equally hard in the opposite direction.'

Professor Lunn's house was in Bloomsbury. Oppressively dark, dusty and book-laden it seemed the typical lair of an academic. Physically speaking, Lunn the professor was straight out of central casting. Woolly, bearded, a hint of a shuffle. Opera was booming from behind the closed door when I rang the bell and once inside I nearly gagged on the air quality. He sat me down formally in front of a desk covered in overflowing ashtrays, and I expected a lot of good-natured preambling, but luckily he got straight to the point.

'If I understood correctly you're interested in the connection between pre-war Germany and the aristocracy,' he said, squeezing a roll-up between his thumb and forefinger.

'That's right.'

'In that case allow me give you the clipboard version,' he lit the cigarette. 'The prime minister of England, Chamberlain it was at the time, thought England was ill-prepared for war . . . there was the famous debate at the Oxford Union.'

'This house will not fight for king and country.' I'd actually found and read the transcript on the Internet.

'That's right,' the professor nodded approvingly. 'Word of this inevitably found its way to Hitler who therefore believed that he could take England without a fight,' he paused to allow ash to drop into the china saucer on his desk. 'These were the days when Edward and Mrs Simpson were an item. No doubt you've seen one of the many films,' he added, faintly disdainful.

I nodded.

'Edward was under the impression he could have a morganatic marriage, that he could be king, although she would never be queen. When it was made clear to him this was not the case, he was forced to renounce the throne. It is well documented that he met with Hitler's people in Portugal and the assumption was quite simply that Hitler offered him a deal. Edward would help Hitler get England and in return he would be put back on the throne complete with Mrs Simpson – as a puppet king to be sure, but still . . .'

'But after the First World War,' I said, 'how could he think of doing such a thing?'

'Those who do not learn the lessons of history are doomed to repeat them,' Lunn quoted.

'And there were others involved?'

'There would have to have been. People inside England, influential but "safe" people who Edward was in touch with. Help on the inside.'

'And who is safer and more on the inside than Viscount Lytton-Jones?' Wolf said. We were still mulling it over days later, 'You can see how it might happen, Edward calls his favourite cousin and arranges for him to come and visit his nice new friend in Germany.' He hoisted the camera onto the stand and screwed it down. The Bancrofts, whose house we were currently invading, sat on their couch and stared fearfully into the black depths of the lens. 'Bring the family, nursemaid and kids, why not? All very kosher.'

'Exactly, though *kosher* might not be the tip-top choice of word to use when weekending with Nazis,' I added.

I'd asked Lunn why nothing had ever been written about these cohorts.

'Because it was hushed up,' Lunn said simply. 'In those days the aristocracy had the money and power to hush anything up. The royals knew of course, but it was a family affair. No washing of dirty linen in public etc. You must understand – the idea that a member of the royal family had collaborated was *unthinkable* and by the time it might have come out . . . well . . . England had already declared war on Germany.'

'But keeping it quiet. It's an amazing abuse of power. Dealing with Hitler, I'm sorry but these people were out-and-out traitors.'

'Nobody ever knew exactly who was involved,' said Lunn, 'and besides, this all happened nearly seventy years ago, they're probably all long since dead.'

'Yes, I'm sure you're right,' I said resigned, 'but if they weren't . . .?'

'. . . Then it would be an even bigger scandal than Ted Turner having a sex change.' Dwight uncoiled the wire of his microphone and blew a ball of fluff from its head.

'That wasn't exactly the way he put it, but . . .'

'So what now?' Wolf asked.

'If all the players are dead,' I said grudgingly, 'nothing I guess. Without a warm body, it's just old news.'

daniel

Poor Lord Bancroft, born on a Monday, packed off to the nursery Tuesday, prep school Wednesday, Eton, Thursday, Friday to Oxford, where he graduated with a respectable 2.1. Saturday he enrolled in the army. Sunday entered the bank, then on Monday he inherited the family home by which time, like Solomon Grundy, he was already dead.

Thank God the house was of manageable size as long as he was conservative with his money. And Lord Bancroft was nothing if not conservative. A truly sober fellow, in the non-alcoholic sense of the word, he lived a quiet life; a few friends, a spot of shooting, the odd weekend party. But he'd never ridden on a motorbike, travelled with a backpack, had outdoor sex, or sex anywhere for that matter except in bed with the lights firmly off. He'd never eaten in a Thai restaurant, stayed up all night, had a take-away, watched an American sitcom. He'd never used a mobile, worked a fax, turned on a video or taped a show. He might have enjoyed many of these activities but they belonged to a different world, a world that didn't understand him, didn't particularly want him, a world of which he was thoroughly scared.

He met his wife at a point-to-point. They had interests

in common; gardening, country living. Their life stretched before them as cosy and predictable as a cup of Earl Grey . . .

Lloyds seized everything they had, bar the house and contents. Lord Bancroft took it on the chin, but his world shrank a little further. Money grew tight. Eventually he let his faithful butler go. Mr Nieve surprised him by opening up shop in a town, 30 miles away, selling antiques. He offered to work one day a fortnight for which Lord Bancroft was grateful.

It was a few months later when Lady Bancroft first noticed something.

'Have you seen my earrings, darling? The ones your mother gave me?'

'You wore them only the other night,' he reassured her, 'I remember it quite distinctly.'

But Lady Bancroft was meticulous with her belongings. She had a jewellery box lined in velvet in which she kept everything that was precious to her. She was sure she'd put them back.

One day the wicker seat on the dining-room chair wore through. The set was eighteenth-century English – six spares were kept in the cellar and only used when the table was extended for special occasions. In the cellar Lord Bancroft found only four. He rang Mr Nieve. 'I think you'll find there were only ever four, sir,' Mr Nieve said smoothly. The matter was dropped.

On it went, a pair of hunting boots, a vase, surprisingly valuable, or had it been broken a while back? The awful spectre of Alzheimer's crossed both their minds. They began keeping incidents from each other, but finally the inevitable happened. Lady Bancroft's brother came from America to visit. Lady Bancroft's Boston-bred sister-in-law liked nothing better than picking up antiques in English country towns. She returned, late Saturday afternoon, excited to be in possession of a pair of beautiful dining room chairs . . .

maggie

'The butler had been stealing from them!'

'He stocked his shop straight from their house,' Rory had said.

'And they never suspected?'

'Did they strike you as the type that would?'

The answer to that had so far been an emphatic no. Now I looked over to where Dwight was feeding the microphone under Lord Bancroft's sweater. Despite Rory's build-up, I couldn't think of a single question to ask them. After the prospect of Bevan and a real story, anything even approaching *Newsline*'s original brief seemed about as fresh as over-warmed takeout.

'These people are like waxworks,' I hissed to Wolf. 'Look at them, are they even alive? I mean how the hell are we going to make this interesting?'

'Ask them about their sex life,' Wolf said.

'Ask them about their sex life? Why, that's just brilliant.'

'Why not.' Rory appeared in the doorway, 'Go on, ask them. I dare you.'

'You dare me?'

'Why, can't you handle it?'

'This should be interesting.' Wolf sighed.

Most people are painfully self-conscious when you film them. They make a little joke, play to the camera, poke fun at themselves and Bancroft was no anomaly. He looked as if he'd rather have a tooth pulled than answer the question I'd asked him.

'Frightfully bad form,' he faltered, 'not the sort of thing one talks about at all,' and I felt bad. He was too uptight to give up much but at least he was willing. The question had been a cheap shot for a laugh and I wish I hadn't let myself been goaded into taking Rory's dare. 'You can kick me out any time, you know.' I told him, genuinely hoping he might, 'I really won't be offended.'

Lord Bancroft sighed ponderously. 'Well, my dear, you have to understand that for a certain class of Englishman, sex, as such, is not stumbled upon until much later on in life. Boarding school, the army, the bank. For Americans I'm sure it's as commonplace as going to supermarket – "recreational" I've heard you young people call it, but I don't believe I actually encountered a creature of the opposite sex before the age of twenty-five.'

'Oh come on, Lord Bancroft, surely you had one of those nannies?' I tried to jolly him along.

'Ah indeed I did,' he said.

'Scary things your British nannies, they beat you with a wooden spoon, make you eat cod liver oil and don't they tell you that you go blind if . . .' From the doorway, Rory groaned and shook his head. I fluttered my eyelashes demurely at him.

'As a matter of fact,' said Lord Bancroft, and suddenly I realized that something interesting was about to happen. Self-consciousness can be exhausting and in the end it's invariably easier to relax. The harder people find it to talk about themselves the more revealing the moment of total capitulation can be and as a reporter you learn to look out for it because get this moment on tape and you've hit the jackpot. As Lord Bancroft lost himself in some memory, his every muscle seemed to loosen up and when he sighed it was like the final breath going out of a dying body. Wolf saw it too and he zoomed in close on his face.

'. . . it was my twelfth birthday,' Lord Bancroft wasn't looking at the camera any more, but straight through it, back to some forgotten picture of his childhood, 'I was just recovering from the flu, if I remember correctly. No, no, she never beat me, dear Nanny, in fact . . . well, in fact . . . she . . .'

'She . . . yes? She . . .' I prompted.

'She seduced me.'

There was a stunned silence. Lady Bancroft turned to her husband, aghast. Rory's jaw dropped.

I was shocked. I hadn't been waiting for a moment of revelation, just a moment of . . . I don't know, *intimacy* maybe, or television intimacy at least. 'That's terrible,' I said, praying he'd go on. There was a pregnant silence.

'No, no, no,' Lord Bancroft said finally, 'Not so terrible . . .' another agonizing pause. 'In actual fact, I quite enjoyed it. You see,' he said cautiously, as though testing whether the thin ice he was already skating on might carry a little more weight, 'personally I'm rather partial to sex.'

'You are?' Lady Bancroft turned sharply.

Wolf quickly pulled back to include her in the frame.

'Yes, my dear,' Lord Bancroft turned to her. 'I'm terribly sorry, but I'm afraid I am.'

She lowered her gaze but when she raised it again, there was a flash in those pale green eyes. 'Well' she said crossly, 'You really might have told me because . . . so am I.'

'Cut.' I said.

Rory and Dwight were playing tennis on the Bancrofts' woefully unmaintained court. Rory was serving and I had to laugh. No American would be seen dead on a tennis court without the appropriate Nike shoes and Aggassi-sponsored Head racquet that Dwight was scampering around with. Rory was wearing faded shorts, a striped woolly scarf and, despite the cold, a mildewed pair of sneakers with no socks. His wooden racket was old and warped but he might have been playing with a frying pan for all the difference it made. He was a natural athlete, serving balls with absolute precision at poor hapless Dwight, who sent one after the other into orbit before Rory eventually dispatched him to poke around in a field of nettles outside the court to retrieve them.

'Ah, Maggie Monroe,' Rory caught sight of me, 'the woman that brought tantric sex to the upper class—'

But somehow I just wasn't in the mood for it.

'You know what, I dare *you* to say something nice for a change.'

Rory looked at me quizzically, then stuck his finger through the wire.

'What's that?'

'Truce?'

I hesitated then linked my finger with his.

'Truce,' I said and shook it.

'So I couldn't help looking at them after the interview and wondering . . .'

'What?'

'Well how they go about it.'

'*It* being sex?'

'What else?'

'You're thinking he has to make a noise like a capercaillie and she must respond like a terrified hen pheasant?'

'It's that whole politeness thing . . . go ahead, darling . . . no, I shouldn't really . . . oh go on, treat yourself, you come first . . . no, I insist . . . after you, my dear.'

'Thanks to you,' Rory said, 'now they're more likely be mounting each other neighing like warthogs.'

I burst out laughing. 'OK, so whose turn?'

'Mine unfortunately.'

'OK, truth or dare?'

For the first time since embarking on this oddball journey, Rory and I had managed to spend two hours in the car together without exchanging a single snitty remark. We'd come off the highway a while back and were now beetling through a series of small country lanes. A strong northerly wind was sending needles of rain across the windscreen of the Rover.

'I'm not up to another dare from you.'

'So truth then. Tell me one personal thing about your life.'

'Uh . . . name three birds of prey,' he said. 'How about we play that instead?'

'Coward.'

'Well what do you want to know?'

'I don't know. Anything . . . brothers . . . sisters, where you went to school. What do your parents do for example?'

'Uh . . . they're retired.'

'And before?'

'Unemployed.'

'They're retired from being unemployed?'

'See that?' Rory wound his window down.

'What?'

'Over there, church.'

The red herring was so obvious it might as well have been wearing a false beard.

'That heap of old stone you mean?' Actually it was beautiful. Tall and elegant, the church was built of honey-coloured brick.

'That is one of the few remaining sixteenth-century churches in England.'

'No kidding?' I said. Rory back-pedalled every time he came close to talking about himself so I was becoming an expert on ruined monuments of the English countryside.

'In 1537 Cromwell ordered the church to be plundered then burnt. When his soldiers came over the hill, Lord Haven, who owned the estate, set fire to his own house. The soldiers thought it was the church burning and so they left it standing. It has survived to this day.'

'Fascinating,' I executed a giant yawn.

'The sincerity of your sarcasm is impressive.'

'No, really,' I folded my jacket under my head and closed my eyes, but like all other personal fragments I'd wheedled out of him, I stored away the unemployed/retired family comment like a credit note to be redeemed later.

Rory Jones' car was a wreck. Stylish, sure, but mechanically a piece of junk – and it died on us without warning. Wolf and Dwight were ahead of us in the van, so no help there and the steep banks on either side of the road were too high to get a signal on my cell. We pushed the Rover onto the grass and waited for someone to come along and rescue us.

'Why do you drive around in something that doesn't work properly?' I pulled the collar up on my coat.

'I like old cars, they're romantic.'

'How can it be romantic to be standing in the rain waiting for a pick-up truck?'

'The English have a very strange definition of romantic. You wouldn't understand.'

'Try me.'

'Oh I don't know,' he sighed, 'extreme discomfort is romantic, crazy ideas are romantic, insane optimism is romantic, noble hopelessness is romantic – oh for Goodness sake, what is it now?'

'What?' I said.

'You've got that irritating face on again.'

'What irritating face?'

'Sort of smug, knowing incredulity.'

There was this great stand-up routine Bob Newhart did in the sixties, you probably remember it. Sir Walter Raleigh calls from America to try to sell the head of the West Indies Company on the idea of tobacco and this guy is not exactly convinced. 'It's a kind of leaf . . .? Uhuh . . . Let me get this straight Walt, you put *leaves* in your mouth? . . . and you do what? *You set fire to them?* What can I say, Walt, don't call us, we'll call you.'

Bob Newhart, Lenny Bruce, Mort Sahl, these were all names I grew up with. When Jay found a signed copy of Mort Sahl's 'Iconaclast' in my loft, he said, 'Aha . . . when satire and America coincided for the first and only time to my certain knowledge.' Jay claimed that Mort Sahl's tragedy was that he was brilliant with Eisenhower, but when Kennedy came in he was so happy that he ran out of material.

Anyway, every time Rory started with his how to be English lessons I'd say, 'Let me get this straight. What age are your children sent away to boarding school? Seven????????' Then he'd drop in something about these little seven year olds being made to fag and I'd say, 'Yeah, sure I knew it all along.' He'd say, 'No, no it's a kind of slavery of younger boys to older boys.'

'Uhuh?' I'd say. 'Well don't call us, we'll call you,' then give him my Bob Newhart face just to see how crazy I could make him.

'What can I say,' I shrugged helplessly, 'I feel it's my duty to more fully understand your people.'

'Well *my* people feel they have to romanticize trials and tribulations in order to accept them. Once they're accepted, we can have a nice cup of tea and forget all about them.'

'Aha, as in a nice cup of tea solves everything?'

'Exactly, as in when the Second World War was announced over the radio there was a power cut over the entire country because tens of millions of people rushed from their armchairs to boil the kettle for a nice cup of tea.'

'That's a great story. Is that true?'

'Perfectly true – war, by the way,' Rory added, 'being the embodiment of romanticism for the English, combining as it does discomfort, hopelessness, crazy ideas *and* insane optimism.'

War again. I couldn't get away from it. Not long after we started seeing each other I asked Jay whether he considered himself a war junkie. I'd spent most of the evening in his flat reading articles he'd written for Doctors without Borders. The articles were brutal but nothing to what being there must have been like. I wanted to understand what took him back time and time again. He'd been angry at the question. He took his coffee into the bedroom and didn't come back. I didn't know what to do. We hadn't known each other long enough to have laid down rules of engagement. I ended up staying because I had no idea how to leave. I fell asleep in his leather armchair and woke to find him removing the coffee cup from my hand.

'I'm sorry. I didn't mean to sound flip,' I told him.

'You're just young enough to think that love makes the world go round, Maggie,' he said heavily. 'Well it doesn't.'

'What does make the world go round then?' I knew what he would say; hate, war, grief, pain. Maybe he saw it in my face because he laughed. 'I don't know, kiddo . . . Pepsi probably. Could be Pepsi makes the world go round.'

He said he didn't like the word junkie, but was prepared to admit to being a recidivist. He told me war and danger held a hypnotic lure for him, and that for most people who got involved this was also true – until they burnt out. Most people in Jay's line of work burnt out a lot quicker than he did, so I wondered then, where were the scars from Jay's wars? Where was the blood?

My mother had two great theories. The first was her Scotch tape theory. She liked to mend things with it. This applied to everything. If it was broke it got Scotch taped. Items that were badly damaged got the double Scotch tape treatment; anything unScotch-tapable just got thrown away. It became a good joke for my father when I started dating.

'Is it Scotch-tapable?' he'd ask, finding me in tears over a boyfriend.

'I don't think so,' I'd sniffle.

'So throw him away.'

My mother's other theory was the blood. As a little girl, whenever I fell down and started bawling my mother would say, 'Is it bleeding?' as I presented her with my wound. 'Because if it's not bleeding it's OK.' Blood was her sole criterion for concern. No blood meant no crying allowed. This trick, believe it or not, worked until the day a neighbour's dog was hit by a car right outside our front door. Dad and I joined the small crowd that gathered. After a while the dog was pronounced dead. I looked for blood but there was none. That evening I asked my father what the dog had died of. 'Internal injuries,' he replied and this had profoundly scared me.

I had told Jay about my mother's blood theory and he

thought it very funny. He remembered it that night in his apartment.

'I'm not going to die from internal injuries if that's what you're worried about.' He laughed when he said it, but for some reason it made me want to cry.

'Now I come to think of it,' Rory was saying, 'your obsessive and rather tragic preoccupation with the repressed British and their stiff upper lips is simply an extension of this form of romanticism.'

'Oh,' I smiled, 'how do you work that one out?'

Rory pulled an old paper bag from the side pocket of the car and smoothed it against the bonnet. 'I'll make you a graph.'

Jay had sounded exhausted the last time I'd spoken to him. I asked him how he was and he said, 'Well behaved in many a doctor's office,' but I heard the tension tighten every word. We had one last gap coming up in the filming schedule, only a couple of days away. When Jay told me being in Bosnia made dealing with mudslides in Northern Pakistan seem like a stroll in the park, I told him he needed a break. We agreed to meet in Paris.

'Please do me the courtesy of paying attention,' Rory was saying. He'd drawn a circle on the paper bag, 'Extreme discomfort equals romantic equals insane optimism (because we believe a cup of tea will make everything all right) equals we bear with fortitude equals a stiff upper lip – ergo you think we're repressed.'

'Ergo?'

'Latin, ergo equals therefore.'

'Ergo,' I looked at the empty road, the broken-down car, the rain slicking his hair flat to his forehead and began laughing. 'You know, maybe it's not that all Englishman are hopelessly romantic, I think it could just be you.'

'What do you mean by "netting the sea"? Could you be a bit more specific?'

'Fishing,' Rory said, 'as in the deliberate trapping of the denizens of the deep.' He hauled a tangle of netting from the back of the Land Rover he'd borrowed.

'Fishing, as in poor harmless creatures flip-flopping around before they die a horrible painful death?'

Rory shook his head. 'Where does this appalling PC attitude come from? You wear leather, you pig out on steak.'

'Pig out on a steak – surely another very unfortunate mixed animal metaph—'

'Besides who was it who killed two beloved family pets in one afternoon?'

'That was accidental death—'

'And do you not eat fish?'

'Of course, I eat fish, I just think that whole hook in mouth thing is icky.'

'What's your preferred method of slaughter then? Shoot them with a rifle, electrocution? Or you could just question them to death perhaps?'

'Jesus,' Wolf rolled his eyes. 'Don't tempt her.'

A few gulls wheeled over the sea, squawking some unidentifiable warning to each other as we slid down the dunes. A group of tiny birds bowed their heads against the wind. Their legs, skinny as toothpicks, were mirrored on the wet sand. 'Dotterel,' Rory said, barely glancing at them.

It was a beautiful afternoon, sunny, crisp, the sky darkening to orange as dusk approached. By the time we'd had the Rover towed to our next pit stop, it had been too late to start filming. 'Netting the sea' had been Rory's alternative form of entertainment.

'For your next "how to be English lesson",' he announced, 'you have to be cold and wet for two hours without once complaining.'

'Oh God no,' I'd said, 'anything but that.'

We trudged along the beach. 'It's dead low tide,' Rory shouted over his shoulder. 'Perfect timing.' He turned and walked backwards, leaning against the wind.

'This can't be legal,' Dwight muttered. He looked apprehensively down the length of the deserted beach. Dwight was strictly a dry-dock boy, viewing the sea like some sixteenth-century Bruegel painting, dark, oily and filled with all kinds of scary monsters.

'It's highly illegal,' Rory said, 'but great fun. Sure you don't want to try?'

'Positive,' I said. 'I'll film.'

'Make a base over there.' Rory pointed at a small bay of rocks. 'You'll get some shelter. 'Take my coat if you're cold.'

'I'm fine, thanks.' But holding onto the camera, my hands were stiff as baseball mitts. He draped his coat over my shoulders. 'Keep this dry for me, would you?' He pulled it together under my chin and I was uncomfortably aware of his touch.

'This is what?' I said breezily, 'the North Sea? Famous for its oil rigs and freezing temperatures?'

'As opposed to – say the Pacific, famous for its balmy waters and palm trees?' Rory pulled off his boots and slung them towards me. 'Look after these too could you?' He rolled up his pant legs, picked up the wooden pole at the end of the net and stepped over a low breaker. He forged on as if walking fully clothed into the sea was normal and he was just running a little late for an appointment with King Canute. When the net was taut he stopped, waist high in water.

'Wolf, you come in halfway,' he shouted, 'and tell Lady Bracknell over there, he'd better stay on the break-line.'

Only then did I catch sight of Dwight's outfit glowing underneath the oilskin jacket he'd borrowed. Some sort of knickerbocker thing in garish check tweed cinched in at the knee. He saw me staring and had the grace to look faintly embarrassed.

'My grandfather's,' he said defensively.

'Oh yeah, sure they are, Smallboy.' Wolf stepped gingerly into the soapy water. I saw the shock of the temperature hit him. Resolutely he pushed on, waves breaking below his waist. Rory motioned for him to stop. Wolf groped in his shirt pocket for a half smoked joint and jabbed it into his mouth. He got a match to it and took a long hit.

From somewhere a cloud had snuck up on us. It was now starting to rain and I had to laugh. If this was Rory's attempt at bonding with his American brothers, it was going to backfire badly. Dwight and Wolf looked the very picture of horrified urbanites. I know my crew and let me tell you, ground cement runs in their veins. Besides, from the way

he was pulling at his crotch, I guessed that Dwight's pants
were already shrinking painfully. The rain soon became
relentless. Water seeped through the coat, through both
sweaters I'd put on and I could feel it cold on my skin. I
kept the three boys in the viewfinder as they moved forwards, parallel to the beach. Dwight was still hovering on
the break-line, dolefully clutching his corner of the net.

'They swim out into the shallows to feed,' Rory yelled,
'they'll come back in when the tide turns.' He wiped spray
off his face with his shoulder. 'When I say now, pull the
net round as hard as you can.'

I ran along the water's edge to keep up. The weather
had cleared for an instant to reveal the sun, dipped low in
the sky. Gallantly it tried to hang on but eventually yielded,
slipping into the ocean as if the effort of suspending itself
all day had finally proved too exhausting.

'Now,' Rory bellowed. He curled the net in a high arc.
'Dwight you bloody great poof . . . bring it in closer.'

Cautiously Dwight inched himself out to sea. A wave
broke over the tops of his rubber boots. He looked over at
Wolf, desperate for a little empathy, but Wolf had problems
of his own. Puzzled he stared at the water. His enormous
body jerked, he looked shocked, like he'd had his leg bitten
off by a hammerhead but hadn't yet taken in how serious a
problem that might be.

I watched in amazement as a smile broke over his face.
He hollered something then gripped the net and whooped
with delight. I panned round to Dwight, waist high in water.
His face was flushed with excitement. Rory, holding the
two sides of the net aloft, struck out for shore. I couldn't
believe it. Laughing and shouting the three boys dragged

the net in then collapsed, panting on the sand. Rory was first up. He hauled the net to safety from the advancing tide then peeled back its four sodden corners. Inside was a squirming mass of silver. He turned towards the camera and made an elaborate bow grinning from ear to ear. For a moment he was captive in my sights. He was Mandras from *Captain Corelli*, and his catch was for me and me alone. I found myself looking at him much longer than the image warranted, protected by the camera's clinical lack of emotion. With his fisherman's jumper, bare legs underneath rolled-up trousers and his black hair blowing in the wind, he looked twelve years old. I wanted to pull the camera down to film the fish but I couldn't. I was held by Rory's face and then it struck me why. I felt my heart beat. It was just the one thud, but it was loud enough to make me freeze-frame the image in my head. There was nothing in his face, nothing except pure joy of the moment.

They fuck you up, your mum and dad
They don't mean to, but they do.
They fill you with the faults they had
And add some extra, just for you.

— Philip Larkin

daniel

During the next break in filming when Maggie heads to Paris, Rory drives to Bevan. In the hall he breathes in the musty smell of the house and knots his scarf round the throat of the Chinese Buddha on the stone table. It's Friday evening so as he pushes through the swing doors to the kitchen it occurs to him that this week he could have been on that dig in Turkey. He could be squatting on his haunches and feeling the hot sand sifting through his fingers. He could even be flirting with that lithesome interpreter with the buck teeth from Fez – or maybe he could have talked Maggie into blowing out whatever business she was supposed to be taking care of and dragged her along with him . . .

'Darling, how lovely,' says Audrey unwrapping the fresh bread he has brought from the deli. She puts it straight into the deep freeze and removes a frozen loaf of Mother's Pride for dinner.

Rory has renewed his monthly promise to himself. Tonight he will talk to Alistair about selling Bevan.

But after dinner, Nanny retires upstairs, Grandpa listens

to the radio in his bedroom, Alistair watches the ten o'clock
news and Audrey falls asleep, her feet on top of Lurch.
Rory bunks out and instead sits in Alistair's study and tackles
the pile of unopened mail. He's appalled by how bad the
situation has become. Alistair has always displayed ostrich
tendencies when it comes to financial obligations but these
days it's not just bills he ignores, it's all letters from polling
cards to farm notices. Correspondophobia is what he suffers
from – in my opinion, a perfectly rational fear of any docu-
ment that arrives in a brown envelope.

When Rory first tackled the finances of Bevan he was
optimistic that careful planning and economizing would
make a difference. He soon realized he might as well stand
over the loo and ritually flush down wads of notes with the
Queen's head on. Bevan is a house that *eats* money. It's as
if the architect, as a devilish experiment, set out to see just
how uncost-effective he could possibly make it. A local
paper once wrote an article on Bevan simply quoting statistics. They reported a staggering 240 doors, 75 of which
led directly outside. Multiplying the cumulative draught by
the average winter temperature, they'd come up with one
hell of a heating bill.

So this is the Herculean task Rory has inherited. And
it's not a task meant to be completed, simply carried on.
Even for someone who signs up for it, this job can wear
you down until you have no passion left to burn. If you
don't sign up for it you might as well chain yourself to the
rock and, like Prometheus, wait for that great eagle of
frustration and futility to peck your liver out day after day.

Since the accident, Rory has had a choice to make. The
same choice I had to make a few years ago and one, at the

time, he fought me tooth and nail on. What was the point of keeping Bevan, he argued – if our parents were cold and tired, if they couldn't cope and their backs hurt, if they never took a holiday, didn't want friends to stay, if they had no fun, no bloody fun at all – but what I couldn't drive through his thick head was that if you took them away from Bevan, made them live in a cottage, dwarfed by their possessions, no trees to plant, no clearing to be done in the lake-field, no bonfires to be built, no head scratching about the latest damage to the drains in Bindey's cottage – then they wouldn't be our parents any more, because Bevan is in every breath they take. They cannot exist as separate entities and to force them to do so would be to expose them, to turn them into shadows of their former selves. Rather than being acceptable eccentrics, they'd just be two tragic septuagenarians clashing empty bottles at each other in drunken cheer. Besides, the point of keeping Bevan is that it deserves to remain standing. *Keep the house going for future generations.* You look after your inheritance. You protect the land. That's what primogeniture is all about. And OK, I didn't like it when it was my job, and now it's Rory's, he likes it even less, but decayed, putrid, atrophying though they might be, houses like Bevan are important. Tradition *is* important. If Rory gives up on Bevan, he'd bloody well better understand what's at stake.

But I don't want any favours from my brother. Saturday morning when he takes a walk with Alistair and tries to raise the subject I watch as crippling guilt and misplaced loyalty push him once again into a decision his heart is not in. Well you can stop that Rory, don't bloody lay this thing on my head. Why is it the custom to canonize the dead in the false memory of the living? I wasn't such a great brother half the time, so don't make out that I was some kind of hero, I was crap the last few years. And if you want proof? Remember that beautiful girl with tiger eyes? The one you were sniffing around for ages. The one who was sacked the very first day from her big Opportunity Knocks job, who cried those plaintive little tears on your shoulder? Well know this – I was the one who slept with her.

maggie

I'd been really excited at the prospect of two days in Paris, but when it came to it there was a problem finding a decent room. There was an Internet convention and every hotel in the city was booked. Eventually the concierge from the Cadogan found a room and I took it blind. When I arrived in Paris and walked into the bedroom with its sanitine coverings and general air of beige, I remembered the conversation about the English's warped sense of the romantic. Rory had claimed his ideal hotel in Paris was not the George V but a plain boarding house; a brass bed with an agonizing dip in its centre and an old crone stumping up the stairs with a bowl of steaming black coffee in the morning.

I mean there was nothing wrong with this room apart from it being identical to every other mediocre hotel room in the world. It was the coffee machine that got me – the brown plastic filter machine that stood on the dressing table next to paper packs of sugar and decaf coffee – part of the world's nod to the convenience-seeking Americans. I have been in some real polyester palaces in my time, some swanky hotels too. Extremes are great, but middle of the road? This one just depressed the life out of me.

Several hours later, I found just what I was looking for in the sixteenth quarter. The room was huge and old fashioned with peeling wallpaper and brass fittings. The bathroom had damp in one corner and a couple of the black and white tiles were broken – but there were no pastels, no coffee machine and of course, I realized too late, no CNN for Jay.

'Interesting choice,' he said when he arrived.

Drugged by an afternoon nap, I watched him groggily as he looked round the room.

'Tell me the truth,' he sat on the bed, 'am I too old and out of touch to appreciate that this is a hip hotel?'

'I'm really sorry.'

He laughed and kissed me. 'Did you know that when you're cranky your upper lip gets shorter?'

'Does it?'

'Yes it does.'

'Is it short now?'

'It's retracted almost entirely into your nose.' He kissed me again. 'Oh look here it comes, that's better.'

I laughed but he was right, I was cranky. The room wasn't romantic at all. It was damp and cold. Jay was sweet though. In the spirit of spontaneous bookings we chanced a family-run Italian restaurant he knew. It was only six o'clock when we sat down to eat but even so the restaurant was full. I was amazed by how attentive the service was until Jay, who couldn't keep a straight face any longer, admitted the owners were identical twins.

'So how is snobbery, debauchery and lunacy coming along?' he asked.

I began giving him a suitably witty account, but he soon interrupted.

'And who is this Rory character?'

'Oh just a guy, you know, the agent for the houses.' Saying it though, I felt the same guilt you get walking through the green light at customs when you have something to declare.

'Have you slept with him yet?'

'Give me another day or two.' I picked up the lamb bone and sucked out the marrow.

Jealousy was a relatively uncharted territory for us. I once asked Jay about all the nights he was away.

'Are you getting bourgeois on me, Kiddo?' he'd replied. When he saw this wasn't the answer I was looking for, he said. 'You're asking me whether I am *faithful* to you?' as if this was too high-schooly an attitude for him to dignify with a reply, 'You know what I feel about you.'

I thought the reply ambiguous, so I didn't push it further.

'He's been driving us around, a guide sort of, anyway, don't worry . . . he's just a baby.' I stopped.

Something in Jay's face flickered, but he didn't miss a beat.

'How many months is this baby?'

'A little over four-hundred and fifty would be my guess.'

I watched him as he reversed the calculation. Age was one of the few things I think he was frightened of.

He asked me once what my father missed most about being young.

'I don't know.' I still thought of my father as being young. At sixty-five he had become a sort of guru and consultant to stage lighting designers and could be found telling tales of the good old days when Dylan and Baez were king and queen and when tuning in and turning on was still a middle-class luxury.

I was about to answer 'excitement' but thought better of it. Instead I said, 'His ponytail I guess.'

Jay nodded. 'As good an answer as any.'

After we left the identical twins restaurant, Jay told me he might have to go back to Sierra Leone. He told me he didn't want to but I thought I could hear something else in his voice. We walked for a while. The moon shone on the curves of the cobblestones, black and polished. I heard the sound of a piano being played. We stood still as the notes tumbled out of a window above us, beautiful and melancholy.

'Listen,' I said. 'It could almost be Rubinstein.' I wanted him to kiss me then, just to have a cheesy moment in a narrow street in Paris.

'It ain't though.' Jay turned his coat collar up. I knew he wanted to go back to the hotel so meanly I made him walk on.

I think I needed something in Paris to inspire us. I tried to imagine us living there, just another pair of lovers, shopping for bread in the market, bargaining with crotchety dealers for the tin toys that, for some obscure reason, Jay loved to collect. But it wasn't to be.

On the next street corner Jay stopped and hunched his shoulders around a cough. I thought it looked deliberate, like he was trying to keep it quiet. The cost of a cough could be a bullet, I thought melodramatically. I waved down a cab.

Back in our brass bed with its dip in the centre, Jay reached for his paper and I felt my upper lip shortening. I knew I wanted more out of the evening but I couldn't isolate exactly what.

'What is this revisionist trash they're endlessly spouting?' Jay was shaking his head. It wasn't a question that required an answer and though he went on to explain what had enraged him – something in local government – all I heard was nationalism, fascism, interventionism on an eternal loop.

'Can we not talk politics for once?' I horrified myself by saying.

He turned to look at me. 'OK,' he said evenly, 'what shall we talk about?'

'I don't know.' His tone had made me feel five years old. 'Something light. Something *fluffy*.'

'I'm sorry, Maggie, I don't do Martha Stewart.'

I should have laughed but I couldn't. I curled up, away from him. I heard the rustle of newspapers being opened, but I don't think he was reading because I didn't hear the pages turning. After a while he put his fingers through my hair and rubbed my scalp gently.

'Please turn round,' he said. And I did. Blotting the dampness on my cheeks on the pillow first.

'Do you have any idea how lucky we are? Our relation-ship is made up of perfect free-standing moments . . . we get to travel light, no baggage, duty-free.' He put his arms around me and kissed the top of my head. Then he read me excerpts from the *Washington Post* in his Truman Capote voice which he did so brilliantly I laughed till my stomach ached.

'So Duchess of Roxmere, or the barmaid?' Wolf asked.

'Neither,' Dwight said.

'You can't have neither.'

'Suicide then.'

'You can't have suicide, you have to choose.'

'I'm telling you, neither.'

'My rules.'

'Sorry,' Dwight was outraged, 'my dick.'

We were having a pub lunch in a small village in Somerset. We'd unloaded our equipment and settled into Stamford, whose owner, the deeply conservative Duke of Normouth, more or less owned the county. His son Miles was due to arrive that night with a weekend party of younger guests. As this was the last house on the Stately Locations itinerary and as we seemed to have filmed nothing but middle-aged couples we'd decided to stay on.

Rory returned from the bar clutching bottles of coke and beer. 'What about you, Rory?' Wolf said. 'Who'd you'd sleep with – the barmaid, or the Duchess of Roxmere?'

'The Duchess is a client, so it would have to be the barmaid, who oddly enough,' he craned his head to give her a closer look, 'is rather sexy – in a terrifying sort of way.'

'OK,' Wolf said, 'now the barmaid or . . .' he looked around, but apart from the odd gnarled local the pub was deserted. His eye settled on me, 'Maggie!'

'Hey leave me out of this.'

'Hmmm.' Rory made a big show of chewing it over. I was about to protest again but Wolf put his hand over mine.

'American girls don't really find English men attractive.' Rory said.

'Oh and you know this because?'

'Ruined by their mothers, emotionally castrated, and ultimately gay.' These were my own words he was quoting back to me and to my disgust I felt my face redden up. 'I'm not saying Maggie's not passable looking but who wants to be put under the microscope and dissected?'

'Like I said,' I played for indifference. 'No passion.'

'We have passion. We just don't talk about it. You're not going to find an Englishman who'll declare himself on the first date.'

'Well why not?'

'Because an Englishman is obliged to play the game. He must follow the rules. To ask you out is to declare a romantic interest. To declare a romantic interest is to expose himself. In order to avoid that horror he is forced to insult you.'

'Insult you?'

'Yes, it's how an Englishman courts.'

'Oh,' I said faintly.

'First he must embarrass himself horribly, then it's advisable to highlight his own worst faults, finally it's important to be as rude as possible to the girl he longs to marry.'

'Jesus,' I said, 'no wonder you weirdos sleep with your dogs and take your wives for walks in the countryside.'

*

En route back to Stamford I asked him whether he followed his own rules.

'Of course.'

'So you insult all the girls you like.'

'I have a Ph.D. in verbal abuse.'

'And have you found this successful?'

'Actually I got as far as the proposal stage.'

'You're *married*?' It hadn't even occurred to me.

'Actually. No.'

I felt stupidly glad. 'Uh, divorced?'

'She left before the wedding.'

'*Before* the wedding?'

'She didn't take to the weather.'

'Jeez, where'd she been living all her life,' I matched his flippant tone, 'down a rabbit hole?'

'Rome.'

I tried conjuring up a picture of Rory sauntering through the Colosseum with a dark-eyed Italian girl but for some reason I kept superimposing my own image in her place.

'So . . . uh . . . what was she like?'

Rory's look said, *Enough of these tiresome questions.*

'Come on,' I wheedled, 'I'm just making conversation.'

'Why don't you just shine a bright light in my eyes?'

'Oh I see, you're a little uptight about this.'

'Not a *little* uptight. I am *very* uptight.'

'OK I'm sorry,' I relented. 'End of interview, I swear.'

The Rover hummed in neutral, stationary in front of a level crossing. The arm of the barrier was down. We waited . . . and we waited some more.

'So was she pretty?'

He ignored me.

'C'mon, tell me if she was pretty at least.'

'There's the train now.' Over to Rory's right, white smoke was rising through the trees.

'Are not Italian girls usually pretty?' I mused.

A muscle was working in his cheek.

'Was she smart? Funny? Did she have enormous breasts?' The train drew into the station.

'I mean you never know, she could have regretted dumping you. She could be pining for you, obsessing over you. She could even be stalking you, waiting for just that right moment to strike.' I peered through the window. 'If your ex-girlfriend's a psycho, I really need to know what she looks like . . . for my own self-protection if nothing else.'

I stole a look at him. He was laughing.

'Wait. Over there,' I pointed, 'is that her?' A woman had clambered off the train. Fifty years old or so, she strutted along the platform wearing the tightest of red suits. She had peroxide hair, orange make-up and impossible white stilettos.

Rory peered through the windscreen. 'Are you quite mad?' he said regretfully. 'You think I'd let someone like that go?' He gripped the steering wheel forcefully, 'I'd be a *fool*.'

I was laughing. He turned to me and his grin was huge and so was mine. Then like someone else entirely was pulling our strings we leant into each other and I knew that in a nanosecond we would be kissing. My whole body fizzed with how good that would be.

I pulled back abruptly. What the hell was I thinking?

*

Stella arrived with the rest of the house party. She was an artist of some kind. That she and Rory knew each other was obvious. When she walked into the drawing room she draped her arms around his neck and pressed her body against his. She kissed him on the mouth then watched his face as he talked.

She must have asked him what he was doing because they both glanced in my direction and she nodded, swinging a small sheepskin handbag fastened with a horn button. Her eyes said, *Watch it toots, this one's mine.* She had long dark hair which waved in the right places and despite her height, tiny elfin ears. Everything about the way she moved said waif, coltish, gamine. You could almost see her pheromones flying through the air, and even they were designer.

For the last three weeks we'd been filming our various aristocrats without the hindrance of guests and, as with any small group of people, you establish a familiarity that everyone becomes comfortable with. Now surrounded by these interlopers with their expensive bohemian clothes, jobs in theatre, art and fashion, it struck me again how little I belonged here. They were Wonder Women and I was Danger Mouse.

Looking at these girls and myself, we were different creatures altogether. Stella, for instance, was stick thin, I'm skinny too, but it was as though her limbs had been carved from a different category of tree to mine. I couldn't stop looking at her, so I could hardly blame Rory for doing the same. I hid behind Wolf and Dwight, shrubs from my own forest, until a gong proclaimed dinner. I worked on automatic pilot, Wolf and Dwight moved about the table with the camera, I asked questions, listened to answers, but all the time aware that I was watching Stella watching Rory.

Ever since the moment at the train crossing, things had changed. I felt knocked off centre, no longer sure how to look at Rory, unable to remember how I'd treated him the day before or even two hours earlier. This unwelcome feeling of unease and desire had crept up on me, self-inflated in my head and like a sleeping bag I couldn't roll it up tightly enough to stow it away. I don't know if he was aware of it, but I was. Very aware. Much too aware.

After dinner, the men drank port and the women congregated in the drawing room. All the girls smoked, but Stella was the one I sought out to ask for a light.

'Of course,' she said politely.

I told her I'd once heard this great urban myth. Some girl from LA had gone to stay with her fiancé in England in an incredibly grand house party like this one. The girl had been nervous and lit up a cigarette before dessert. The Duchess or whoever it was stood up abruptly and rung the bell for the servants.

' "The American appears to believe the meal is at an end," the Duchess had said and remained standing. Everybody was forced to stop eating and leave the room. Unreal huh?'

'That was my mother,' Stella said quietly.

We had been warned there would be after-dinner games. 'Kick the pot' was to be played in the pitch dark — which meant we wouldn't be able to film. We reached a compromise. There would be just enough light to film but not enough to ruin the tension. That tension could exist in a game of hide and seek played by adults was news to me but I kept quiet and listened while the guests downed brandies and rules were explained.

'The point of the game is for HE to catch and identify all the players. HE may identify players by touch, or trick players into identifying themselves. If HE identifies a player wrongly, that player is free to go.'

I went into a huddle with Wolf to work out shots. I hadn't yet figured out this English obsession with games, but my best guess was that it was their way of opting out of talking to each other so when Rory passed I chirruped, 'The lengths you people go to to avoid intimacy.'

'You think so?' he grabbed my hand and pulled me into the circle of guests. 'Then time you came in from the sidelines for a change.'

Straws were drawn for He and it was Rory who pulled the short one out. He began counting and we all scurried off. Within seconds the house was silent except for a stealthy footstep or creak of a door as hiding places were found and abandoned. 'One hundred,' Rory yelled, 'ready or not, here I come.'

Soon the game was being played in earnest. Behind a curtain, curled up on a wide window sill in an upstairs room I waited, feeling more than a little foolish. I thought of Jay and of what an absurd parallel we were making. He was in a country where people were playing their own after-dark games of hide and seek for real. I tried to imagine what he was doing at that moment. Having a beer with a

NATO rep in some motel, or discussing fundamentalism with an over-eager first-time journalist. At a pinch he could be playing bridge – a game he loved and claimed an addict could find a fix for in any country – but one thing was for sure, he would not be playing 'kick the pot' in the middle of the English countryside with a bunch of junked-up ex-public schoolboys. It was almost shaming, then, how much I was enjoying it.

The stillness in the house was punctuated by the occasional scuffle as someone was cornered, and ongoing wails from imprisoned Hoorays. Good-natured warnings were howled from the prisoners' den. 'Do not attempt rescue. HE is sitting on the pot. Get off the bloody pot you filthy cheat.'

Finally, after a prolonged silence, I heard footsteps powering down the stairs and a blood-curdling scream of, 'Pot's Out!' There was a roar from freed prisoners. A fellow guest burst by me, panting heavily. I could dimly make out his shape as he squeezed himself into an oversized umbrella stand. My legs were badly cramped, I had to move, it was now or never. I crept stealthily along the corridor. 'Pot's in,' someone shouted. Feet again thundered up the stairs like HVO troops on the rampage. More shouting. Chaos, then it was all quiet on the western front. I was out in the open – sorely in need of a hiding place. I dropped to my knees by the wall. Ha! I would fight and die a soldier's death but the wall I was leaning against gave way. I reached out with my hand. It wasn't a wall, but a tall heavy screen. Perfect. I slipped behind and forced my breathing under control. Enveloped by the darkness and silence, I soon lost track of time and place. My ears tuned to every noise, however insignificant, analysing it for danger. It was really unnerving just how real the game felt. The sense of being hunted was genuinely creepy. I could have been the last Christian on the run from Islamic killers. The hairs on my arm rose as I heard a creak. I froze then felt a stab of real fear. I peered between the hinges of the screen, but through the blackness saw nothing. I relaxed but then moments later, there it was again. Somebody was heading my way. My heart drummed. I shrank against the wall, trying not to breathe. It was hot. My shirt was damp with sweat – with a terrible jolt I realized that the screen was being peeled back, panel by panel.

'Aha,' said a voice softly.

The pads of Rory's fingertips touched the side of my head, moved slowly down my face then round the back of my neck. I said nothing, I would not talk and give myself away but the game Rory was playing was breaching every rule in the Geneva Convention. His fingers found the edge of my T-shirt, brushed against my rib cage. I was barely breathing, running out of oxygen, running out of resolve. My face was burning. When he kissed me it was like a ghost kissing a ghost because I couldn't see him and I certainly couldn't recognize myself. I slid down the wall, his grip tightened on my shoulders then let go – and suddenly, abruptly – I was alone.

Stella needed a lift to London. We'd finished packing the equipment into the van after breakfast when she came down the steps with her suede bag and threw it into the boot of the Rover.

'You don't mind do you, Rory?'

Rory glanced at me.

'No problem,' I said mechanically, 'there's plenty of room with the crew.'

And suddenly it was all over. There Rory was, shaking Wolf's hand. 'I'm sorry I won't be around over the weekend,' and it was only then I remembered he'd warned us – right at the start – of another commitment. 'Parents' anniversary,' he now explained, and gave Wolf a pained look.

'No problem, man,' Wolf clapped him on the back. 'Come to New York sometime. Anytime. I'll take you to a Rangers match.'

I stood a short distance away, eyes itchy from the dust of a sleepless night. After 'kick the pot' had petered out everyone had drifted around, talking, swilling brandy round glasses. Stella had ensnared Rory on a couch built for two. She kicked off her kitten heels and curled her legs up underneath her. She twirled her hair around her little finger as she meowed.

I went to bed.

Rory caught my arm halfway up the stairs. 'Maggie . . . don't go . . . the night is still young . . . we could, er, let's see . . . do a thousand-piece puzzle . . . read *War and Peace* out loud, alternatively . . .'

'Rory. I don't think I should.'

'Should . . .' he said carefully, 'for such a small and uninspiring word, "should" has so many tiresome impli-cations.'

'Yes it does.'

'Why?' he demanded. 'Because you're a lefty liberal

New York feminist and I'm a sexist, emotionally castrated Englishman?'

'Something like that.'

'Minor problems.'

'Rory?' We both turned.

Stella was at the foot of the stairs smoking a cigarette. Property rights were printed all over her face.

And now it was too late. The morning after the night that never was.

'Call me of course if you need anything urgently, otherwise . . .' Rory was standing in front of me, 'otherwise, good luck . . . and, er, send me a tape, if you remember.'

'Sure.' I stuck out my hand and, painfully aware of Dwight and Wolf hovering, said my professional thank yous. Rory climbed into his car. I busied myself with equipment shuffling as the engine of the Rover fired up. He hooted the horn.

'Bye,' I said and gave a mock salute of sorts.

'Bye-bye,' Stella called out of the window. She waved gaily as Rory drove out of my life.

daniel

Talk about spineless. What the hell is he thinking? Actually, that I can tell you. He's thinking why, oh why does he specialize in flighty foreign girls. He's thinking hopeless, no future, not even as a temporary refuge because, for certain whacky reasons of principle, Rory believes it's wrong to use people to stop up the holes in your soul. In other words he's retreating behind those stuffy Anglo Saxon sensibilities of honour and fairplay. If it had been me, I'd have tossed Stella out of the window and given Maggie a damn good shagging but seduction is an oblique art and Rory has never fully been aware quite how to practise it to its greatest effect. Once I accused him of having an old-fashioned attitude to women. He told me he was sick of having to compensate for my behaviour. It was true, I had a tendency to drop girlfriends at his feet like roadkill, sweet bloodied doves with their feathers all sticky and matted and proudly say, 'Now look what I've done.'

Back in London, Rory mopes on the sofa in Benj's flat whilst Benj, Pimlico's resident gastronomic genius, prepares him a 'snack.' Carefully positioned on the kitchen worktop stands a jar of sandwich spread, a bottle of salad cream and a pork pie. Benj cuts slices of Mother's Pride into triangles, spreads them with butter, then places them on the dusty blow heater to harden. Those of you who were sent to that great institution known as the British boarding school will recognize these Red Cross items. The rest of you unfortunate enough to have been kept at home, fed with your mother's home cooking, unable to experience either the pleasures of paedophiliac gym teachers or the rigorous beatings of assorted sadomasochistic masters will not appreciate why boarding school is to thank for England being a nation reduced to rapture by Marmite on toast.

'God I miss it sometimes,' Benj says. He smears sandwich spread on the bread and balances a wedge of pork pie on top. 'Great food, parental escape.'

He takes a bite. 'Frankly, school was everything a boy could want.'

'A little short on female company perhaps.'

'You are surely forgetting the twin marvels of matron's bosoms.'

'Thankfully I am.'

'For years after I left I used to ring sick bay just to imagine those vast mammary glands rubbing against each other as Matron ran to answer the phone.' Benj looks dreamy.

'No doubt she's still single,' Rory says dryly. 'Why don't you give her a call.'

'Talking of single women,' Benj passes over a morsel, 'how was your jaunt with the fragrant Miss Munroe?'

'It had its moments.'

'She boil anybody else's rabbit?'

'Actually,' Rory says, 'she showed remarkable restraint.'

'Was Miles's sister in residence?'

'I saw her.'

'Did you sleep with her?'

'Are you insane?' Rory nearly chokes on his pork pie.

'Why, what's wrong? She's nice, well . . . when I say nice what I mean is, she's available, she's handsome—'

'Quite. I'd be more inclined to feed her a sugar lump than sleep with her.'

'And Stella?' Benj says slyly.

'Stella.' Rory sighs. 'Stella should come with an "emotional vacuum" warning round her neck.'

Benj snorts. 'You're getting ridiculously hard to please in your old age.'

'As a matter of fact,' Rory says moodily, 'that's not strictly true.'

maggie

'*Madrid.*' Wolf reads out loud from a copy of the *Week* magazine in my bedroom, '*Jose Astoreka set a new world record by crushing thirty walnuts between his buttocks in fifty-seven seconds.*' He chuckles. '*Dortmund. A top German surgeon was fined four thousand pounds for making his patients do Hitler salutes. Claims that he was trying to improve their shoulder mobility was thrown out of court.*'

Dwight picked up another reel of film and checked its code against his list. 'Half of these are labelled wrong, Wolf.' He scratched out a number and corrected it with a resigned sigh.

'*Seattle. Lovelorn woman is accused of eating twenty red roses in a flower shop.*'

'Is the Duke of Normouth also Baron Normouth?' Dwight was poring over the wedge of notes that Massey had provided us with, pedantically checking the spelling and titles against the film's labels.

I pressed my knuckles into my temples. The drive to London had been long and snagged with thick traffic. I'd been silent the whole journey nursing a wall-to-wall headache.

'What about Bevan?' Dwight looked up, 'Seventh or the eighth Earl?'

'Who cares.' Wolf threw the magazine onto the bed. 'Let's go eat.'

'Here we go,' Dwight flicked the page. 'Bevan, Eighth Earl of, Alistair Joclyn, Jesus, look at the amount of other names he has, Ramsay, also Danby, Reevesdale, Lytton-Jones. Oh wait, here we go, Viscount Lytton-Jones, Daniel, deceased 1999 . . .' He squinted at the page. 'Hang on, Maggie. This is weird, Viscount Lytton-Jones was Alistair Bevan's father, right?'

'Mmmm.'

'But he can't be.'

'Why not?' Idly I picked up Wolf's discarded magazine.

'Because it says here he was born in 1961.'

'Let me see that,' I snatched the piece of paper from him and scanned down the tiny print, 'Viscount Lytton-Jones. Daniel, born 1961 . . . Wolf he's right . . .' The silly poker rhyme I'd invented to remember the hierarchy of titles came back to me. 'Dwight, when is a viscount not a viscount?'

'When he becomes an earl,' Dwight said promptly.

'On his father's death . . . exactly! That's it, we're not looking for a viscount at all.

'But we have an earl — Alistair Bevan is the earl.'

'Yes, but don't you see? That photograph was taken in 1938 when our traitor was still a young man — at that time it's conceivable his father *and* grandfather were still alive.'

'She's babbling,' Wolf said.

'No, she's right,' Dwight's face was pink with excitement. 'When one generation dies, everyone inherits the next title up. If the grandfather and father both died *after* that photo was taken, the viscount would have moved up two rungs – he'd be a marquess or a duke or something—'

Danby, Marquess of Danby . . . got it,' I stabbed at the page with my finger. 'Issue: Alistair, Con, Dinah, William, Robert.'

'Born 1904.' Dwight read over my shoulder. 'I cannot believe we didn't check this before.'

'And died?' I hardly dared breathe.

'Not died.' Dwight stabbed at the spot with his finger.

'Not died as in . . . not dead?' Wolf was now peering over my other shoulder.

'Not died as in alive,' Dwight said.

'Holy Toledo,' I turned and stared at them both, 'a warm body.'

daniel

'But where did you meet her?' Benj asks puzzled.

'In the country.'

'Perfect! See? Daniel was naturally attracted to the hare in the race, but you, Rory, will end up with the tortoise — of course a tortoise who's got enormous style and flair. Just think of the advantages. Country girls are tough, they're used to the weather, it's what I've always thought you needed — a nice solid English girl.'

'She's not English.'

Benj digests this.

'Perhaps Scottish then?'

Rory shakes his head.

'Er, Welsh would have to be my third choice.'

Rory just grunts at him.

Benj clatters the plates into the sink. 'Tell me it's not the bloody American.'

'It's the bloody American.'

'Terrific, Rory. Your brother dies, your fiancée runs screaming when you inherit the coldest house in England, you've been in a foul temper ever since, and now,' he draws breath, '*now* you go falling for the perfectly formed Miss

Munroe, whose advantages as far as I can see are . . .' he taps off on his fingers, 'a) not overly fond of this country, b) not overly fond of the people and c) not at all fond of the weather for that matter, so it's fortunate really that you're absolutely free from all responsibility to follow her when she leaves on?'

'Monday,' Rory says sulkily.

'Thank you, yes, Monday, in two days' time. For?'

'New York,' Rory mutters.

'Where, by the way, she also *lives*.' Benj runs out of steam. 'Christ, Rory, shag her if you must, but if you had an ounce of feeling for your friends you'd forget all about her.'

'I've kissed her.'

'What!' Outraged, Benj drops his cigarette.

'I've kissed her,' Rory repeats mutinously.

'And what else, might I enquire?' Benj stamps on the smouldering carpet.

'And nothing else. I just kissed her, all right. I wanted to kiss her and I'm thinking I'd quite like to kiss her again.'

Benj sinks onto the sofa. 'Bloody hell.' He shakes another cigarette from the pack directly into his mouth, 'Go home, Rory, I beg you,' he mumbles. 'Go straight home and take a cold shower before you do yourself some serious damage.'

From up here the light changes in London are sublime exercise in kinetic art. Brake lights, headlights, traffic lights all vie for supremacy as the four million cars that make up the giant dodgems of London streets weave their way through each other – and it seems a miracle given the sheer volume of traffic that so few of them actually bump and collide. In Sloane Square, where incidentally I did once bump and collide my moped, destroying much of the charming Victorian municipal fountain in the square's centre whilst *oh dear me, Judge, severely under the influence*, the lights have just completed another circuit from red to orange to green. Cars, jettisoning exhaust from their backsides, surge forth, breaking right and left around that comforting bastion of mediocrity, the Peter Jones department store.

All cars except one, that is.

The Rover remains resolutely at a standstill. Inside Rory sits motionless.

It doesn't take a genius to see that pushing things further with Maggie is a bad idea. It's not simply that everything Benj says is true, there's also the fact that Rory doesn't wholly trust her, all those nagging doubts he has conveniently pushed aside in the last few weeks. Who knows what draws him so strongly to this girl but let's just say on their first meeting he suffered something of a *coup de foudre*. Love is the drug, as they say, or maybe love will be Rory's drug of choice because when he thinks about Maggie he feels, well, literally sick – and he hasn't felt that good about anybody in a very long time. So he's running scared. He had decided to take Benj's advice and go home, maybe even ring Stella for the full emotion-free fuck experience. Now as he grips the steering wheel, the traffic continues to split around him. Ignoring the hooting of horns and the gnashing of roadrage teeth, he wrestles the Rover's clutch into reverse and performs a neat U-turn.

maggie

Wolf and Dwight hit the town. My guess was dinner, lap dancing and a friendly brothel. They made a big effort not to look relieved when I told them I wasn't coming but I was grateful to them anyway. I should have felt excited about the Bevan story being back on track but instead I felt confused and uneasy. I was glad to be on my own. It was only while I was swiping the card through my bedroom's security box that I realized Jay might be waiting inside. For the first time I disliked the uncertainty of it, then hated myself for feeling that way.

Alone in my room I tried twisting my hair round my finger Stella style, but I just felt silly. 'Rory,' I miowed. Then cut myself off. What a loser. The message light was flashing on the phone. I felt elated as I dialled nine to access voicemail then dashed when a voice announced my dry cleaning was ready. Finally I stood under the shower and let the water run over my head at full pressure but I knew that Rory was unfinished business and I'd go crazy if I didn't do something about it.

The operator informed me with some sympathy that there were 139 R. Jones in the central London area and did I not have an actual address? Of course I didn't have an address. I had no idea about his life, let alone where he lived or what might happen if I showed up on his doorstep. Would he offer me a Coke? Glass of wine? A tequila slammer? Would he invite me in to sit on a sofa? Or a beanbag? While he leapt up and put on some – Jesus, what? *what?* The Mamas and the Papas? Puff Daddy? Verdi's greatest hits? I knew *nothing* about him. Fretfully I read through the leather-bound file of hotel services cover to cover. Then I read them through again in Spanish, French and German. After that I ordered a club sandwich. It appeared in a miraculously short time because when I heard the knock, I was still sitting in my underwear clutching the soggy bath towel to my knees. I wrapped it round my waist and opened the door but there was no trolley waiting for me, no smiling waiter holding a pen and a room service chit. Instead, in the corridor outside, arms crossed casually, Rory Jones was leaning against the yellow wallpaper.

'This is *the* famous chippie of north London,' Rory said. 'People come for *miles* to this place. Look.' He pointed to the queue of people stamping their feet in the cold outside. Inside, the fish and chip shop was decorated with tiles of sea life and lit with brilliant gaudy striplights. The front counter thronged with people holding out their hands for warm newspaper parcels of takeout. In the seating area it was hot and steamy in contrast to the freeze creeping over the city. 'Unbelievably for England,' Rory had said as we parked the Rover, 'it's actually going to snow.'

Flakes dropped silently past the window, blurring from

white to blue to pink as they floated across the strobed restaurant sign. The smell of batter was overpowering, the feeling of goodwill overwhelming, and at that moment there was no place else on earth I would rather have been.

'I used to have a fish you know,' I told Rory between mouthfuls.

'Really,' he said. 'Barracuda?'

'A little tropical thing.' In fact what I'd wanted was a sister. When that idea was shot down, I'd begged for a dog. The fish was a compromise. My father took me to the pet shop on West 67th Street. My heart was set on something exotic and colourful. We were directed to the tropical tank where the fish swam around like neon sweets – striped peppermints and rock candy with fins. I couldn't choose between them, then I saw this creature under the plastic shipwreck at the bottom of the tank. It looked so persecuted with its sad bulbous eyes. It was on special offer for two dollars.

'It was so cute, all black and velvety. I named it Magic Johnson . . . you know after the basketball player, but my parents told me it was racist.'

'It was?'

'I never really worked it out either.' I sighed. 'My parents are . . . well . . . it was always something; Vietnam, the plight of the Idaho potato pickers, support Lesbian Mothers.'

'My mother wouldn't know what to do with a lesbian. "Darling," ' he mimics, ' "Do peel this magnificent lesbian and pop it into the fruit salad." '

I laughed. 'You an only child as well?'

'Brother . . . one.'

'Yeah? Older . . . younger?'

'Daniel was a year older.'

I picked up on the tense straight away. 'Rory . . . Oh God . . . I'm so sorry.'

'Yes,' he said. He turned away, seemed to steady himself then turned back and said casually, 'Ah well, let's face it – as tragedies go, there are a lot worse.'

I was shocked by his tone.' *Oh no*, I thought, *no blood here, just terrible internal injuries.*

But he'd already begun talking.

'Number one bereavement hot spot is losing a child. Two is a wife or a husband – although there must be a qualifying factor of youth and major heart-wrenching element such as victim was mother/father of twins or died after a long period of suffering. Next we have losing a fiancée which scores extra points because of 'blighted life' syndrome. Your parents dying doesn't cut the mustard if you're over the age of twenty-five – it's not tragedy if it's not before its time – and losing a sibling if they're under twenty is definitely considered losing a child for the parents, see category number one. After all those we move onto losing a sibling *over* twenty, in which case parents and other siblings get equal billing rights. Rock bottom on the list you get losing the sibling who's not a child, who's well over twenty – but neither a husband, nor a father, not anybody's fiancé, and then when of course that person is naturally self-destructive . . .' He broke off, put his head in his hands. 'I'm sorry.'

'It's OK, you should talk about it.' I put my hand on his arm but he shook it off angrily.

'I don't want to fucking talk about it.'

After a second or two he said, 'He liked to drink. One

night he got into an argument with a bus.' Rory's voice had a shrug in it. 'He lost . . . I lost him.'

I twisted the napkin in my lap. 'What was he like?'

'Oh you know, charming, clever, funny, wicked. Everybody adored him. I did everything he told me to, of course.'

'You adored him too, huh?'

'Naaa, he was just a lot bigger than me.'

I smiled.

'When we were small he was always in trouble, *we* were always in trouble. Then he'd hide in the linen cupboard and I'd get the blame.'

'The linen cupboard?'

'English word for the only warm room in the house – in our house to be more specific. We used to take our books, stay there for hours curled up on the shelf.'

'God, I can't imagine. You must really miss him.'

'You know,' Rory picked up the vinegar bottle and absently twisted its top. 'I still shout at him for scratching my car when he hasn't borrowed it. I get irritated when he leaves the top off the toothpaste, then I remember it wasn't him, and I still celebrate his birthday every year even though he will never get any older.'

I looked down at my shredded napkin, moved beyond anything.

'Of course,' he said brightly, 'he was also a right bastard. Nicked all my clothes and most of my girlfriends. Never even considered giving either back.'

I listened to him as he talked on and I breathed easier. The internal injuries weren't fatal. He might still be bleeding heavily but I reckoned he'd pull through.

*

We walked to the car. Snow was settling in a milky film on the sidewalk. 'You know if all British institutions are as delicious as fish and chips, I might have to change my opinion of your people.'

'Oh?' Rory raised his eyebrows. 'Do you still need that much persuading?'

'Why? You think you're all so loveable?'

'Actually, yes, I think on the whole the British are pretty nice people.'

'*Nice* . . . Oh sure, just ask an Irishman.' I broke off. Rory was scowling at me.

'If there's one thing I can't stand it's that facile American attitude that the IRA are just romantic freedom fighters on a jihad . . . they're nothing but a bunch of murderous thugs.'

'Whoah, I'm sorry.' I'd been teasing, nothing more.

'Maybe you just had too much vinegar with your chips.' Rory said nastily.

'Maybe I did,' I said, stung.

'Maybe I should take you home.'

'I guess maybe you should,' I said stubbornly.

There was silence in the car.

'You're not going to sulk the whole journey are you?' I said eventually. Rory looked at me suspiciously.

'Because if you are, I'm going to have to talk . . . I mean haven't you heard, it's a question of manners.'

He laughed. 'OK, OK, OK, I'm sorry. Now do you want to see something I'm really passionate about?'

*

He parked the Rover in front of an arched stone entrance next to a security box. Rory knocked on the window. The guard inside was old and had a grizzled crew cut. He turned reluctantly from his miniature television to the hatch.

Rory handed him a twenty-pound note.

'You're a very sick gentleman Mr Rory.' He rubbed the money between dry fingers.

'Thank you, John.'

He ushered us through the hut and out the other side.

'Where are we?' I asked.

'Highgate Cemetery. Your parents would love it. Karl Marx is buried here.'

I gazed round in wonder. The whole world suddenly looked like it had been sprinkled with icing sugar. Snow had settled everywhere – it powdered the topside of red berries. It lay like a chalky overscore on the stone of gothic chapels and was piled into the crevices of gargoyles' mouths.

'We're in Narnia!' I said.

Rory squeezed my hand. 'This is the west side, the wild-west side. Normally people aren't allowed in here.'

'Except us.' I looked down at my hand in Rory's and tried not to think of it as the betrayal it was.

'Tonight we are exceptionally abnormal people.'

We wandered along the path, Rory pointing out sleeping stone lions, obelisks, headstones with funky engravings.

'Look,' he stopped in front of a tomb with an enormous effigy of a dog carved on top.

' "Tom Sayers," ' I read the inscription, ' "last of the bare-fisted fighters." '

'The dog was the chief mourner at Tom's funeral. Not a popular fellow it seems.'

He knelt beside another grave and swept the snow off with his arm. 'Look at this.' It was a cheap headstone, all the more poignant when compared with the elaborate splendour of its neighbours. A woman who had died in the plague was buried with her seven children.

'Shit, "I heard myself saying softly, and I looked at it for a long time.

We walked on. Snow continued to fall heavily. A fox stopped and stared at us from the middle of a pathway, his front paw raised questioningly. I was dazzled and in awe and I told Rory so.

'They say that in a place this beautiful, the disappointment of death is softened,' he said wistfully.

'How come you know so much about it?'

'I did some work here once.'

'Grave robber?'

'Archaeological work.'

'What do you mean?' I said curiously.

'I worked for the V and A . . . still do occasionally, when not squiring unhousetrained Americans round the country.'

'Whoah, wait a minute. You're an *archaeologist*?'

'Don't ask.' He gave a bitter laugh, 'Let's just say I got waylaid by family business. What? Now you hate archaeologists?'

'Oh no, nothing like that.' I'd been wringing my hands, trying to jump-start circulation. 'Bit cold that's all.' I pressed them under my armpits.

'We should have brought gloves . . . stupid of me.'

'Oh wait,' I said, struck by the brilliance of this notion.

I patted the gloves in the inside pocket of my coat. But when I tried to undo the buttons, my fingers were about as dextrous as raw sausages. I held them up helplessly.

'They don't seem to work.'

Rory took hold of my coat lapels. 'Cold hands, that's bad.' He pushed the first button through the buttonhole. 'Could lead to frostbite.' He undid the second.

'Frostbite's bad.' I couldn't drag my eyes from his.

'Very bad,' he whispered, 'before you know it your fingers turn green, drop off into the snow one by one—'

'Surely that's leprosy,' I said.

We kissed. His hands were inside my coat, wrapped round my back. Snowflakes dissolved against my burning face.

'Look at you. What a mess. Your ponytail's all over the place, your cheeks are red, you look like one of the wild things.' He pulled me to him. 'A wild thing from the wild side.' We kissed again.

'Give me your hands.' Obediently I stuck them out.

'Rory . . . I.' All evening I'd been wondering what to say.

'What?' He began putting on my gloves for me.

'Nothing . . . hey you know, just don't think I don't do this all the time.'

'What? Kiss Englishmen?'

'Every time I'm in a graveyard, sure.'

'OK.' He kissed me again and I knew I couldn't say it. Figured instead Jay was my problem and I would confront it later, when things were different, when my head wasn't dazzled by snow, when my heart had stopped buzzing, when my – wait a second, why was my heart buzzing?

'Your phone's ringing.'

'Leave it,' I said shakily, but he was already feeling for it under my coat.

'Seems rude not to get it while I'm here.'

'Hey stop that . . .'

'Stop what?'

'That,' I whispered.

'Just trying to give you a hand.'

'I hate to put you to so much trouble.'

'Believe me,' he said, 'it's my pleasure.'

I swayed against him. His hands found bare skin.

'Rory, uh . . .'

The cell buzzed so violently I jumped. Rory plucked it out of the breast pocket of my coat. 'You're absolutely right,' he said, mock surprised. 'It was here all the time.'

It continued to vibrate in his hand. 'What's more it appears to be rather sexually excited. No wonder you're so attached to the damn thing.'

I laughed and made a grab for it, but it slipped from my woollied hands onto the ground. Rory dove for it. Pushed me down. Rolled me over in the snow. I squirmed and broke free, he grabbed my leg, pulled me back, I kicked him.

'Christ, you fight dirty.' He pinned me to the ground. I stopped struggling. 'Come home with me, Maggie. Now, tomorrow, come up to my parents for the weekend.' I lay on the snow, grinning, nodding my head. Of course I would come. And I didn't care about Jay, I didn't care about anything much until I remembered.

'Oh Jesus,' I sat up abruptly. 'I can't.'

'What do you mean you can't?'

'I can't.'

'Why not?'

'I've got an interview.'

'An *interview*? I thought you'd finished. With whom?'

Sheer instinct kept my mouth shut.

'Can't you cancel it?'

'I can't, it's really important.'

'Wait a minute,' he joked, 'what could possibly be more important than spending a whole weekend with me and my adorable family?'

I was silent.

'Ouch,' he said and his eyes had grown wary.

Inside my hotel room the phone was ringing. 'I've just had a call from Washington,' Jay said, 'I think I could get to you by Sunday, so at least we could fly home together.'

Wherever he was calling from the reception was bad. 'Where have you been hiding the last week?' I could only just hear his voice through the crackle. 'I've been leaving messages.'

'I've tried to get hold of you too,' I said lamely, but Jay was far too savvy.

'I'll see you Sunday.'

'Yes.' There was a pause.

'I have wanted to be with you,' he said heavily.

I hesitated. 'Me too.'

I couldn't sleep. Thoughts crowded and turned in my mind like colliding planets. Finally I took the comforter off the bed and opened the doors to the terrace. It was a desolately beautiful night. There was a half-moon, a dense stillness despite the icy wind which swayed the leafless branches of trees. Hunched up, I stared out over the railing. At two a.m. in New York, the city would be sleeping with its eyes open and its heart beating. People would be talking, fighting, eating, fucking. But London was truly asleep.

I felt lonely, out of sync with where I was, with who I was. A stranger to myself. I struggled for a little perspective but I was appalled at how much grey area Rory had introduced into the black and white of my objective. I cursed myself for committing the most heinous of crimes. Never get involved. Never. This . . . *thing* with Rory, whatever it was, had no foundations, no future, it made no sense. Jay made sense. Getting this story made sense.

The middle of the night is a dangerous time to put your life in order. As minutes concertina, hours spin away and the possibility of sleep recedes ever further, it's easy to make a pact with any devil who's on hand. Forget the sentimental soliloquy, I had no choice but to chase this story. I would get it and pump it for all it was worth and then I would get the hell out of England.

Three dirty Germans crossed the Rhine, *parlez vous* —
Three dirty Germans crossed the Rhine, *parlez vous* —
Three dirty Germans crossed the Rhine,
Fucking the women and drinking the wine,
Inky pinky, *parlez vous*.

— Bawdy trench song

daniel

Where had Grandpa been when she was up before? Surely there all the time? In the house, in his bedroom – sitting in his green wing-backed chair listening to his Beethoven and books on tapes. No, wait, I remember now, he'd been out for the day somewhere, but it doesn't matter. All I can tell you is that when my father picked up the telephone to find Maggie Monroe on the other end, it took him less than fifteen seconds to confirm that the Marquess of Danby was alive and well and living at Bevan. As soon as she asked the question, you might have thought my father would smell a rat. However there is no one less Machiavellian, thus he is incapable of recognizing the telltale signs in anyone else. Besides it's thrown into the conversation casually enough and when she goes on to tell him whatever fib she's invented about needing more footage, he's happy for her to return to Bevan. Moreover, unaware that all sorts of gaskets are about to blow, he insists that this time she and the crew spend the night.

It's not that he's pathologically naïve. It's just that he's lived with this particular family secret for sixty-odd years and hasn't thought about it for thirty. Within his circle of

acquaintances there are plenty of skeletons in many a promi-
nent closet. The baby in the bathwater, Lucan, the Beast of
Glamys. There are countless stories of incest and bad
behaviour about which our family, like many others, have
closed ranks. It would never occur to my father that hushing
up a scandal was an abuse of power and class. He considers
it a matter of loyalty. He's as likely to betray family or
friends as – let's say – be made Chancellor of the Exchequer.
Despite the scorn universally heaped upon it this is one of
the plus sides to old school tie nepotism.

As a child my father had played with his royal cousins.
He could vividly remember having to be on time for every
meal. After the 'unpleasantness', as his mother had called
it, he never saw them again. He has no shame about his
father's role in the scandal. Everyone knew that Edward was
weak and had flaws but Grandpa had loved him and the idea
of him being exiled was the worst possible thing he could
have imagined. Home and hearth are what make the English
function. My father believes, as Rory and I do, as my
grandfather does, that it is right to make sacrifices for those
you love. He understands, too, that there exists a time
before any war when the spy, the ally and the enemy are
indistinguishable from one another.

So when Maggie and her crew turn up, his overriding
concern is simply one of temperature – that they be warm
for the bonfire that evening. After giving them mugs of
Nescafé, he herds them into the cloakroom and is rifling
through the dozens of mismatched boots and coats that hang
by the gun cupboard when Grandpa himself pushes through
the outside door.

'Ah, here's my father now,' Alistair says.

And Maggie exchanges a look with her crew.

Grandpa, as is customary, is dressed in full military outfit. His trousers are beautifully pressed by Nanny, and he wears a jacket buttoned over a shirt and tie, all in the same khaki brown. A leather strap is fastened diagonally over one shoulder. His boots are polished and three medals are pinned in vertical symmetry down the length of his chest.

'Just landed, just landed,' he announces to no one in particular. He puts one foot in the bootpull and leans stiffly against the wall for balance.

'Any action?' He peers beadily around the cloakroom.

'Good journey, Pa?' enquires my father.

'Little bumpy,' Grandpa says. 'Otherwise, a damn good bit of flying.'

He notices the presence of strangers and his eyes light up. 'Prisoners of war?' he asks hopefully.

maggie

The Marquess of Danby strode around the drawing room picking out various objects of interest for our inspection. Two grand pianos, surfaces muddled with sheet music faced each other across the room, and from underneath he pulled out a box of musical instruments: a ukulele, a mouth organ, a guitar, its guts snapped and curled, some cymbals and a tambourine. 'We all used to play in the old days,' he turned them over nostalgically in his hands, 'the girls painted beautifully, everyone danced. Once a troupe of Russian gymnasts came to stay, awfully limber they were.' He unlocked a display case and removed a pair of Chinese figurines from the glass shelves. 'See these?' The Marquess had pianist's hands, his fingers were long and tapered, but the knuckles were crudely distorted by age. 'Collected by my grandfather on his grand tour . . .'

I was about to make appropriate noises about their beauty when he added, 'Hideous aren't they? Always longed to smash them.'

'Why don't you then?'

'Perhaps I will one day.' He turned the two figures to face each other. 'Hello there charming little Oriental lady,' he mimicked. 'What a very pretty fan you're carrying.' He dipped the female figure in coquettish deference. 'Oh how kind you are Honourable Sir.' The pitch of his voice changed to female, 'but not nearly as pretty as my drawers.'

Wolf and Dwight caught my eye.

'Perhaps,' continued the old man, advancing the male figure closer, 'If Honourable Lady could just lift her skirt then Honourable War Lord can—' He broke off. 'Good God,' he exclaimed in disgust as rain splattered against the windows, 'this weather really makes you want to go to Tahiti and horse about with one of those Wahinis like whichever one of those painter fellows it was . . . Gauguin, I think.'

'Why are you wearing a uniform?' I said.

'Plane crashed on the lawn once to great excitement,' he looked out dreamily at the darkening sky. 'Kept Italian prisoners here for a while. Nice bunch of fellows, good with the tractor. My mother taught them to play Up Jenkins. They don't teach young people about the war,' he said sadly, 'they just don't think it's important, I suppose,' his eyes became fierce, 'but I think it's important, don't you?'

'Yes,' I said truthfully, 'I do.'

'Good girl.' He patted my shoulder clumsily. 'I have rather good memorabilia you know – travelled all over the place, the Japanese were awful,' he waved his hand in Wolf's direction, 'Pearl Harbour – long before your day of course. So many stories . . . but most people are no longer interested in such things.'

'Try me,' I said.

'Where shall I start?' the Marquess said eagerly. He winked and like a spider casting out its sticky web, I smiled back encouragingly.

'With your trips to Germany before the war.'

daniel

My mother sits at the green baize card table, a large gin and tonic in her hand. She finishes off the last three clues of the *Telegraph* crossword while Nanny completes her weekly lottery ticket. Grandpa sleeps, head lolling against the winged edge of his favourite chair, his feet resting on the matted dreadlocks of Lurch's back.

A small bird, a starling, is flying round the room. Trapped, it bumps itself against the heavy damask curtains then flies in increasingly frenzied circles until Alistair unlocks the window latch and pulls down on the sash. The bird smells freedom in the cold air and makes its bid. Reluctantly Alistair closes the window after it.

'Sun's over the yardarm,' says Alistair, surveying the uniformly beige sky outside, 'so how about a drink?' He pours a glass of whisky from a decanter and hands it to Maggie.

He's worried his guests are bored and doesn't know what to do with them. He's also nervous about the imminent arrival of Rory and begins only now to question the balance of money against the wisdom of inviting a television crew actually to stay the night – however much they are prepared to pay for the pleasure.

'Now,' he says, 'how many for supper?' He begins counting heads, 'One, two, three of us . . . then there's you lot, four, five, six.' He whips the glasses off Grandpa's nose then casually holds them to Grandpa's open mouth. 'Seven,' he announces, apparently satisfied from an inspection of the lens, that Grandpa is still alive. 'Seven for dinner is that right? Oh, and Robert,' he says, 'with Robert that makes eight.'

maggie

We sat on the twin beds up in Wolf's bedroom and studiously avoided eye contact.

'And you're sure you got it?' I asked.

'Quite sure.' Wolf nodded his big head.

'His reaction and the photograph in the same shot?'

'It's all there, Maggie.'

'Good,' I said, 'great.'

'Well, you wanted a story,' Wolf looked at me, 'and now you've got one.'

'I did, didn't I.' I scraped the toe of my shoe against the floor, 'which you know . . . is great, so, um, high five and all that.'

'Yeah, high five, crack open the champagne, let's smoke a cigar,' Wolf said.

Now it was Dwight's turn to look accusingly at me, 'But . . .'

'But what?' I snarled.

'He's so . . .'

'Sweet.' I finished it for him. 'Yeah, I know.' I sighed, rubbing the goosebumps on my arms. 'Hey, life's a bitch, right?' But a quote of Don Hewitt's, creator of 60 *Minutes* kept popping unbidden into my head. 'The public's right to know doesn't translate into the media's obligation to broadcast.' The Marquess and his family were not the only people I'd found myself liking over the last few weeks. I didn't know what to think any more. Were the English aristocracy a class that deserved to be wiped out or an eccentric but splendid remnant of a tribe under threat? For some reason I remembered a story Alan once told me. Why, I don't know, because it was hardly a parallel – the son of a friend of his, a young soldier had been in Bosnia only forty-eight hours before he was sent into a building. The Serbs inside were taken by surprise. This boy, terrified, shot wildly around the room, killing everyone. He'd run into the kitchen to find another soldier facing him. The man had no gun. Instead he held a crumpled picture of his child and pushed it into the boy's face with shaking fingers. Overcome with guilt and horror at what he'd already done, the boy let him go. In the basement of that building they'd found three girls, dead, covered in ejaculate. The boy had gone after the Serb, found him and shot him dead. 'Try people fairly,' Alan said, 'then you needn't shed tears for them.' The Marquess of Danby might be a sweet old man now but he was also a Nazi sympathizer and a traitor.

Dwight and Wolf were still looking at me. I shivered, 'Jesus,' I dragged myself to my feet, 'I'm going to find a sweater before I die.'

The gunshots came moments after I'd left the room. I headed towards the noise, along a corridor, up a staircase, through a passageway. There was another shot, this time louder. At the end of the passageway was a closed door, a faded picture nailed to it. It was a child's drawing of a skull and crossbones – or what was left of it. Droplets of blood were crayoned around the warning. 'Enter here at your peril.'

I turned the key, took a step into the room and then the floor just swallowed me up. My legs buckled and my arm ripped against something sharp. A stinging pain, then my feet made contact with something solid. When my eyes acclimatized to the dark I realized I'd fallen through the floorboards to a half level below. Cautiously I hoisted myself back up to the floor and sat down, dabbing at my bleeding forearm and looking around. In this part of the house there could be no pretence at normal living. Wallpaper hung off the walls in great brownish curls. It was bitterly cold, but not hard to see why. The room had shadows of furniture but the walls beyond them ended in disjointed brickwork – there was no roof. Birds wheeled and squawked in the night sky above. I craned my neck up but there was another crack from a gun and something thudded onto the floor close to where I was sitting. 'Hey,' I yelled. From the other side of the ruin a man stepped out. He lowered his gun, the scanty light from the moon caught his face and I stopped breathing.

'Maggie,' he said. 'Maggie! You're here, you came, I don't believe it!' He hurried across the room.

I didn't get it. Didn't even come close. 'What are you doing here?' I clutched at my arm as the memory of Rory appearing bootfaced at Roxmere came back to me. 'Oh no, they didn't send for you did they?'

He stopped. 'No, they didn't send for me.'

And still I didn't get it.

'Then why are you here?'

He gave me a measured look, then he opened the gun and dropped the cartridges into his hand.

'I live here, Maggie.'

I stared at him stupidly. Then, like live wires crossing, snippets of information began sparking through my brain. *Pop*, Rory's determination for us not to come to Bevan. *Pop*, Massey reading from Burke's peerage, *eldest son recently deceased. Pop*, Rory in the fish and chip restaurant, *he had a fight with a bus, he lost, I lost him.* Nanny saying, *there's only the baby left now.* Oh for Christ's sake, Rory's agency contacts, the foot through all those doors. Robert, Rory for short, was the 38-year-old baby. I didn't want it to be true but it seemed so obvious. A radish could have put it together quicker than I had.

'Your last name's different . . . that's why I didn't get it, Bevan's the . . .'

'Title . . . one of them. The family name is Lytton-Jones. I dropped the Lytton. It does tend to confuse.'

'So the Viscount Lytton-Jones who died tragically—'

'Was my brother. Daniel.'

For some reason I just felt angry. 'All that time . . . All those things I said to you, and all the time you were . . . you were . . . well, one of them.'

'One of *them*,' he repeated flatly.

'But why didn't you tell me?'

'Wait a minute.' He took a step towards me. 'Who didn't tell whom? Why would you come here when I specifically told you not to?'

'Everyone told me this was one of the great houses,' I faltered, 'I was just doing my job.'

And only then did realization slam into me. My job . . . *my job*. For crying out loud, how could I have been be so stupid? I'd put the growing unease I'd felt over the last week down to confusion over my feelings, down to guilt about Jay, my lack of loyalty, spending too much time rooting around in other people's lives, down to anything but its real cause. 'Give them enough rope and they'll hang themselves,' Jay had said. I thought of all the footage sitting in its neatly marked reels back in our hotel room. I'd gone out of my way to get the most controversial footage I could. Anything I could make satirical or mocking. Leaving aside Rory's grandfather, I hadn't a single frame I could possibly describe as the puff piece I had sold Stately Locations and Rory on.

In this business, there's always a certain amount of professional crapping on people, but you have to keep some kind of integrity. You have to believe in some kind of truth. My justification was that I believed something about these people and I had sought out and found behaviour to prove my point. But in the way witnesses at a murder trial will have conflicting accounts of the same event, the truth is mercurial. '*If there's more than one version of the truth, there is no truth.*'

'Maggie, this is my family home for Christ's sake, and you're a journalist.'

'Meaning what?' I turned on him defensively, 'I can't be trusted?'

'Well can you? Why are you here? How long have you been here? And just what have you filmed so far?'

I felt my face morph into a blank screen, incriminating footage running all over it.

'My parents? My grandfather?'

'Your dad showed us around. We had tea with Nanny. Nanny made me drink milk. I haven't drunk milk since the fourth grade.' But even as I said it guilt flooded through me, because there is one thing I do know – however many different kinds of truth there are in this world, there is only one kind of lie – and that's a dirty one.

'You've seen how we work. We don't really set anything up. We don't tell people how to behave, we just film what we see.'

'So you keep telling me, Maggie,' he said tightly. 'But what exactly is it that you *do* see?'

I film what I see.

What a load of BS that is. The truth is angles and shadows. In an editing room the truth can be moulded and squeezed into whatever shape you want it to be. As a journalist, you are as responsible as your subject for how they appear on film.

The choices were clear – wing it, or run. It felt like two storm clouds had collided over my head but running is for sissies and whatever else you can say about me, I hope I ain't no sissy.

The look on Dwight's and Wolf's face was comical as Rory virtually marched me into the dining room. I smiled wryly at them and when Alistair Bevan looked puzzled and said, 'Oh so you have met Robert,' Rory said grimly, 'Yes, but it turns out we don't know each other all that well after all.'

At dinner, picking over the fragile bones of some bird on my plate I tried to imagine what it was like growing up in the lost splendour of that house. While Rory's grandfather regaled Wolf and Dwight with war stories using the salt and pepper as tanks, while Rory's parents drank and steadily became more removed, I watched, I opened my eyes and I tried to see. How Rory's mother surreptitiously pushed the heater closer our way when she thought we weren't looking. How only Wolf, Dwight and myself were offered a second helping. How Rory watched over his family so proprietarily, and God help me, I felt ashamed.

There had to be a way out of this mess but I couldn't see it. Whatever happened, I needed to talk to Rory before things got any worse – confession is a lot better than admission but it seemed I wasn't even to be allowed that luxury.

'We're so pleased you're all staying for the night this time,' Alistair said and I closed my eyes.

'*This time?*' Rory said. 'You've been here before?' he hissed. 'What exactly are you doing here again?'

'I was invited by your father.'

'That's not very likely is it?' and the biting sarcasm of his tone made me defensive.

'Well ask him if you don't believe me.'

But Rory's parents were unwrapping their anniversary gifts to one another. The packages were identical. A pair of police breathalysers. The Earl breathed into the tube then looked at the bag, eagerly awaiting the results. The indicator on the bag turned bright green; maximum over the limit.

'Marvellous,' Alistair said, 'they work!' He beamed at his wife. Rory's mother looked indulgent. Rory just looked exasperated.

'I *will* ask him,' he said, 'but in the meantime you don't film one more thing in my home.'

'Come on everyone,' Audrey pushed back her chair, 'let's light the bonfire.'

'And *don't* think we're finished with this conversation either.' Rory added.

In the parklands, standing in huddles around the bonfire, many of Bevan's old retainers and their families had ventured from cottages on the estate to celebrate the Earl's anniversary. The Earl greeted them all, some with a handshake, others with a rough hug. Everyone arranged themselves in a loose circle around the base of the bonfire as the farm manager's grandson, a thin sallow boy no more than sixteen, positioned himself at the top of the ladder and doused the 20-foot structure – looking more than ever like a witch's hat – with petrol. The ladder was taken away and the tractor driven a safe distance from the bonfire while Rory and Alistair walked around its edge, tossing more petrol from watering cans onto the hacked off branches and twisted boughs. When that job was done, they retreated fifty yards or so. The circle of onlookers moved outwards. A bow and arrow covered in a rag was produced. Alistair tested the tautness of string with a finger then handed it to Rory.

Rory pulled back his arm and took aim. Alistair held a match to the end of the arrow and Rory let fly. The burning cloth of the arrow cut through the darkness and buried itself into the hay piled around the brim of the hat. The bonfire whispered, crackled furtively, then to the cheers of the crowd, ignited with a sharp burst of light.

I stood alone, a short distance from Wolf and Dwight, mesmerized by the flames. Onlookers howled appreciation as burning sap caused the occasional explosion. Sparks zigzagged like miniature fireworks up into the night sky. Children ran around brandishing smouldering twigs like swords and it occurred to me that had this been America, there would have been safety ropes and warning signs posted and the occasion would have lost its charm. The heat from the fire was intense, I turned one cold cheek towards it then the other. The whole scene was so far removed from anything I'd ever been a part of and I wondered how it would feel to be there under any other circumstances rather than hostile. Someone put a mug of hot whisky into my hands and I accepted it dreamily, strangely in love with everything that was going on. Eventually the structure of the bonfire gave up on itself and collapsed in a heap of sparks. Children who'd been steadily creeping closer jumped back squealing with excitement and I came back to reality. I scanned the outlines of woolly hats and lumpy coats for Rory's rangy figure but he had gone.

Inside the house the sound of the piano led me to the drawing room. Rory and his father were playing a duet, one at each piano. It was a classical piece, which they played musically but very erratically. One after the other, chords jarred. I stayed hidden in the doorway and watched them.

'You're out of time, Rory,' Alistair shouted good-naturedly. But even with my non-musical ear, I could hear it was Alistair who didn't have the dexterity to keep up.

'Rubbish,' Rory shouted back. 'We're enormously talented.'

Alistair missed another chord. 'Goddamnit!' He crashed his hands onto the keys.

'Come on, Pa,' Rory said.

But his father stopped playing. 'It's no good,' he said, putting his hands into his lap. 'Too old.'

Rory went to sit next to his father. He picked up Alistair's hand and began rubbing his fingers with the bottom of his jumper, as if Alistair were a child who'd lost his mittens. I thought then of a proverb I'd once heard 'When a father helps the son, both laugh: When the son helps the father, both cry.'

'Not old,' Rory said. 'Just cold.'

They began the piece again, one hand each, laughing, making mistakes, teasing one another. I felt a stab of something unfamiliar. I guess it was envy but there was something else – I'd spent my whole life revelling in the fact that I didn't have to belong. Now whether I had any right to or not, I felt part of something and in a few days I was supposed to go home and betray them all. Nice one, Maggie.

I was no longer alone. Wolf stood behind me, camera raised. I blocked the lens then took the camera from him. Wolf looked at me, then to Rory and his father. He gently touched my cheek with his big hand and walked away.

Alistair and Rory were still playing. Every so often Alistair executed a fast whirly diddly movement. You could hear how good he must have been before arthritis had thickened his joints and bones.

'Who's going to look after your mother when I'm not around?' he shouted.

'Come on, Dad.'

'No, I'm serious.'

'Perhaps we can arrange something at auction.'

Alistair laughed but stopped playing. He put his hand on Rory's shoulder.

'Maybe,' he said, 'well . . . maybe when Daniel died,' he stopped short, as if he'd set himself a verbal mountain to climb but didn't know whether he'd brought the right equipment. Rory sat perfectly still.

Alistair took a deep breath, 'Well, maybe we should sell this house.'

Rory stared at his father, astonished.

'Yes, yes, I know,' Alistair said heavily, 'impossible, of course, absolutely impossible. Rory, I'm so sorry about everything.'

'It doesn't matter,' Rory said, and I could see he was struggling. 'Really, Dad, it doesn't matter.'

They looked at each other, a million words unsaid between them, then Alistair broke the spell with a snort. He grabbed his beaker from the side of the piano, removed the lid, poured the brandy down his throat, then turned back to the piano and broke into a solo of vigorous chopsticks.

I know cold. I have been cold in many places. I've slept on floors, in the back of pickups, I've slept under horse blankets on the frozen earth. The body is prepared to put up with all kinds of discomfort for all kinds of bullshit reasons, but this cold was different. This cold was ungodly.

It took all my will power to strip to my underwear. In the bathroom a sign on the toilet read 'No sharp yanks' which made me laugh until I understood that the reason the toilet didn't flush, sharp yanks or not, was because the water inside was *actually frozen*. I peered at it almost expecting to see miniature skaters in furry earmuffs gliding over its surface. The basin next to it was marbled brown with stains but at least there was a comforting dribble of water with which I brushed my teeth. This scanty hygiene routine chilled me to such a degree I put all my clothes back on, coat and socks included and was about to jump into bed when I noticed the electric heater in the fireplace. I flicked the switch and crouched expectantly in front of it. Nothing. On examination the flex led to the back of a dresser but it was too heavy to move. On my stomach I fumbled the plug towards the socket but it wouldn't go in. I looked at the plug in my hand – three square prongs, I looked at the socket in the wall – three round holes. The two were entirely sexually incompatible. I gave up. I got into bed trying to dispel the image of myself being found the next morning, stiff, dead, frozen as solid as a Good Humor popsicle.

daniel

Rory sits in Pa's office and works steadily through the mail. He slaps stamps onto twenty or so envelopes, flicking the bulb of the light to keep it going. He knows Maggie has gone to bed and wonders what she is thinking.

Leona said that Bevan reminded her of a mausoleum. She'd shivered when she said it. That was the second time he took her home. The first time she'd said Bevan was 'romantic', 'so pretty', 'like a castle in a storybook'. The cellar with its toads and chains was 'amazing'. Later it was as though she watched those chains being attached to Rory's ankle. It had been the day after the funeral and Rory suggested they took a walk. They'd got a quarter of the way down the drive before Leona looked sadly at the bottom of her camel trousers, lightly splattered with mud, and announced she'd try to do better next time. At supper she'd wrestled valiantly with the pheasant, but she'd stared at the bread sauce as though it was vomit. Rory promised she'd never have to live there, but she hadn't believed him.

Rory continues with his quest for fiscal law and order but his concentration is shot to pieces. Lethargic from boredom he slows to a crawl. He's finally admitting to himself that his motive for keeping Maggie from Bevan has shifted, it's never been the so called 'unpleasantness'. As with Alistair, our grandfather's secret has been so long buried, Rory doesn't even consider it, it's no longer to do with the threat of exposing the family to the derision of millions of viewers. That was his *excuse*. His *reason* is that increasingly he's finding it hard to see himself independently of Bevan and he knows full well that acceptance is nine tenths of defeat.

He imagines Maggie upstairs in bed, naked and pale against the bitter darkness of the room. He remembers the touch of her lips, the smoothness of her skin. He runs an imaginary finger along the line of her body, feels her ribs dipping into the curve of her waist. He traces his finger out over her hip, across her leg to the inside of her thigh, but his fantasy is somewhat moderated by the sure knowledge that Maggie naked and prone in a room in which the temperature barely reaches above freezing point even in summer, is highly improbable. The fire is gasping in the fireplace, the wood basket empty. In a burst of frustration, Rory picks up the remaining bills on the desk and shovels them into the grate.

maggie

This was crazy, I climbed out of bed. Somewhere in the house, there must be blankets. Blankets would be made of wool and right then wool was what I needed. I prowled the narrow corridors. A trunk in the upstairs hall looked hopeful but was full of antique Chinese baby clothes all beautifully wrapped in tissue paper. I opened a door into a room with a rocking horse in the corner. More of a nursery than a bedroom, the floor was stacked with boxes of broken toys and a line of silver cups sat on one of the bookshelves. The cups had been awarded for every kind of sport from running to cricket. I picked up a yellowing cutting of two teenage boys, their arms linked, tennis rackets raised. The heading read 'The Fabulous Bevan Boys'. I crept out. The room was too sad, too full of ghosts. How much of himself had Rory left behind in that nursery? Distracted, I opened the next door I came across and was mortified to find Alistair and Audrey inside, huddled up in bed. Alistair was wearing an overcoat over his pyjamas and reading out loud from a paperback. Audrey was laughing up at him. On their bedside tables instead of the standard Evian water stood two bottles of Famous Grouse Whisky.

'I'm so sorry,' I backed out hurriedly, 'I was just looking for a blanket.'

'Linen cupboard, dear,' Audrey called after me. 'Down the hall, over the half landing, right at the side table with the serpents' heads, second door on your left.'

It was less of a closet, more of a room. Heat blasted from the boiler in its corner. I can truthfully say I'd never felt so emotional about an inanimate object my entire life. I wrapped my arms around it, pressing my face to its hot dry surface.

'Hey there.'

I jumped. Rory's angular body was curled up between the slatted shelves, his head resting on a stack of paisley quilts.

'Rory! Jesus, you scared me.'

He swung his legs to the floor, dropping the book off his lap.

I retrieved it, mumbling something about hypothermia, lack of blankets, broken radiators and frozen fingertips.

'You're right,' he interrupted gently. 'It's not exactly Claridges.' He removed the book from my hand.

'I'm sorry.'

'Don't be, your fee will go towards repairing the central heating.'

'Rory, we should—'

'If you're thinking this is a good time to talk, it's—' he cut himself off. 'Look, you came for a blanket didn't you?'

He sifted through the shelves, forcing me back against the door. It swung open and a gust of icy air blew in. I leapt back inside, collided with Rory. Steadying me with one hand he reached slowly behind me for the handle.

'Best to keep it shut,' he said, pulling the door firmly to. 'Purely for health reasons of course.'

We stood close, swaying, not quite touching, until I felt myself start to burn round the edges.

He dropped my coat to the floor, ran his hands up under my T-shirt and in one swift movement hitched me onto the slatted shelf behind, hand resting lightly at the base of my spine as he unbuckled his jeans.

He pinned my wrists against the shelf, moving slowly inside me. My skin was slicked with sweat, the muscles on his shoulders shone under the light. I closed my eyes, but when I opened them again I caught him looking at me, and what I saw in his face wasn't what I expected. The exposure felt painful, confusing, so I closed my eyes again. I didn't want everything laid out so bare and raw in front of me, because what I'd seen in his face was anger.

'Look at the state of you.' Rory gently rubbed at the lines indented onto my skin by the shelf.

We were lying in a damp heap of tangled limbs and clothes on the floor. The ceiling blurred into focus above me. The cold, the heat, the sex all had a soporific effect. My whole body felt like it was slow cooking to sleep – just a small raw centre of emotion left.

'Look, I'm sorry,' he said curtly.

I felt my eyes slide away, but he held my face in his hands.

'No, I mean it. I'm sorry.'

'You looked straight through me. You scared me.'

'Maybe, but you've been scaring me for weeks.'

'That sounds bad.'

'It's bad in the only way that bad can be good,' he said.

Back in my bedroom I traced a finger over his eyelids. 'Don't sleep.'

'Uh oh,' he groaned. 'High maintenance. I knew it'

'No, no, you're wrong,' I protested. 'I maintain myself. I'm zero maintenance.'

'Of course you are, you're Maggie the Cat.'

I didn't recognize the reference.

'*Cat on a Hot Tin Roof*. Tennessee Williams. You're Kipling's cat who walks by herself, he said softly, 'and all places are alike to you . . .'

I woke sometime near dawn. The night had washed out to lavender and the air was chilled and still. Morning was biding its time, waiting for the sun to come along and warm it. Rory was wrapped around me, our bodies interlocked.

I lay awake, just wondering. When you tilt the axis of your world even a fraction off centre, the degree of fallout can be colossal. It's fatuous to make comparisons but I had become so used to sex with the emotional contraception of barriers and checkpoints, I'd become so good at sanding down my expectations to match Jay's. Don't take much, don't feel much, don't depend at all. Here with Rory there was no future to consider, no rules to abide by, so the strength of my feelings took me by surprise. I stayed awake a long time, content, limp, slothful, dazed, I turned these unfamiliar words over in my head, all antonyms for my usual edgy self. It was as though somebody had pulled out a stopper and all the jumping beans had drained from my body. I felt like hurling them in the air and shouting hallelujah.

'The first earl had a penchant for little boys, the second liked nothing better than sleeping in all his wife's jewels . . .' Rory was propped up on one elbow, 'The third was scorned by his love, a pickled-onion heiress, and so became passionate about the plight of seagulls, and the fourth, my grandfather's grandfather, was sexually obsessed with the queen.'

'Oh please,' I laughed.

'Truly. He was endlessly writing her filthy letters, "I must report that I dream of you, Sire, naked and dripping as you emerge from your bubble-bath," . . . although in his younger days he liked to object at weddings.'

'Now I know you're making all this up.'

'Absolutely not. You know that moment when the vicar says, "Speak now or forever hold your peace?" For a time he was the scourge of every young bride in the north of England.'

'And you?'

'And me what?'

'What's your passion? Bevan?'

'God,' he said heavily, 'not really. Buildings, yes, grave-yards, monuments, sites, stones, bones, anything old, crumbling, decaying.'

'But still, you gave up something you loved doing to keep *this* going?' I looked around the room. 'Why? For your father?'

'Don't sound so horrified. Have you never given up anything for somebody you loved?'

Jay had been married once. His wife was beautiful but highly strung. She loathed his job. For five years Jay followed her map, redrew his. It had broken up their marriage. Jay believed that if you loved someone, you shouldn't force them to give up something they were passionate about. Never make a career choice for someone else's reasons.

'Why would you ever put anyone in that position?' I said, but the words had sounded a lot more convincing coming out of Jay's mouth.

'Because love is selfish, Maggie. Love is *Top of the Pops*, number one emotion on the selfish chart. Love is a messy and inherently sad emotion, which is why so many people live in mortal terror of it.'

'So the one thing you're dedicating your life to preserving is the one thing that will prevent you from being happy?'

'Maybe, I don't know. All I do know is that I haven't done the thing yet that I'm most proud of.'

'Which is?'

'Who knows. Could be anything. Maybe I'll write a great song or save a kitten from drowning, maybe I will just preserve Bevan for my father . . . Look, I'm not sure I could possibly make you understand.'

'I sort of understand, I do. I think it's kind of noble . . . nutty but noble.'

'Which is, ironically, also our family motto.'

'It's not so bad – where I come from you'd be a real catch.'

'Where you come from any male who's single, can sit up and take nourishment is a real catch.'

I laughed. 'Well I hope at least you get an enormously important title as compensation.'

'Oh sure. Right up there between Master of the Horse and Companion to the Bath.'

'Oh boy.' I sighed.

'Oh boy, *sir*, to you.' He tipped me onto my stomach and slid down the bed.

Later he said, 'Surely it's unethical to sleep with your victims?'

'I consider it a perk. Anyway you're not my victim.'

'I am closely related to him.'

'I could always sleep with your father if that makes you more comfortable.' Classical music was coming from somewhere. I strained to hear it better.

'Don't be disgusting.' He pushed his leg between mine. Now, from somewhere else in the house, a telephone had begun ringing. 'Oh Christ,' Rory said resignedly. 'It's bound to be for me, Nanny will answer it, she'll come in, see I have an erection and there'll be hell to pay.'

I burst out laughing. 'The thirty-eight-year-old baby.'

'I don't think you'll find many babies with one of these,' he muttered, lowering himself on top of me.

'Does Nanny think you're not old enough to have sex?'

'Nanny believes you are *never* old enough to have sex.'

'Well she's not going to know you're in here.'

'Nanny knows everything,' he said darkly.

I assumed he was joking but as he said it, there was a sharp rapping on the door. I looked at him disbelievingly. He yanked the covers over our heads as I dissolved into helpless giggles. 'Quiet, wench,' he hissed. The door opened and small neat footsteps crossed the room. Rory clamped his hand firmly over my mouth.

'Your cousin Benjamin called with your office messages, Robert,' Nanny said. Rory inched his fingers up my thigh. I stifled a gasp. 'I've written them on a piece of paper,' Nanny continued, her tone of voice implying that young Benjamin had left a small dog poop in her hand rather than a note.

Rory's shoulders were heaving with silent laughter.

'Rory!' Nanny said warningly.

Rory stuck his hand out from under the bedclothes. 'Thank you, Nanny,' he said meekly.

daniel

Rory lies in bed, catatonic with goodwill towards the world. Next door Maggie is running a bath. The immersion heater flares on and off as she vainly adjusts the hot and cold taps. He's about to warn her about the scalding temperature of the water when there's a squeal. He nearly laughs out loud until he remembers it was at this point Leona started packing, remembers how he saw escape reflected in her eyes long before the train drew into Skimpton station.

'You know something,' Maggie shouts from the bathroom, 'I guess England's not so bad after all. I mean, two inches of hot water is really quite a luxury when you think about it.'

Rory stretches out contentedly. Benj's note scratches against his foot. He attempts to retrieve it with his toes, but it drops to the floor. He feels around under the bed but his fingertips brush against something else. Whatever it is, it doesn't have the putrid consistency of your average Neolithic Bevan lost property item so instead of recoiling in horror he closes his hand around it and finds himself pulling Wolf's camera onto the bed.

'So Nanny never married?' Maggie shouts from the bathroom. 'No steamy affairs with the local priest?'

'She was in love with a soldier. He died in the war.'

'Poor thing.'

Rory fiddles absent-mindedly with the controls. He powers on the camera and presses the rewind button. 'What did you say you got on film yesterday?' he asks and at the same time wishes he hadn't. In the bathroom, Maggie sits bolt upright. 'I told you,' she says warily, 'just background stuff.'

But Rory has already pressed the play button. There is no sound but the images are more than enough. As he fast-forwards and backtracks through footage from the last twenty-four hours, the viewfinder presents him with the all-too-familiar scenes from the Bevan comedy drama.

'Not even my grandfather?' he asks, watching Grandpa's puppet show with the Chinese figurines. Anger starts boiling in his head as he watches Alistair showing off the breathalyser he's preparing to wrap, Audrey sucking whisky through her curly-wurly straw and then finally there is Grandpa again, turning the knife over in his hand. As Rory stares, realization building, the camera zooms in close until there is nothing in the frame but Grandpa's thumb smoothing over and over the swastika embossed on the knife's handle and Rory's anger turns to cold hard fury.

'Rory.' Maggie stands in the doorway, she's thrown on her clothes without drying herself and water seeps through the thin cotton of her T-shirt like blood from an exit wound.

maggie

'God damn you to hell, Maggie,' he said softly. 'God damm you.' I walked over and took the camera out of his hands.

I gave a sort of helpless shrug, but he was having none of it. He grabbed me at the elbow and propelled me towards the door. I struggled, but his grip only tightened. The music we'd heard earlier became louder as Rory marched me along the corridor, down the stairs and into his grandfather's bedroom. The old man was sitting in his armchair, eyes shut despite the ear-splitting volume of the music. On his lap a photograph book was open and resting on top of a tartan blanket.

'Rory, please don't do this.'

'What do you see here, Maggie?' he demanded.

'It's not—'

'What little pigeonhole best fits your prejudice today. Lunatic? Worthless peer? Nazi collaborator?'

'It's not like that—'

'You're damn right it's not like that. How dare you think by filming you have *any* understanding?'

'Is that you, Alistair?' the old man yelled above the din.

I rubbed my forearm where Rory had held it. He turned

down the volume on the stereo and kissed his grandfather on the forehead. The Marquess's eyes flickered open. He felt for the book on his lap. Rory bent down to pick up a photograph that had fallen to the floor.

'Not lunch yet, is it?' the Marquess asked.

Rory shook his head. He tried to manoeuvre the photograph back into its mount but the Marquess took it from his hand.

'Know who this is, Rory?' The photo showed a young man in uniform standing erect and smiling.

'Cavendish,' Rory said gently.

'Yes,' the Marquess traced his finger across the browning image, 'Cavendish.'

He closed his eyes. I thought he had drifted off, but he started speaking. 'Knew he'd been shot because there was a hole in his head. There were brains coming out of the hole so I pushed them back inside.' He looked at Rory, 'Somehow I thought that might help, do you see?'

'I know,' Rory put his hand on the old man's shoulder.

'Carried him for ten miles,' the Marquess said, 'I suppose I knew he was dead, but I had to do something.' He touched the photograph dreamily, 'He was my friend, do you see?' He felt down the side of his chair and pulled out a pair of headphones.

Rory turned on me, 'As soon as war was declared, he fought, he was the first to realize he'd made a terrible mistake . . .'

'Rory. I was following a legitimate story,' I pleaded.

'*Legitimate*,' he practically spat the word. 'Christ, do you people realize or even care about the damage you do in your self-righteous pursuit of the truth? It would be hugely upsetting to my family, they would be hounded by the press. What *is* the point, just before he dies?'

'Rory you have to believe me, when I came here, I had no idea it was your family.'

He slammed his fist into the side of the chair. 'Don't you get it — it's always somebody's family. God, what an idiot I've been. I, of all people should have known better. In fact, what am I talking about?' He looked at me scathingly. 'I did know better.'

'Maybe you did,' I said, 'but I didn't, I really didn't, things have changed now—'

'Now what?' he said bitterly. 'Now that you screwed *every* member of the family?'

'Rory, that's not fair.'

'Oh don't tell me, last night you had an epiphany. How sweet.'

'You're not listening,' I said angrily.

He put his hands up, 'Spare me the bullshit, Maggie.'

'It isn't bullshit. It's the truth.'

'Well if that's the case, you should have no problem giving me the film.'

I stared at him. 'I can't,' I stammered.

'Won't you mean,' he stated flatly. 'Besides, you can't use it without the release forms.'

'Rory you can trust me.' I didn't know what else to say. I needed time and the tapes were my only hostages. 'You *have* to trust me.'

'Trust you!' he said and the scorn in his voice nearly made me walk. I wanted to get as far away from him, as far away from myself as possible. Rory made a visible effort to keep a hold on his temper.

'I won't sign the release forms, Maggie.'

And I thought, *Just when you think it can't get any worse.*

He was waiting for me to say something, to be the person he now knew I was. I badly wanted to disappoint him but it seems I couldn't.

'Your father signed them yesterday.'

He looked at me then like I was someone he didn't want to know any more.

'At the time my grandfather was acting out of a fierce sense of family, tradition and loyalty, three things you know absolutely nothing about, Maggie.'

It was like my brain had its eyes wide open but refused to let my mouth speak.

'I see,' he said. 'Well in that case, I suggest you take the money and run. Go on, get out.'

'I'm already gone.' I turned. Got to the door. Saw how easy it would be to walk straight through it. Turned back.

'Rory, I don't want to run, I always run.'

'Why are you telling me this?'

'I'm telling you this because, because if you were to ask me to stay . . .' My voice was so low I could barely hear it, '. . . I would stay.'

He looked at me steadily.

'Turn the bloody music thingy up would you, Robert,' Grandpa shouted from his chair. His headphones were still clamped over his ears.

'Maggie,' Rory said helplessly, 'every time I think I know who you are, you turn out to be someone else.'

'Please try to understand.'

He shook his head sadly but there was no softness left in his eyes. 'I really don't think that's possible,' he said.

daniel

If it were me, still lobbing pebbles into that waste-paper basket two hours after she'd left, I'd get off my arse and go after her, because what does it really matter? Why is it we're so good at allowing every petty, mean-spirited emotion to stand in the way of the bigger picture? Paper covers stone, stone blunts scissors, scissors cut paper. Round and round it goes. If I've learnt anything, it's that life really *is* too short — it wasn't just a tired old cliché after all. Too many times the things we get side-tracked by are no more than false trails. In the final reckoning the only emotions that truly hold water are the incontestable ones. So I will Rory to snap out of it, because let me tell you something: you can live in a broken home, you can play with a broken toy, but you cannot love with a broken heart.

And amazingly enough he does snap out of it. He stuffs his clothes into a suitcase, jumps in his car and I think, *Good God, this has a chance of ending well after all.*

Rory drives like Toad of Toad Hall, all horns and swerves and brakes. As he pulls up opposite the Cadogan Hotel, it occurs to him that in the last couple of hours he cannot remember turning right, left, on or off the motorway and wonders how the hell he got here. Now he wonders what the hell to do next. The narrow road he must cross to walk through that hotel entrance widens into a six-lane motorway. Maggie's film has held a mirror up to his own attitude and to confront her means he must first confront himself. He doesn't recognize any of this yet but I hope he will before too long, in the meantime he's stymied by indecision.

He knows one thing for sure, that when the moment comes he will not let her go.

Then the moment is upon him. And anybody who says God does not have perfect timing should watch this space because Maggie is walking down the steps of the hotel. She's pale and her hair is caught up in a rough ponytail. She tips the doorman, who touches his cap and smiles. A porter wheels a trolley full of luggage down the ramp. Rory's out of the Rover, hand raised, mouth open to shout, when a tall man with a shock of grey hair lollops down the steps and catches up with her. He squeezes her arm, says something, teasing maybe, certainly flirtatious, because when she replies he laughs and kisses her – an easy kiss of possession.

Oh Rory. I see the look on his face, watch his arm drop, watch him shrink, climb back into himself, then into his car and drive off without a backward glance. And my heart aches for him.

Why was he born so beautiful?
Why was he born at all?
He's no bloody use to anyone,
He's no bloody use at all.

— Anonymous

maggie

Jay was tired. He fell asleep as soon as the plane took off and didn't wake until the pilot announced we were flying over New Jersey. I sat in the airless vacuum of my seat and stared blindly at the miniature screen in front of me.

Jay stirred only once. I looked at him. He was breathing with his mouth open and the deep worry crease between his eyes was even deeper than ever.

In the cab home I feigned a stomach bug.

'How about some treatment at the renowned Alder clinic?' Jay asked. I shook my head and he didn't push it. 'I've got to go to Washington for a few days,' he said, 'but when I get back let's try to grab a little time together.'

I nodded. 'That would be nice.'

When we got to the Bowery, Jay carried my suitcase into my building. I looked around at the industrial grey paint and graffiti. I was home. The last few weeks seemed surreal, only twenty-four hours earlier I had been in the middle of the English countryside telling a man I barely knew that I would stay if he wanted me to. What was surreal was that I had meant it.

'Talk to me, Maggie,' Jay said. 'Ever since Paris you've had this expression on your face.'

'Like what?'

'Like I've been auditioning for a part that you don't know how to tell me I haven't got.'

'Jay, can I ask you a question?'

'Is it multiple choice?'

'Why did you start seeing me, do you think?'

'Let me see now,' he started ticking off an imaginary checklist on his fingers.

'Jay, I'm serious.'

He pressed his knuckles into the crease of his frown. 'So we're going to have this discussion now.'

'I think so.'

He paid off the cab and we sat on the steps of the building. He took my hand and began separating the fingers.

'We believe in the same things, we want the same things from each other, you're independent, entirely low maintenance—'

'You make me sound like a package.'

'Didn't you just ask me to gift-wrap you?' he said lightly.

'The thing is, I don't think I can be a package any more.'

'Not even if you can have satin ribbon and hand-turned edges?'

He was hedging and we both knew it. These were the discussions we had agreed not to have. Our anti-nuptial contract.

'Was it because you didn't need me to need anything from you?'

He took off his glasses. 'It was because I didn't want to

take more from you than you could give,' he corrected gently.

'How does anyone know how much they're capable of giving?'

'Where is this coming from, Maggie, what's making you unhappy?'

'What if I wanted to give you *everything*.'

'You do give me everything . . . everything I want.'

'What if I wanted to give you more.'

'What "more" are we talking about here?' Jay asked.

'I don't know. A child?' As soon as the words were out of my mouth, I was almost paralysed with shock. Couldn't believe I'd said it. Didn't even know where it had come from.

He was quiet. 'You couldn't give me a child,' he said eventually.

'Am I that selfish?' My laugh sounded false.

He didn't reply.

'Because you don't want one?'

'Because I can't have one.'

I automatically thought, low-sperm count, weak swimmers. I thought adoption, baby from China, love in a Petri dish . . .

'I *won't* have children, Maggie. I can't.'

There was something in the way he said it which made my whole body go still.

'You never told me.'

He rubbed his eyes wearily. 'It's not the sort of thing you go round telling someone on a first date. "Hey, shall we go to dinner, and by the way I've had a vasectomy." '

'It's not funny.'

'No', he said. 'It's not funny. Why is this an issue all of a sudden? You told me you didn't want children.'

'I don't.' Jay had asked me once. I'd said no and he'd said good. I hadn't realized the question had an invisible 'ever' attached to it.

'What is this really about then, Maggie?'

I couldn't explain, wasn't sure myself. Maybe subconsciously I'd just used the one thing against Jay I knew he couldn't come back from. You can't extort commitment out of somebody, it's not a tangible thing to be handed over or promised.

'Look at me, Maggie.' He spread out his hands and they trembled a little. 'This isn't from drink, or because I'm an old fuck, there are things I have seen that will never leave me. Try to understand. What have I got to offer a child? What have I got to offer anyone?'

I didn't answer. In my head, the moment just crystallized into how differently we thought about the future.

'You're idealistic now, you'll be less idealistic in twenty years. Look around you, Maggie. The world isn't a particularly nice place. Love doesn't conquer everything.'

'I know, you told me, love doesn't make the world go round, Pepsi does.'

'Hate,' he said, 'rage, grief, greed, war – those are the things that make the world go around. Love just makes it all a little less painful.' His voice was harsh and I felt numb.

'Can we Scotch tape this?'

'I don't know.' I was crying.

'Don't give up on me, Maggie,' he breathed into my

damp hair and kissed me. 'Please, please don't give up on me,' but all I understood was that he'd given up on himself.

The oldest possession in my loft is an egg. When the stainless-steel boys delivered my fridge, the egg was already in it. For a long time it was the only thing in my fridge – save a few cans of spaghetti hoops for which I have a weakness (cold and preferably out of the tin). After a while there seemed no way of ridding myself of the egg without the risk of it breaking and the stench would have been apocalyptic. So for safety, I drew a face on it with a red felt marker and left it there. That was three years ago.

Staring into the fridge, standing on the bare boards of my kitchen I was struck by the spartan decor of my loft. It didn't look minimalist, it looked studenty, but after I had slept for a couple of hours at least it felt more like home. I opened one of the spaghetti cans and organized the videos from England in sequence in front of the television.

On *Newsline* you get the first edit. Initially you present the material as you want. If that doesn't wash, it becomes a question of give and take – more specifically they take and you try as hard as possible not to give. If you mess up totally Alan can and will put someone else onto it but this doesn't happen all that often. One of the great things about Alan is that once he hands out an assignment, he generally doesn't interfere in the creative process until you screen the finished product for him. Alan likes to be sure of coming to the material fresh and remaining objective enough to gauge whether the final story is solid in terms of content, whether it makes for compelling viewing, and more crucially whether it is a '*Newsline*' story.

Usually I get as much footage as I can then try to find a route through the material after. I know that the end result is a puzzle to which you have the key as long as you are prepared to worry and jiggle the pieces enough. Working for *Newsline* I learnt to edit in my head as I went along, but in order to do this you need to keep a clear view of what you want to say. And that was my problem. I no longer knew what that was.

When you grow up with absolutes, there are good guys and bad guys. There is the pure and simple truth and a self-righteousness that goes with believing you're with the angels on every issue, but let's face it, the truth is rarely pure and it's never simple.

I rewound the tapes over and over again, looking at the faces of the Bancrofts, Lady Roxmere, heard my own indictments, *cold, repressed, snobbish*, remembered Rory's retorts, *shy, scared, lonely*.

I paused on Montague. '*Some say inheriting a large house is a cruel burden, but I say if you've got a family that's been in possession of a house for a very long time you want to keep the bloody thing going. I mean that's what primogeniture is all about. It is the duty of the eldest son to keep the place intact.*'

'Bevan was my father's private war,' Rory had told me. 'The elms were his casualties. He's spent the last twenty-five years planting trees. My father has earned the right to his land.'

I freeze-framed on the Earl of Bevan himself. '*We are dinosaurs. We have clung to tradition even though it has driven us to bankruptcy but of course the knowledge that we are passing on a huge burden to our eldest child is less attractive than it used to be.'*

My confusion meant that I had no idea where to start or end. The set of moral values with which I used to define right and wrong, fairness and decency, had been skewed. I had lost my ground rules, and with no ground rules I didn't feel safe enough to tell a story, and with no story, there would be no film. I finally pinpointed why this was such a scary admission – the implication being that if I'd got this project so wrong I had to question so many other judgements. I wondered about past programs I'd made, how passionately I'd felt about issues, how fairly I'd manoeuvred edits, manipulated questioning or back-to-backed two non-consecutive incidents to make a point. The film-maker can be as guilty of planting evidence as any bent cop. It's no fun shining a torch in your own eyes and, as I watched the tapes, I wondered how many people had been burnt by the flare of my unswerving certainty.

Dawn broke over the city, two, three, four times. Sun glinted off the fire escapes outside the window. The sewing machines whirred beneath my floor. When I ventured out to the deli to pick up some food I noticed that someone had painted a row of watermelons on the inside of the lift. Everything was as it used to be yet nothing felt the same and time continued to run on and out.

On the fifth day, I made the mistake of picking up the phone without screening the call. Alan was on the other end. I bargained with him for a little more time. He knew, because I'd told him, exactly what story I had on tape and he thought what I was going to produce would be worth it, but I heard the warning in his voice. Not long after my stay of execution was granted I got into a crying jag and couldn't get out. When it was over, I thought that by rights, I should feel purged. Rory was a bug I caught in England, a particularly virulent one. Now I was rid of it. But it wasn't like that at all. Instead, never had I felt such a failure, both as a journalist and as a human being.

daniel

Rory's in a blue funk and I reckon if ever there was a time for a Dionysiac moment this would be it. If it were me, *exampli gratia*, I would be wallowing like a hippo in a river of alcohol by now but, as we've seen, Rory's made of sterner stuff. He does not succumb. Instead, curiously, he takes to cushion scattering with a vengeance, stripping bare the mews house in a burst of feverish energy. Even the moose head comes off the wall and gets chucked into the back of the car along with the rhino bin and Bevan's other artefacts of the past. When Rory delivers them home he gives no explanation for their return and Alistair does not ask for one.

Upstairs in the nursery he dumps everything on the floor. He has every intention of leaving them there without a backward glance, but he does give a backward glance and some bird charts stacked in the corner catch his eye. There are three of them, old and warped. Seabirds, Birds of Prey, Marsh Dwellers. When we were children we were given two pounds a chart to memorize them. Rory moves aside a stack of cardboard boxes and squats down.

'Greater Black-backed Gull, Gannet, Kittiwake,' he

closes his eyes and whispers. 'Arctic Skewer, Herring Gull, Little Tern.' He opens his eyes and sits down on the floor staring numbly at the posters. 'Latin name for wren?' he can hear Alistair asking. 'Troglodytes, Troglodytes, Troglodytes,' he hears my reply. You see, I want to point out to him – all the snippets of other people you absorb as a child will, one day, absorb you.

After a while Rory notices that one of the cardboard boxes he has moved is full of papers from my room. Hesitantly he sticks his hand into this lucky dip of memories. Out come letters, bills, photographs; Rory and me, mouths smeared with orange ice lollies. Another; I am dressed as Robin Hood and he, Maid Marion. A picture of my grandmother, holding the newborn Rory in his christening robe. Her bosom is so massive, he looks like a tiny brooch pinned to it. He unfurls a school photograph. There I am at the back, shockingly good looking even in the midst of spotty puberty, and there is Rory, one row, one year and, as yet, two undropped bollocks away. He crams the photos in his pocket and keeps digging.

I know he will find the map sooner or later and he does. He recognizes my handwriting and looks at the big envelope, undecided, before opening it.

There's a field at Bevan, to the far left of the farm road, which climbs a hill directly west then drops rather anticlimatically away leaving nothing more dramatic than a horizon of stunted fencing. I have always had a notion to plant a wood there quite from scratch and I thought it would be rather romantic to do this at the beginning of a new century. Everyone has their own idea of a legacy whether it's a book, a film or a child – it's not that I'm competitive but trees outlast most of them. 'The thing I am most proud of.' This was a silly game Rory and I used to play. Well, the Millennium wood was to have been it for me.

Most people when they design a wood draw it rectangular, but I wanted this one to be more interesting so I drew a shape at random. Bordered naturally on three sides by the paddock, the old orchard and the fox cover, I gave the fourth edge a curvaceous sweep which lent it a whimsical look. The idea was to create a wide ride running through the wood with statues and tree houses along the way, before eventually opening out into two clearings in the centre. The clearings would be planted with all sorts of odd and rare trees, 'Liquid Amber' and pear trees for example, both more usually associated with gardens than woods, then evergreens planted behind for a dark backdrop. I thought of putting a bench in the middle where one day mine or Rory's teenage boys might sit and catch a smoke. Rory turns the map over to cross-reference the tree plan on the other side. I'd chosen things that turn lovely colours; there was a red cedar or two, some *sorbus* for their berries – and a lot of ash which goes umber in the summer, a dried reddish haze in winter and does well in boggy ground like we have at Bevan.

My plan had been to enlist everyone's help; get the children up from the village, teach them about plants, give everyone who ever worked at Bevan a tree with their name on it . . . but look, I'm getting carried away by my own genius. Rory's not studying the map any more – he's staring at the floor, more and more anguished, his face all screwed up, then before you know it he's started crying and I see that the poor bastard is in a lot more trouble than I thought.

maggie

I opened the fridge and stood hopefully in front of it. All that was left was a can of clam chowder, a bottle of red wine with a corkscrew embedded in its top and, of course, the egg. I must throw out the egg. The egg was symbolic – a sign of something rotten in my life. As I heated the chowder I wondered how to achieve its eviction without breaking it. An egg carton seemed logical, but that meant buying more eggs and then what to do with the rest? They'd sit in the freezer for ever and my problem would have multiplied. Eventually I decided to wrap it in an old pair of briefs and put it – well not in the trash can, from where it could be traced back to me by angry neighbours, but somewhere safe, where it would be dealt with swiftly, where there were other competing putrid smells – a hospital for example. So that was the plan. Swaddle the egg in warm clothes and leave it at the hospital. No doubt when it was found dozens of depressed post-partum chickens all over New York would be questioned. *Please come forward, you obviously need help, you will receive sympathetic treatment.*

I'd still not edited my footage, hadn't even left the house for the last two days. Now I was definitely losing it. I took a walk. Though night, the cold bite was fading from the air. Winter would soon turn to spring. I headed west along Rivington Street, aware as I always am on returning home how different this place is to any other. People are loud and sharp, the air buzzes with tangible energy. It was after midnight but the streets were packed and lights were blazing. Even the traffic was snarled. When I hit Broadway I saw why. A car had crashed up on the pavement; its door jammed open against the kerb. It had knocked down a trash can and the pavement was decorated with the waste of city. There were the usual disco lights of cops and ambulances and the street was being cordoned off. I detoured into the all-night record store which was deserted save for a few music addicts patrolling the second-hand aisles. In world music I picked out some Cuban tapes I'd been meaning to get for ever. Heading downstairs to checkout, a man was pushing out of the classical section, a bunch of CDs in his arms. Music boomed through the glass door as I held it back for him and I stiffened. I know nothing about classical music, but this I recognized.

Beethoven's ninth symphony. The music Rory's grandfather had been playing at such ear-splitting volume that morning at Bevan. I bought it, feeling a little foolish. At home I slipped it out of the case and fast-forwarded to the passage I was looking for. It was a short piece of music, but very powerful. I don't know what it's supposed to be written about, but to me it seemed to be about courage, about death, pain and glory. I turned up the volume, played it loud. Opened all the windows and played it louder still until it had chased all the other stuff out of my head. Then everything was clear.

In the morning, I rang a contact of mine and arranged to rent a small editing suite with a technician thrown in. I headed downtown, the film packed tightly into two cardboard boxes. For the first time in a week I felt completely calm – OK so maybe there is no truth, but you've got to believe in something.

daniel

Benj's father dies. Suddenly and unexpectedly. He gets no chance to make his old man amends, no time for the usual last-minute pact with the living before he faces the dead – and a punishment, I believe, richly deserved as was his tumour in the stomach while we're on the subject of karma. One minute he has indigestion, the next they're slicing him open and there it is – the big C – nurtured on his internal river of bile, sprouting like watercress in and around every organ in his body. He doesn't survive the operation.

The effect on Benj is predictable. He disintegrates, regresses, ages, weeps, jumps a generation, celebrates and mourns all with varying degrees of confusion and guilt. At the funeral he stands by his mother in the church wearing a suit which looks like it has been made for a much fatter man. Benj maintains his composure for most of the service then walks unsteadily to the lectern brushing Rory's finger-tips as he passes. As he stands up there, gazing out over a sea of expectantly mournful faces, I wonder whether he will go off at the deep end, take this opportunity for an exquisitely timed revenge – out his father for the emotional and physical abusing shit of a man that he was. Instead Benj delivers an address so touching, so wry, so fucking true, that it reduces most of the family to tears.

After the service Benj gets drunk and stays that way for a month. Rory makes no attempt to stop him, simply monitoring him closely, occasionally feeding him and when not delegating the job of babysitting him to Alison, sleeping on the sofa himself in Benj's sitting room. This is all quite good for Rory, leaving him little time for his other favoured pastime – obsessing about Maggie. When he does obsess about her, he still fails to appreciate the simplicity of the situation which is no more complicated than this: Maggie is attached to nothing and nobody while he is attached to everybody and everything. Instead he executes a competent job of convincing himself he's motivated by nothing more than pique. She had got under his skin in the same way that another driver stealing a parking place from under your nose leaves you with a seething murderous resentment wholly out of proportion with the crime. He is convinced these feelings will, given time, pass – but is not particularly surprised when they don't.

When Benj comes out of his stupor he makes an announcement. For the first time ever he feels in control. He feels all powerful and will take steps to change his life. He tells Rory that he knows he can achieve anything. Rory is mildly impressed until Benj adds that these accomplishments include the scaling of rooftops and soaring through the air unassisted by wires. 'Things are about to change,' Benj says, the frightening gleam of the converted in his eyes. 'We're in the dawning of a new era. Someone will have to lead the people and show them the light, that person could be me and I could be well paid for it.' At which juncture Rory checks him into the Priory clinic and goes back to work.

maggie

I have always had a secret passion for Central Park zoo. The noise, the smell, the meeting of furtive lovers and chatterings of school kids exchanging baseball cards. When I was in third grade, my school organized a day trip there but my mom wouldn't sign the permission form. The rest of the class went and I was sent home early. Of course I knew my mother was right to disapprove of caged animals, but when other teenagers were smoking their first illicit cigarettes, I was rebelliously throwing bread at penguins.

Wolf was waiting for me at the entrance, leaning his considerable bulk against the railings. I bumped him.

'Hey.'

'Hey yourself.'

We wandered through the park. It was April now and during the time I'd spent editing, the cherry trees had blossomed. The Bowery, Little Italy, Chinatown were all ablaze with marigolds and pansies. I've noticed something amazing about New Yorkers. They'll steal the hub caps off your car and the spokes out of your bicycle wheels but they have the sensibility to leave the public flowers alone. They want the city to smell and look nice while they pick over its bones.

In the park, people were draped over benches, laid out on the grass or leaning against trees reading books, pitching into mitts and generally enjoying the first real warm sun of the year. A frisbee came spinning our way. Wolf sent it back, cutting low through the air.

'You know who you reminded me of when I first met you?' I told him.

'Who?'

'Chief.'

'Chief?'

'The Indian in *One flew over the Cuckoo's Nest*.'

'Deaf and dumb?'

'I may have found it disconcerting how little you talked.'

'Did it ever occur to you I couldn't get a word in?'

I grinned. I was afraid to ask him so I didn't.

You hear of those screenings for Hollywood turkeys when executives sit down for the first time and take a look at where their dollars have gone. Apparently the air takes on a certain quality as if the fumes of so much disappointment actually pollute it. They say there's a smell. Well, of course it wasn't quite like that after I showed the edit, but up on the tenth floor of the *Newsline* building, there was definitely a vibe – and it was not a good one. I guess I shouldn't have been surprised. The CBS suits who had become a fixture at *Newsline* wouldn't know a good story from a shoe shine.

Alan eased himself up and out of his chair, 'What happened to this hot story you were chasing?'

'It didn't pan out.'

'Aha.'

'It was a hot story, but the trail was cold.'

'I see. So this is the piece you're expecting us to run?'

I met his look squarely. 'This is the piece I'm handing in.'

Alan cleared his throat. 'This might be fine work, Maggie, but it's not the fine work I was expecting, in fact let's be clear, it's twice not what I was expecting. What happened to your original brief?'

'Yes.' One of the CBS execs had joined us. 'Where are the beautiful gardens, the pomp and circumstance, what about all that royal stuff we suggested you include?'

You could see why he was disappointed. I mean there was no sex, no celebrity, no ground-breaking scandal – but it was a good story, it was a touching story and I told him I thought people would want to watch it.

'But they're all so . . . well . . . so shabby these people,' the executive looked at the blank screen. 'The female demographic wants glamour, it wants something to aspire to. No one's interested in downtrodden.'

I reminded him that Lesley Stahl from *60 Minutes* once did a story about divorced wives living out of their cars in Beverly Hills. She shot it, loved it, but *60 Minutes* refused to air it. They said no one would be interested. She kicked and screamed and eventually got it shown. It had huge ratings. I told Alan I thought he should air my piece exactly the way it was and I kicked and screamed but it didn't do a lot of good. Alan listened throughout, but I could tell the argument was academic. It didn't matter whether he agreed with me or not. He wasn't running the show any longer.

'The material should go to someone else,' the executive said when I'd finished.

I looked down. My sneakers were covered in subway dust. I had a flash of Rory in his greying tennis shoes throwing the ball up in a perfect arc. If I handed the footage over to *Newsline*, ironically it would be edited according to my own original brief of snobbery, debauchery, lunacy. If I refused to hand it over, I would probably be fired. Alan put his hand on my shoulder, 'Everything you've got, Maggie, give it to either Ed or Neil today and we'll see what they can do with it.'

I nodded and Alan looked relieved.

I got out of there quick. Alan eviscerated by bean counters was something I never thought I'd see.

'Hungry?' Wolf asked.

'I could eat a horse.'

'Settle for a dog?'

At the stand he waved away my dollars. I didn't mean to look surprised. It's not that Wolf was ungenerous with money but small acts of chivalry had never been his style. He lathered on mustard and sauerkraut and handed me the frankfurter.

'A) you've quit,' he said, 'and will therefore soon be on welfare and B),' he soused his own bun in mustard, 'well . . . talk round the building is you damaged the tapes on purpose.'

'Well let's just say personally, professionally, technically, I've truly messed everything up.'

'Aha . . .there you go again,' Wolf said. 'As George Bush said to Geraldine Ferraro, "Snatching defeat out of the jaws of victory".' He grinned at me, a blob of mustard on the side of his mouth.

'Oh Chief . . . so you *did* like it?'

'Yeah well. I thought it had real heart.'

I didn't trust myself to speak. We sat down on a bench.

'Talk is they could sue you,' he said.

'They could.'

'But you don't think they will?'

'Naa, I don't think they'll bother.'

'So what are you going to do?'

I gave an elaborate sigh. 'I don't know. Nothing for a bit, see how that feels. Then look for another job, maybe think about doing that documentary we always talked about.'

'I meant about your love life,' he said.

When Jay returned from Washington he took me out to an Indian restaurant near his apartment. 'You're wearing a black hat,' he said. He touched the spark of electricity on my hair as I pulled off my beanie. 'Any chance there's a white one in your bag?'

We sat down awkwardly. One of Jay's president stories was when Reagan was woken in the middle of the night to make decisions on some knotty foreign problem he would ask, 'Do they have white hats or black hats?' before making a decision, turning over and going back to sleep. 'Just think,' I could hear Jay saying, 'the entire foreign policy and maybe the history of the world hung on what colour hat the baddies were wearing. Incredible.'

The food arrived and I watched it jumping and splattering on the plates in front of us as if it were too spicy even for itself. We both waited for one of us to have the courage to begin.

'I could have it reversed,' Jay said eventually, but I heard the *if you really wanted me to*, in his voice. I reminded him that you were never supposed to force someone into giving up something they believed in.

'It's a low blow to use a man's own bullshit against him.' He took my hand.

'You are not the real you when you're with me,' I said desperately.

'The real me?' He raised his eyebrows.

The thing was, Jay wasn't a recidivist. He was a war junkie. He needed to stand close to someone who was dying in order to feel alive – that was his addiction. I wanted to tell him I understood but I couldn't find the right words. 'I feel like time you spend with me is time taken out from being you,' I said. 'Your reality kicks in when you leave me in the morning. Well I can't just be your treat when the going gets rough.'

'I think that's a little unfair.' When I said nothing he added, 'Ain't no pot of gold at the end of the rainbow, kiddo.'

'Maybe there is, Jay, maybe I just need a different map to get to it.'

'Tell me about him,' was all he said.

When I finally got around to saying the name, he looked

up from his plate. 'Lytton-Jones? Wait a minute . . . is there a Daniel?'

'Yes,' I was amazed.

'I know him.'

'I don't believe it.'

'Yes, I do, well I don't know him exactly, but I met him. Ethiopia, I think it was. Very English, funny. He told me he took a homeopathic approach to drugs, i.e. anything that was plant-based was fine – heroin, marijuana, cocaine, "If God put it there it must be OK".' Jay chuckled. 'It really made me laugh at the time.' He was doing a piece for some English satirical magazine – I don't know how seriously he was actually taking it.'

'He's dead now.'

Jay nodded like this didn't surprise him.

When the cheque came he said, 'I feel like I've been run over.' He put fifty dollars on the plate. 'And so you leave me, bloodied by the side of the road.'

You feel run over, I thought. *While you're in hospital, look me up. I'll be on the women's ward across the corridor.*

I stretched over the table and kissed him on the cheek. He caught my hand. 'If that's your idea of a Band-Aid,' he said softly, 'I'm going to need a larger one.'

'I'm so sorry, Jay.'

He sighed. 'You know what we are, Maggie? Just two people maturing on a different schedule . . . I read that somewhere and I thought of us.' He took my hand and turned it over in his like he was examining it for signs of the future. 'Two people maturing on a different schedule –

at least that's the way my old man's pride is going to sell
it to my young man's ego.'

'We've been together a long time now,' I told Wolf. 'I don't
know, he's everything I always wanted. He's grown-up and
decent, he's serious about things that really matter, he
believes in the things I believe in, he's a really good guy, a
good man. He has all the right heroes – God, he's virtually
a hero himself and well . . . well the truth is I've finished
it with Jay.'

'Actually I meant Rory.' Wolf wiped the ketchup from
his mouth.

There was such an expression of tenderness in those
heavy features I felt my face crumple. While I cried, Wolf
ate the rest of my hot dog.

When I finished, he handed me the paper napkin.

'I have nothing to say to Rory.' I blew my nose

Wolf shook his head slowly. 'You see, this is why you
will be great at making documentaries. You'll never have to
worry about thinking up happy endings.'

I had no idea what he was talking about.

'You don't have to say anything to him, Maggie,' Wolf
said, as though instructing a first year film student. '*Show*
him.'

'What do you mean?'

'Send it.'

'The film?'

'Yes, of course the film.'

'What's the point, he hates me,' I said sulkily.

'Send it anyway,' Wolf said.

daniel

A few days before Benj's get out of jail card becomes valid
Rory goes down with a bad case of flu. Its sheer spite takes
him by surprise and he finds himself in bed with a high
temperature watching a succession of Carole Lombard
movies which he only partially manages to follow. When
Benj appears on the doorstep, the event is notable only
because for the first time in his life Benj is four shades less
green than his cousin.

They lie sprawled on the floor, take-away menus scattered
between them, watching *Miss Universe* on the telly. The
mews house is bare and cold without the furniture. Rory
misses the moose head; despite the obvious drawback of
it being dead, the moose had actually been quite good
company – a low maintenance virtual pet – and Rory quite
often finds himself talking to its blank space on the wall,
which has done little to improve his temper.

'And a number ten,' Benj says into the phone.

'Park or bif?' demands the voice on the other end.

'Which is it?' Benj is confused.

'That's why ask. Park of bif. Which you wan?'

Benj sighs, he has always assumed the point of numbered

menus is to avoid confusion of this sort but he's far too good-natured to say so.

'Rory,' Benj nudges him with his foot, 'see what number ten is would you?'

Rory grunts. On screen the Miss Universe candidates, holding their numbered placards, parade their teeth, bikinis, hopes and dreams across the stage.

'Rory! Number ten?'

'For fuck's sake . . . Miss Uruguay.'

'Oh thank you very much, so very helpful. Right, my friend would like one Miss Uruguay . . . yes with hot sauce . . .yes cash on delivery is fine. Yes, thank you too.'

'You're a real wag . . . a natural vaudevillian,' Rory says sourly as Benj hangs up the phone. 'I mean, are these witticisms spontaneous or do you practise them beforehand?'

'Sorry, I wasn't listening.' Benj is a little offended. Having traditionally been the recipient of efforts to raise the level of his own happiness rather than someone else's, he is ill trained for the job in hand.

'I was just wondering what kind of wit you were,' Rory says grouchily.

'Just your average halfwit.' Benj sighs again. He stares at the television. 'Hey, you know, I've got it. Stella's having a party in Suffolk this weekend. Some fantastic possibilities there.'

'Such as?'

'Wine, women, song.'

Rory doesn't bother to acknowledge this.

'Um . . . well,' Benj stumbles, 'women, girls . . . er, sex?'

Rory gives him a withering look.

'Sex!' Benj rallies. 'Come on, surely you remember. That strenuous activity where a woman puts her naked body at your disposal. Sometimes for as long as five whole minutes consecutively.'

'Sorry,' Rory says. 'Doesn't ring a bell.'

On screen Miss Chile is being crowned. She bursts into tears and adjusts her Grecian-style gown around her Brazilian-style boobs.

'Anyway, I'd better go home this weekend. I haven't been for months. My father has bought a seaweed-extracting machine.'

'But Bevan isn't by the sea.'

Yes,' Rory says wryly. 'Well spotted.'

maggie

The waxy orange flakes floated on top of the water. The fish's bulbous head quivered with excitement, his little mouth opening and shutting like, well, a fish, I supposed. He gobbled up the flakes. Wolf eyed me over the top of his *New York Times*.

'Another four weeks,' he said, 'and that fish'll be floating.' He stretched his feet out on the ottoman and flipped the page.

I grabbed the handykit off the table and dragged a chair over to the wall. Aimed the hammer at the nail. 'Shit.' The nail dropped, twisted, to the ground; I sucked my thumb.

'Still haven't heard anything, huh?' Wolf searched out the sports section. I glared at him then chose a larger nail from the metal box and executed a repeat performance. The picture was a little crooked, but it was good enough. The loft looked completely different furnished, though I couldn't decide whether better or worse – I kept tripping over things which I hadn't remembered buying, but once I'd tripped over them, turned out they were quite comfortable to lie on.

'Maggie?'

'You know something, Wolf, it's so much safer in life to be a cynic. Santa Claus, the infallibility of your parents, a believable religion – they all fall by the wayside sooner or later. We're told stories of monsters in the woods, then scolded for having nightmares. We're drip-fed fantasy then taught to be suspicious of anything that has no roots in reality so why, oh why are we still conditioned to believe in romantic love?'

Wolf grunted and went back to his reading.

I wrenched open the window. Manhattan was in the throes of a freak heatwave. It was so damn hot it steamed at night. The air hung over the city, hazy and polluted. Yesterday in Washington Square a girl tore off her shirt in protest. Both her nipples were multiple pierced and she had 'fuck me' tattooed across her belly button. Later in the day a large scantily clad Hawaiian reeled into me on the subway and asked, 'Have you ever been raped?' As opening gambits go I guess it left a lot to be desired. Luckily a group of Asians came aboard causing him to bellow, 'CHINKS!' every few seconds. The Asians just nodded their heads politely. God, New York in the spring. The city was lurching from 99 degrees to 49 on an hourly basis which was interesting as my internal emotional temperature had been doing roughly the same thing.

It took me days to post Rory the film. The problem was I didn't know what to put in the note. I tried flippant, casual, professional but none of them seemed right so in the end I just sent the film on its own, figuring that if it didn't say what I felt then nothing I could put on paper would help much anyway.

After I sealed the package, it sat on my desk for days.

Finally, Wolf came round one morning with bagels and juice. He saw it there, stamped and addressed, and simply picked it up without saying a word and lumbered off to FedEx.

For a week I was on a high. Whatever Rory thought of the film at least a line of communication would be opened. After two weeks, I tracked the package and received confirmation that it had been delivered. I kept giving Rory new deadlines to get in touch and the weeks started to pile up on top of each other like unreturned library books. As soon as I realized he wasn't going to get in touch I tried to fill myself up with hate, hate, hate for the slimy boy germ that had exposed me to all this emotional garbage. Well to hell with him, at least I had tried.

'So just how much longer are you going to give him?' Wolf said.

Out of the window I watched the last of the trestle tables being carried through the doors of the building. The Chinese sweatshop below was closing, their lease up. They invited me to their goodbye party. I hadn't intended to go but at the last minute I changed my mind. Most of the racks had disappeared along with plastic bags, sewing machines, and accompanying loops of electrical cabling from the ceiling. The space looked completely different – well, not unlike what my loft used to look like. The centre of the floor had been chalked out as a dancing zone. I don't think I'd ever thought about the kind of dancing that Chinese tailors liked but these guys were into waltzing big time, beautiful old-fashioned tunes like the *Blue Danube*. I forked noodles off a paper plate and watched the seamstresses move dreamily through the airless room. I liked the party at first, assuming its mellow, drifting atmosphere was out of choice, then it occurred to me that it was because all these people had lost their livelihood and had no idea where their next pay cheque was coming from.

'I've been offered a job,' I told Wolf. A young NBC journalist working in Cambodia had committed suicide. Her papers had finally been found, along with her diary. The network wanted someone to retrace her journey and cover the MIA story at the same time. It was something I was really interested in doing it but I'd been finding excuses to put off the decision for as long as possible.

'You could come too now that you've quit and are on welfare.'

Wolf looked up questioningly.

'I already agreed to go,' I told him.

daniel

As soon as Bevan appears round a bend in the drive, Rory stops the Rover and gets out. From here the house is still magnificent. When he shuts his eyes he can conjure up the drive before the elms were cut down. Their replacements, limes and turkey oaks, stand nearly 15 feet high. One day, not in Rory's lifetime perhaps, but one day, the drive will look like it did when we were boys. The trees will outlive us all.

Spring is on its way. The buds are swelling on the horse chestnuts. The grass around my headstone has shot up to knee-high. Rory slings the dead flowers into the nettles then opens the plastic bag that he's brought with him from London. Inside is a photograph frame: a picture of a fantastically sexy girl wielding a whip – he leans it against the headstone. He crouches down and scrawls a message across the glass with a felt tip. 'Daniel, you fucker, thought you could do with a change.'

Rory waits for Alistair in the office where he reads the crumpled remains of the *Telegraph*. It's not that he's worried about getting the money back for the seaweed machine, it's just that it's so brain-damaging, the relentlessness of the whole thing. Trying to pre-empt Dad's financial gaffes is like trying to second guess the direction a frog will jump next. He reads a biographical account of Ted Hughes's marriage, occasionally, Eeyore-like, surveying the bulging pile on the desk, but old habits die hard. Furious with himself, he throws the *Telegraph* down and works the mail methodically until he hears a door slam and his name being shouted.

'Office,' he shouts back.

The buckles of Alistair's gumboots make a clicking noise as he walks down the hall.

'The fence to the old paddock needs replacing,' he says from the doorway, as though he'd seen his son at breakfast rather than nearly two months previously. 'Come take a look at it with me?'

'Dad, we need to talk.'

'And bring that farming catalogue, would you?' Alistair flutters his hand. 'Padded thingy near the bottom, could have something useful in it.'

Rory hands over the catalogue.

'Dad.'

'Deer have been a bloody nuisance this spring.' Alistair slices through the envelope with his letter opener. 'We're going to have to fence all the new trees as well.'

'Pa,' Rory says very quietly.

Nervous, Alistair fumbles with the envelope, dropping its contents to the floor.

Rory bends down, 'I need you to listen, please just for a minute—' then he breaks off. What he's handing his father is not a farming catalogue with its comforting photographs of ploughed fields and Massey Fergusons but a copy of a video with the words 'For your next bonfire' scrawled over a *Newsline* label.

'Something the matter, Rory?' Alistair queries innocently.

Rory is looking thunderous. He paces back and forth across the small room. Nanny, Grandpa, Ma and Pa sit in Nanny's room, all glued to the small screen.

'It's just that you seem a little ill at ease,' Alistair says, enjoying his son's discomfort hugely.

'I didn't particularly want you to see this,' Rory says through gritted teeth. 'I didn't particularly want *anyone* to see it for that matter.'

'Shame about the twenty million Americans then,' Alistair quips cheerfully. He turns his attention back to the television and gives a tremendous guffaw. He pats Nanny's knee.

'Oh Nanny, you have such screen presence, I've always thought so.'

Nanny looks deliciously pleased with herself. She carefully fingers another almond slice on the plate in front of her.

'Too bad our nice Miss Munroe wasn't around when Rory cut up the dining room curtains so he could dress like Julie Andrews in the *Sound of Music*,' Alistair says.

Audrey glances at Rory apprehensively.

'Remember, Nanny?' Alistair gently removes the remains of Nanny's paper napkin from her mouth.

'I do, yes indeed.'

Rory stops pacing and looks at the screen just in time to catch Alistair and Audrey sipping whisky through their curly-wurly straws. The shot cuts to Grandpa holding the Chinese figurines in his hands. Rory has already seen the sequence of this footage and is terrified of what's coming next. He thinks of the weeks ahead spent fending off journalists, his grandfather in the spotlight, his family humiliated and ridiculed.

'Right, we're not watching this any more.' He leaps up and attempts to switch off the television, cursing himself for not warning his father about Maggie.

Alistair grips his arm, 'Shut up and stop being a bore.'

'And do sit down,' Nanny commands.

On screen, Alistair is leaning on the dairy door, the baby beaker clipped to his dirty Barbour, painstakingly describing his recipe for buffalo face packs. The dread footage of Grandpa, or even any reference to it is not yet evident, nevertheless Rory can hardly bear to watch. His own commentary, rather than Maggie's, is running over the visuals so he cannot see that somehow she has achieved something rather remarkable. She has caught the eccentricity and yet the charm, she has shown the snobbery but also the sadness but as still no sign of Grandpa and his swastika knife appear on screen, Rory's relief gives way to other less noble emotions. Alistair looks closely at his son and quite correctly reads embarrassment hidden behind the scowl on his face.

And at that moment, something dawns on me – what Maggie must have known all along and Rory has singularly failed to understand – that however bizarre our parents' moral codes and way of life might seem to the rest of the world, they are perfectly ordinary to them. People can be happy with the way they're portrayed as long as you show them just the way they are and judging from my father's response Maggie has succeeded in doing just this.

'What a pompous twit you turned out to be, Rory,' Alistair says lightly. 'I rather thought we'd brought you up better than that.'

Rory looks wildly at him.

'I may not be the world's most successful businessman, but at least I try. In fact, your mother and I spend *all* our time trying to keep Bevan going for you.'

'For me?' Rory finally loses it. 'For *me*?' He jumps to his feet again. 'How can you say that. I hate this bloody house,' he howls.

'No,' Alistair shouts, '*I* hate this bloody house.'

'What are you *talking* about, Dad?' Rory's totally wrong-footed. 'What do you mean?'

'Exactly what I said. I hate this bloody house.'

'Dad, this is your home, this has always been your home.'

'Yes, it's my home,' Alistair says vehemently, 'but God knows it's no fun any more. Has it never occurred to you that we kept it going for Daniel, that we keep it going for *you*? For *your* children?'

This hits Rory low in the guts and winds him totally. 'But why did you never say anything?' he eventually manages.

'Oh, I don't know,' Alistair says wearily. 'I don't suppose you ever asked.'

In London, Rory shows the film to Benj. Five minutes aren't up before Benj is laughing his head off. He quickly apologizes and snaps opens another can of Coca Cola. When the credits finally roll, he says, 'So she didn't shop Grandpa after all . . . and how guilty out of ten do we feel?'

'All right, all right,' Rory says grudgingly, 'I suppose you think I should go after her.'

'Don't be ridiculous, she's completely unsuitable.' Benj helps himself to another slice of toast and cod's roe. 'You know these American women, they all insist on central heating.' He ignores the dirty look. 'Besides, you can't trust these foreign correspondents, she'd be off with a scud stud in the blink of an eye.'

This is too much for Rory's frayed nerves. 'Screw you,' he takes a swipe at his cousin. Benj ducks. 'That's not to say you shouldn't apologize though.' Benj calmly squeezes more lemon onto the cod's roe. 'You were, after all, particularly vile to her.'

'So you *are* saying I should call her then?' Rory says hopefully.

'Let's not exaggerate,' Benj says. 'A brief note would be more than adequate.'

To say what? Maggie had not sent a note. He'd taken the envelope out of the dustbin at Bevan and given it a good shaking. Why had she sent it? Professional courtesy? Where was the boyfriend and was he still around? Why had she sent it to Bevan and not to London? These questions are all irrelevant but serve as reasonably good excuses not to leave a message every time he calls and gets her answering machine. The fact is Maggie's film has made him think. She's reached a kind of truth he has been unwilling to face. She's presented his life to him, everything he stands for, and he's unsure how he feels about such painful exposure. He knows too that his anger is misdirected. The real culprits were around long before she appeared; himself, our father, me for copping out so spectacularly. *Is there anything else you ever wanted to be?* Maggie had asked. *Not the eldest son*, Pa had said. Rory feels a tightness like a rubber band around his heart and the pain sends him underground.

One night about a week later he has a dream. It's after the fire and he's sneaked up to the east wing. The forbidden east wing. He stands by the door, terrified by the blocked shapes of furniture shrouded in dust sheets. I am in the middle of the room wearing my games kit; shorts, an Aertex shirt and scuffed Clarks sandals. He watches me as I walk round in circles, humming the same tune over and over again. I smile at him, he smiles back. Then without warning the floorboards give way and I slip through. My arms are thrown out to him but he is rooted to the spot until the moment I disappear. Only then, as if magically released, is he able to rush to the hole. He looks down and sees me, he stretches out his arms but I am still falling. I will fall for ever.

He wakes up in a cold sweat. For a while he lies there, darkness encircling him, then, knowing sleep is impossible, goes to the kitchen for some water. He knocks against the drainer and saucepans clatter to the floor.

Saucepans clatter to the floor. Take the bike, Daniel, take the bike.

The Bevans are a careless family, we lose a lot of people. Alcohol, pills, guns, self-loathing, fear, weakness, guilt . . .

Saucepans clatter to the floor. And now I am there, back in the house. I am with him.

I pick up the pans and stack them one by one on the drainer.

'What's up?' says Rory, sleepy and crumpled from the doorway.

'I'm having a little problem sleeping.' I balance the last saucepan on top of the plate rack.

'It would help if you went to bed,' he says and I can tell how annoyed he is.

'How 'bout I borrow the car?'

'Again?' His tone is sarcastic. 'It's only just back from the body shop.'

'I need to go out.' I try to keep the alcohol from my voice, then I think, *Damn him — why the hell should I?*

'Go out. Where? It's four in the morning.'

'See a man about a dog. Ha.'

'You're drunk.' He takes the bottles from the dustbin. 'Christ, Daniel.'

'Tanked, tiddly, pissed, pie-eyed, bibulous, soused, shaken and stirred but not drunk, so what's new?'

'Daniel you promised.'

'Oh, my friend, be warned by me that Coca Cola, milk and tea are all the human frame requires and with that the wretched brother—'

'Daniel, just go to bed.'

'I want to go to Highgate. To the cemetery.'

'Well I'm not letting you take the car so you'll have to bloody well walk.'

'It's fifty degrees below zero!' I shout at him.

'Take the fucking bike then,' he shouts back.

Take the bike, Daniel, take the bike.
And he hurls the padlock keys at my feet.

In the back of the cupboard, behind the Domestos and the Ajax, Rory finds the bottle of whisky. He unscrews the lid and drinks it. The brown liquid slides down his throat like treacle.

He wakes about six hours later. He makes it to the loo just in time. When he surfaces again it's two o'clock in the afternoon and someone is beating a gong inside his head. He endures another bout of vomiting after the first coffee. After the fourth coffee he takes a cold shower and calls Maggie.

maggie

Ever since I worked for *Newsline* I have kept two packed
suitcases in the closet by my front door. They're there for
quick escapes. One is labelled hot, the other, cold. Inside
the hot suitcase are three pairs of cotton combats, T-shirts,
boots, and plenty of underwear. I searched the loft for some
books to throw in as well. I always seem to take more books
than clothes and leave them wherever they get finished. It's
nice to drop a well-thumbed paperback in places you've
been. It feels a little like carving your name onto a tree.

When the phone rang, I let the machine pick it up.

'I was going to hang up again, but . . .'

I recognized his voice immediately. Held the book tight
in my hand.

'But then I wondered whether all those consecutive hang-
ups might not seem a little creepy even by New York
standards so—'

I grabbed at the portable under my bed.

'Christ, Maggie,' I heard the surprise in his voice, 'I
didn't think . . . you're up early.'

A month ago I would have told him that I was up early
a lot, that I wasn't sleeping too good, but, crouched on the

floor I didn't know what to say. Even the simplest of sentences seemed beyond my power so I just said I was packing.

'You're going somewhere? When are you back?'

'Oh you know, this year, next year, sometime, never.'

'There was a long pause. 'Look I just called to say . . . well . . . how have you been?' His voice took on my own stilted tone.

'Fine . . . you?'

'Good . . . great.'

Wonderful. After three months of silence we were finally speaking, the way two people speak when they know a tree might fall on their head any second.

'Why did you call, Rory?' Three months was a long time. What was I hoping for? I had no idea, an apology? Some kind of acknowledgement that I was not the total bitch he thought. But there was nothing but silence down the end of the line.

'Rory, I'm leaving this evening. I'm going to Cambodia and . . .'

'I'm sorry,' he cut in, 'I'm obviously keeping you.'

'No, no, it's fine,' I trailed off and the conversation drifted even further out of reach.

'OK, well . . . it was nice to talk to you,' he said and I felt pride kicking in. I had got real efficient at not thinking about Rory these days. Keep tearing off the scab and it doesn't heal.

I dug my nails into my hand. 'Yeah, you too,' I said and hung up the phone.

daniel

In the white sunlight of late afternoon, amongst the usual limo hassling and police whistling of JFK airport, Rory throws his holdall into a yellow cab.

'Bowery, corner of Rivington Street,' Rory says, 'and please hurry.'

Maggie had said that her flight was *this evening*. It is now four o'clock. Four o'clock is afternoon. Five o'clock is still afternoon. Six is a hybrid hour, between afternoon and evening. Six is the earliest an evening can reasonably be expected to begin. *This evening* lasts until *tonight*. Seven is this evening, so is eight. Nine is pushing it. Ten o'clock is definitely tonight. Rory does his sums and reasons therefore that Maggie's flight is due to leave between six and ten o'clock, which means she would have to leave the house between three-thirty and seven-thirty giving him a four-hour window of opportunity — except judging by traffic it will probably be four-thirty before he arrives, knocking one pane out of his window. Still, three out of four is a 75 per cent chance, Ladbrokes would give him 3–1. If Maggie were a horse, these would be good odds. But hang on – Maggie didn't say *flying* this evening. She said *leaving*. That could mean leaving the *apartment* this evening which could mean flying *tonight*. This changes the odds considerably. Anything is possible.

As he presses the intercom on the outside of Maggie's building, noises from the real world penetrate his consciousness almost for the first time since he's left London. The air is warm and carries the smell of frying food. Sun gleams off the stainless steel of fridge doors and sink tops along the street. Traffic streams ceaselessly by. Then the door he's leaning against buzzes violently and he stumbles in.

maggie

'Two minutes,' I shouted at the intercom, 'Oh and could you please help me down with my bag?' I left the front door open, suitcase zipped shut in front of it and looked around quickly for my backpack. When, instead of the driver from Tel Aviv cars I'd been expecting, Rory bounded through the door, there was no way my mouth would open, let alone have words come out of it.

'Maggie,' he grabbed my arms. 'Look, tell them you're sick, tell them you're ill, tell them you've lost interest, lost a limb, tell them you can't write, can't film, can't function, tell them anything you like but just please, please, please, Maggie, I beg you, tell them you can't go.'

'Oh my God . . .'

'I mean it, tell them you're not going.'

'And then what?' I was still staring goofily at him.

'I don't know,' he said, 'then we will . . . well . . . we'll . . . uh . . . well obviously, you've got to come home with me. I mean . . . it's the village fête this weekend.'

I shook my head. 'Oh, Rory, why did you have to come now?'

'To stop you from going, of course. Cambodia's a horrible place, hot, wet – the food will be, well probably delicious,' he conceded, 'but you'll get hideously fat . . . wrinkled.'

I laughed, but my laughter nearly turned to tears. Rory pulled me closer.

'Stay. I'm asking you to stay.'

'All this time. You didn't even call—'

'Begging you to stay.'

The buzzer sounded. I looked to the door.

'It's too late, Rory.'

'Maggie, come on, of course it's not too late.'

'Everyone's waiting. I've got a job to do . . . responsibilities.'

'Fuck 'em.'

'*You* of all people.' I said, shocked.

The buzzer sounded again. 'That's my cab.' I pressed the intercom.

'And fuck your cab,' Rory said cheerfully.

'Tel Aviv cars,' scratched the voice.

Rory grabbed my hand. 'Look, I know I may not be even close to what you had in mind—'

'Rory don't.'

'And that probably scares you. I know it scares the hell out of me.'

But what I was scared of was how easy this could be. I felt completely split in two, but it seemed far safer taking my cues from my old self.

'It's too late, Rory.'

'Wasn't it Oscar Wilde who said something like, I will wait for you for ever . . . as long as you're not too long?'

But it just felt like a chastisement.

'You can't just turn up after three months and expect me to drop everything,' I said angrily.

'Maggie, I know I screwed up, I really did – more than you know, but . . . oh fuck it . . . look, the fact is . . . I need you.'

I heard everything I should in his voice but it didn't reach me. Instead I felt overwhelmed by panic, cornered, like I was in a big black box and gradually all the oxygen was being sucked out of it. How convenient it had been to blame Jay – but our relationship had danced as much to my tune as his. Now Rory has laid himself bare, what exactly was I prepared to give up for somebody I loved? Not enough it seemed. I snatched up my backpack. 'Well don't need me. I don't want anyone to need me.'

'Oh yes?' he said wildly. 'Well what about Magic Johnson 2. What's the poor little bastard going to do? Cook for himself?'

I looked round. My poor little fish was doing laps in its bowl on the table, its existence entirely forgotten. I picked it up and dumped it in Rory's arms. 'Present,' I said, then I turned and ran.

He caught up with me as I got into the cab. He was still holding the fish bowl. The water had slopped down the front of his pants.

'Damn it, Maggie, you're running again. It's a bad habit, you said so yourself.'

'Please,' I begged the driver. 'Just go.'

'Promise me, Maggie, when you get there, you'll stop

for a minute, just one minute, and think about whether I'm right.'

I shook my head helplessly. Forget the daydream, look at the two of us, our lives were mutually exclusive. Whatever future there might be would only ever play itself painfully out within the narrow lines we've both drawn around ourselves.

'Actually, let me revise that. One minute might be pushing it, so look, take two.' He got a better hold on the glass surface. 'I mean, who are we fooling here, take as much time as you like. Maggie, please . . .'

The cab jolted forwards with the surge of traffic and moved slowly off. I looked out the back window. Rory's mouth was opening and closing, but I couldn't hear what he was saying. Instead, I carefully focused on Magic Johnson 2, swimming around his bowl, getting smaller and smaller and smaller as the cab gathered speed. Thankfully we turned the corner, and the tears began to leak down my face. Outside in the street, the cherry trees shed blossom like confetti over the city.

daniel

'Two thousand for the weekend but for that you get to sleep in Churchill's bed.' Benj leans back in his chair and props his feet up on the desk. His tea, a boiled egg and a slice of toast, sits in front of him.

Since giving up alcohol, his appetite has become ferocious and the resulting half stone he's put on makes him look and feel well, at least he's assuming that this unusual feeling of energy is what people like to call 'well'. Above all he enjoys the programme and attends religiously. There is no semi-AA for Benj.

'No, no, my dear madam,' he says with exaggerated chivalry, 'It's extremely unlikely that Churchill, or indeed any surviving members of his family, will also be in it. But perhaps for an extra hundred or two I can tempt you with a glimpse of Queen Mary's bloody nightdress?'

Alison appears silently at his elbow and places a cup of tea beside the boiled egg. She notices the toast and without thinking, slices it into neat soldiers.

Rory walks out of his office clutching a leather holdall.

'Rory, stay here this weekend. We can, uh, uh, well . . . we'll take in a couple of reclamation centres . . . go see a cemetery perhaps. Have our legs amputated, you know,' Benj says weakly. 'Have some *fun* for a change.'

Rory laughs. 'It's the fête. I promised I'd go.'

Benj takes his feet off the desk in excitement. 'Oooh, will they have whack the rat?'

'Why, do you want to come?' Rory asks hopefully.

Benj notices his toast. A great smile spreads across his face. 'Actually,' he looks meaningfully at Alison. 'Perhaps I'll stay.'

Alison blushes and fiddles with her hair.

In Skimpton, Rory passes signs for the village fête. On a whim he parks the car near the train station, heads down the slope, and crosses the railway track towards Bevan. When Alistair was a boy, the train would stop at the bridge to allow Grandpa to jump off with his suitcase. Rory scrambles up the bank to the park. A week of sun has finally brought out the full glory of spring. The countryside has metamorphosed from grey to green and it's the best that England can ever look. Primroses and crocuses blanket the ground, the chestnuts are nearly out, the park is full of lambs. By the river the bulrushes are swelling, the weeping willows thickening, herons are nesting. The giant sycamore holds out its massive boughs over a tangled bed of wild garlic plants, their damp pungent smell so comforting. Rory absent-mindedly pulls on the frayed length of rope attached to a branch some thirty foot up the tree, as boys, our means of transport from one side of the brook to the other. The wind feels warm against his face. A day like this he thinks, one perfect day can keep you going for the rest of your life

– and there will always be one more perfect day. Rory sucks the air into his lungs, holds it there for a long time before expelling it and he remembers then what he has always known and so often denied – that Bevan is spectacularly beautiful, a magical place that will always be a part of him. He remembers what I used to tell him; that no matter how hard you try, there will always be something of the father in every son.

The house feels empty. Rory shuts the front door behind him and walks down the hall. Dust spins in the air as light, flooding through the dining room windows, refracts off the glass chandelier. Rory hears noises and opens the door to the drawing room. A stocky fellow in a suit is standing by the wall. He mutters something and a second man, grasping the end of a tape measure, rises off his knees and advances on Rory hesitantly.

'Afternoon,' he says, thrusting out his hand. 'John Fielding of Knight, Frank and Rutley.' He misinterprets Rory's look of astonishment for lack of brand recognition.

'Property Agents,' he explains, handing over his business card.

maggie

If your job is to poke around in others people's affairs, you have to understand that you're living a life of borrowed experiences. In your head you might store thousands of frames, fragments of other people's existence, but the memories these give you are transient. They're facsimiles, carbon copies of the real thing. And because there's no long-lasting emotion behind them, they too, like the ink on fax paper, end up fading with time. And after a while, it makes you wonder, it really does, what tangible moments your own life is actually made up of.

'OK, Maggie,' Wolf said patiently. 'One more time. Take it from the top.'

'Sure, ready,' I adjusted the expression on my face, tried to concentrate. 'In this painful period of er . . . uh . . . American history. Goddamnit,' I broke off again. I was making a real mess of it. From the moment we'd begun the MIA assignment I'd been subject to this helpless day-dreaming.

'Try it again.'

I cleared my throat. 'At last some of the long-sought men Missing In Action will have their remains flown back to their loved ones who perhaps will find, er, closure . . . look, do I have to use the world closure,' I said crossly, 'I hate the word closure.'

'Not like you're looking for it yourself or anything,' Wolf said dryly.

I glowered at him. Took a huge breath, faced his camera, began again. 'At last some of the men long gong, glone, GONE . . . aaargh'

'Let's go get you some lunch,' Wolf was employing his most condescending voice.

There wasn't much to be had in the way of lunch in Phnom Penh. We'd been eating in the same small restaurant on the far side of town for days, but Wolf, impatient to get at his rice and boiled Pepsi, pulled me into a rat run through the town's back alleys. I followed sulkily in his wake, scuffing my boots on the cracked mud. As we reached the end of the alley he stopped abruptly and I bumped into his back.

'Ow.' I said belligerently.

'Look.'

'What?'

'Over there. Look.'

'Where?'

'He must have followed you.'

My breath caught in my throat. I scanned the busy street, but I could not find the face I was looking for in that bustling sea of people.

'There,' Wolf said, and I saw what he was looking at.

On the road facing us was a tattered billboard. Underneath the word 'Restaurant', written in both English and

Cambodian, was a picture of a fish. A black fish, one of those big ugly Chinese ones with bulbous eyes not unlike—

'Magic Johnson 2,' Wolf said. 'Ahhh, sweet. He must have swum all the way just to see you.'

'Wolf. You son of a bitch.'

Wolf retied the elastic on his ponytail. 'I'm sorry to say this, Maggie, but you're a real piece of work yourself.'

'Me?'

'Yeah, you. Fine, go ahead, die a wizened bitter old hag, see if I care.'

'Wait a minute,' I said defensively. 'Whose side are you on?'

'I'm on your side – at least I used to be, but you're stubborn and stupid so now I'm on my side – because anyone that's dumb enough to care about you including and especially me is liable to get an ulcer.'

I stared at the stupid black fish.

'You will go anywhere, attack anything, fight for any cause you think is important but someone actually needing you is more than you can handle.'

'Shut up, Wolf.'

'That's your problem, you're scared to death.'

'That is such bullshit,' I howled. 'I am not.'

'Yeah, you are. You're scared of all the things you want the most.'

'I'm not listening to this.' I stomped off.

I blinked back the tears for the second time that week. I guess when you get lost, it doesn't happen in one go. What happens is you take a series of wrong turnings so small it takes you a while to cotton on to the fact your life is not on the right track any more – well who's going to sit you down and tell you it's too late?

'Who would have thought, Maggie,' Wolf shouted after me. 'You are a goddamn sissy after all.'

daniel

Rory heads cross country towards the cricket pitch. In the distance he can hear the caterwaul of a Wall's ice-cream van. He knots his jumper round his waist and vaults the stile. How just like Pa, he shakes his head. How just like Pa to say nothing.

The fête is teeming with people. The air smells of sawdust. All the familiar stalls are up – coconut shies, bottle stands, guess the weight of the pig. Overturned crates are laden with jars of marmalade and chutneys. Rosie from the village shop is judging the gardens-in-a-tin competition and Bindey's nephew is laying out oversized turnips and marrows for inspection.

At whack the rat a gargantuan man Rory recognizes from the Skimpton darts team brings the heavy mallet down on the rat onto which, this year, somebody has actually bothered to sew a tail. The blow sends the rat scurrying up the pole. His supporters cheer then groan as it stops inches from the bell.

Rory wanders on. A bouncy castle seems to be this year's capitulation to the new century. Scores of grubby toddlers fall over each other in a sticky mess of mucus, tears and ice cream. By the middle of the pitch, the smell of sawdust has been overpowered by a stall frying onions and sausages. Rory sees Nanny holding court on the bingo stand then spots the sign behind her. *Donkey rides 50p.* Two bored donkeys graze mournfully on dandelions while next door to them a line of hysterically excited children and parents queue in front of a second sign. *Buffalo Rides £2.*

Audrey stands behind a long table trying to serve four people at once. The table is piled high with bits and pieces from the house. China, books, pictures, even the Buddha from the hall table is on it. As Rory walks over Alistair pops up from the boxes underneath the table, the moose head in his hands. He dumps it unceremoniously in front of a waiting customer.

'How much for the moose?' Rory elbows his way in.

'I'm bid six pounds by this kind lady.'

'I'll give you four.'

'Do you mind?' the woman says, a little annoyed.

'Ten pounds, not a penny less,' Alistair demands.

'Three,' says Rory.

'Ten,' the woman bids indignantly.

'Right, if that's the way you feel – two pounds fifty,' Rory grins at his father, 'and that's my final offer.'

'Have it for nothing,' Alistair says. 'After all, it belongs to you already.'

The woman finally understands what she's up against. She moves away, smiling faintly.

'On condition you take it away,' Alistair heaves the creature into Rory's arms.

Rory rests it on the table. He's about to open his mouth but Alistair is way ahead of him.

'Not now, Rory.'

'I've just come from Bevan.'

Alistair nods. 'Try to understand,' he says. 'I will miss my trees, I will miss the view over the park probably every day for the rest of my life, but I will survive. We, your mother and I *will* survive.'

'But, Pa—'

'We've had to come to terms with the death of our child,' Alistair says. 'What the hell does a house matter after that?'

Rory nods dumbly.

'So take the damn moose and go and find your grandfather.' Alistair puts his hand on Rory's shoulder and gives it a squeeze, 'You're actually a little in our way right now.'

Towards the end of the cricket pitch the stalls begin to peter out. Behind the tea tent on a patch of grass dotted with empty beer cans, two spotty teenagers are snogging for England. Rory rests the moose on the ground and skims the crowd for Grandpa. He sees the military jacket first, set neatly down on a hay bale outside a stall, then Grandpa marches out, shotgun in hand. He's transferred the medals to his shirt and they flash in the sun when he moves. Rory smiles.

Grandpa looks through the viewfinder of the gun. He makes an impatient gesture as if the sights are not up to scratch then puts the rifle to his shoulder and fires. There's a sound of shattered china.

'Ha!' Grandpa exclaims. 'Loader,' he bellows. An arm,

holding a second rifle, hastily appears from inside the tarpaulin.

As Grandpa merrily continues to obliterate the remainder of Bevan's legacy, Rory closes his eyes. The sun is warm against his forehead. He feels like he could chart his entire life through every fête past and for the first time ever, he feels like this is not a bad thing.

'Loader, where have you got to?' shouts Grandpa. 'Come out here at once and take a turn.' Rory opens his eyes and blinks into the sunlight.

maggie

Grandpa put his arms round me, levelling the rifle in my hands. 'Steady,' he warned, 'Line it up. Steady, *steady*.'

I closed one eye, squeezed against the trigger. The gun smashed painfully against my shoulder. On the bale, one of the Chinese figurines exploded.

'Oh, good girl!' Grandpa took the rifle from me and reloaded.

I saw Rory then, standing by the entrance of the tent, or rather leaning against the guy ropes, arms crossed. He'd seen me too, I could tell, and was watching us, a look on his face I couldn't read. I held my ground. I had come 6,000 miles, I had crossed another continent to be there, so I reckoned the next 40 yards were up to him.

He pushed himself off the ropes and ambled over. People between us sped up and blurred, then he was in front of me.

'So,' he said nonchalantly. 'Just landed?'

'Yeah.'

'Good journey?'

'A little bumpy,' I said, 'otherwise . . . a damn good bit of flying.'

He pulled me close. I could feel his heart pounding.

'Look,' I said. 'I just want to get one thing straight.'

'Yes?' His eyes narrowed suspiciously. 'And what might that be?'

'I'm not going to be one of those weird little women who make cucumber sandwiches and wear flowery hats. I'm not going to join the Women's Institute, or eat bread sauce, I won't share bath water with anyone except you and I will never and I mean never ever live in a house without adequate central heating.'

'Anything else?' he said mildly.

'Yes. I also want to point out . . . well . . . don't think that just because I've come here, I'm here for good or anything like that. It's like . . . I mean you do realize I have a job, or well I'm looking for a new job because it's not like I'm going to give up my work or . . .'

'Or your what?' he demanded.

'Well, my work . . .'

Rory broke into a grin and it was like I'd been waiting my whole life for someone to grin like that at me, 'Well that's a relief,' he said. 'Because following in a long-standing and proud family tradition, I am destined to remain seriously broke.'

daniel

The new owners of Bevan are businessmen. Developers with their eye on commuters from Stockton on Tees. Though not averse to the idea, they utterly fail to understand why Rory, having sold them the house and land, is spending no small percentage of the purchase price planting a wood for them. Needless to say they put it down to eccentricity.

I, of course, know better.

There are fifty shovels in the back of the tractor. The clearing teems with people. Rory has gathered them all together; everyone who has ever worked at Bevan, their families and grandchildren; the Skimpton cricket and darts team, Rosie from the local 7–11, even Doctor Banks from the village. Over the last few weeks most of Rory's clients from Stately Locations have also made the pilgrimage, the Bancrofts, the Harcourts, the Roxmeres, Benj, Alison, my mother, my father, Maggie. Rory methodically ticks them off a list, his list that has been appendaged to my map. They take their trees, carefully labelled in Latin and English, and one by one they plant my wood, and I am proud. I am really proud. Here's what I think, for what it's worth. The land does not belong to the new owners, just as it didn't belong to my father. The land does not belong to the ramblers, the twitchers, picnickers, prospectors, city week-enders, gypsies, Estate owners or farmers, it belongs to those who work it and are passionate about it.

It belongs to those who are prepared to put their soul into it.

Rory has moved off some way from the crowd. Overhead the air darkens, the weather changes fast and furious. Clouds hurtle through the sky. Rory stands in the clearing looking down the valley towards the house. He takes off his boots and the soil feels damp between his toes. He can smell the seed, smell the honeysuckle lifting off the breeze. He sees the woods, the park, the great oak tree bowed in the fox cover. He hears the sound the wind makes as it blows through the flowers of the horse chestnut. He feels the current in the earth, the rain on his skin. He sinks to his knees until the water has seeped through his clothes then he turns his face skywards and I see he's understood.

When Rory drives down the drive of Bevan for the last time, he will have Maggie in his car and the moose head strapped to the roof. God only knows where they think they're going but at least together they might have some fun getting there. As for me . . . well who knows? Bob Dylan said, 'I'll let you be in my dream if I can be in yours,' and I think that's a pretty good trade off. I still don't know where I am, but my hope is I'm only passing through. Meanwhile, finally, jealously, gratefully, tearfully, I can and damn well will raise an imaginary glass to my brother.

To say that the English aristocracy is a spent force is undeniable, but to say it is no longer of value is not necessarily the case. In the end it's family that counts. Our story, depending on who's telling it, is one of irreversible decline or, as I prefer to see it . . . a story of survival against the odds.

— Earl of Bevan

Acknowledgements

Hunting Unicorns originally began life as a screenplay embarked upon by my sister Susie and me as a way of threading together some of the humiliating fates suffered by those to whom the more staid traditions and values of the English are a complete anathema.

My thanks, therefore, to all those people who on hearing of the project flooded us with urban myths, embarrassing anecdotes and deliciously weird stories.

Apart from it being a revelation to discover just how many people had an Alistair or Audrey Bevan somewhere in their family tree, I loved all these stories because they really made me laugh – no bad thing when you find yourself locked into a room with an obstreperous computer. Those urban myths that found their way into *Hunting Unicorns*, namely the bunny, the basin, and the wallpaper, are silly enough but, believe me, fall way short of being the silliest.

My eternal thanks to all those friends who for one reason or another stopped me toppling over the edge whilst writing this book: Nan and Andy for Brooklyn and bagels. John and Emily for their tower of flies. Susie for tuna sandwiches. Carole for

BELLA POLLEN

her wisdom and breakfasts at Balthazar, Sarah and Clare for their
google wizardry and Mr Kipling's almond slices. Nanda for her
tortillas and above all, Dave for the Barn.

Thanks also to the following for their invaluable help: Molly
Dineen, Rebecca Frayn, Catherine Bailey, the London office of
Médecins Sans Frontières, Charles Kidd of *Debrett's Peerage*.

PERMISSIONS ACKNOWLEDGEMENTS

The publishers gratefully acknowledge permission to reproduce
copyright material from:

The Decline and Fall of the British Aristocracy, David Cannadine
Picador (1990)

'The Stately Homes of England', Noël Coward – refrain, Oper-
ette (musical, 1938). *The Columbia World of Quotations*. Copyright
© 1996 Columbia University Press

Christiane Amanpour: 'News is part of our communal experience . . .' Part of a speech made at the Edward R. Murrow
awards ceremony of the Radio Television News Directors Associ-
ation held 13 September 2000 in Minneapolis. Grateful
permission received from Christiane Amanpour, CNN's Chief
Foreign Correspondent.

Every effort has been made to trace all copyright holders but if
any has been inadvertently overlooked the author and publishers
will be pleased to make the necessary arrangements at the first
opportunity.

extracts reading groups
competitions books new
discounts extracts
competitions
books new
events books
extracts
new titles reading groups
interviews
events extracts
discounts
new books events
events new
discounts extracts discounts
www.panmacmillan.com
extracts events reading groups
competitions books extracts new